When Camilla King was summoned to Thunder Heights she did not know she was about to become mistress of her grandfather's huge estate.

Camilla never met her mother's family. Her father had never forgiven them for his wife's mysterious and tragic death, even though Althea had been the old man's favorite.

Now suddenly, years later, Grandfather Judd had left everything to Althea's only child. Overnight Camilla had become a woman of property.

A dream come true? Not to Camilla. For along with this fortune she had inherited a legacy of hate. And violence.

Camilla began to wonder whether her mother's death *was* an accident. Or was it murder?

If so, Camilla knew death would strike again. And that she had been marked as the victim.

Fawcett Crest Books
by Phyllis A. Whitney:

- ☐ BLACK AMBER 23943 $2.25
- ☐ BLUE FIRE 24083 $2.50
- ☐ COLUMBELLA 22919 $2.50
- ☑ DOMINO 24350 $2.75
- ☑ THE GOLDEN UNICORN 23104 $2.50
- ☐ HUNTER'S GREEN 23523 $1.95
- ☑ LISTEN FOR THE WHISPERER 23156 $2.50
- ☐ THE MOONFLOWER 23626 $2.25
- ☐ THE QUICKSILVER POOL 23983 $2.25
- ☐ SEVEN TEARS FOR APOLLO 23428 $2.50
- ☐ SKYE CAMERON 24100 $2.25
- ☑ SPINDRIFT 22746 $2.50
- ☐ THE STONE BULL 23638 $2.50
- ☑ THUNDER HEIGHTS 24143 $2.50
- ☐ THE TREMBLING HILLS 23539 $2.25
- ☑ THE TURQUOISE MASK 23470 $2.95
- ☐ WINDOW ON THE SQUARE 23627 $1.95
- ☐ THE WINTER PEOPLE 23681 $2.25

THUNDER
HEIGHTS

Phyllis A. Whitney

FAWCETT CREST • NEW YORK

THUNDER HEIGHTS

THIS BOOK CONTAINS THE COMPLETE TEXT OF THE
ORIGINAL HARDCOVER EDITION.

Published by Fawcett Crest Books, a unit of CBS Publications,
the Consumer Publishing Division of CBS Inc., by arrangement with Hawthorn Books, Inc.

Selection of the Bargain Book Club, Spring 1970

ISBN: 0-449-24143-2

Printed in the United States of America

25   24   23   22   21   20   19

CAMILLA KING STOOD AT THE WINDOW OF HER SMALL THIRD floor room overlooking Gramercy Park and watched the last windy day of March blow itself out through the streets of New York. A gusty breeze rumpled treetops in the park, tossed the mane of a horse drawing a hackney cab along Twenty-first Street, and sent an unguarded bowler hat tumbling across the sidewalk.

Ordinarily she loved wind and storm. But how bleak and discouraging everything could look on a gray day in New York. The sky was as gray as the streets and as overcast as her life seemed at this moment.

Behind her in the little room Nettie sniffed tearfully as she packed the top tray of Camilla's trunk. This was a labor of love for Nettie. A departing governess had no business using up the parlormaid's time. But the Hodges had gone out and there was no one about to complain.

"You'll find a better place than this, Miss Camilla," Nettie said, wiping away tears with the back of her hand. "You being so pretty and clever and all."

Camilla smiled wryly without turning. "And with such a fine outspoken way about me that it has lost me the second position in a row?"

"A good thing, too," Nettie muttered. "With himself so high and mighty that—"

"It was the children I was thinking of," Camilla broke in. "They're darlings and I had to speak up against his harshness. But Mr. Hodges said I was too easy with them and perhaps he should employ an older woman for governess."

"You're twenty-three and that's a great age!" Nettie protested. "At twenty-three I'd been married to my Tom for five years and had two babes of my own. That's the bad thing, Miss Camilla—you being so alone."

Camilla had visited Nettie's home and had seen—and envied a little—the joyous welter of family life in which Nettie thrived. She had never known such a life, but she could still remember the warm affection and gaiety of those years before she was eight, the years before her mother's death. At times, when the moment was right, her mother's image still returned to her mind full and clear and vital. Then she could remember the way Althea King had moved, light and lovely as a dancer, her dark head carried with such proud grace. She could recall the very line of her thick black hair coming to the point of a widow's peak at her forehead. Wherever Althea King was, there excitement had burgeoned. The strangeness of her death had wiped out so much. And now it grew increasingly difficult for Camilla to bring that bright image back to mind.

For the years that John King, her father, had been married to Althea, he had come out of his books and his scholar's reverie a little, and had known a quiet joy in her company. But after her mother had died in that faraway place up the Hudson, he had lost himself more than ever in his writings, his study, his teaching.

A housekeeper had been brought in to take charge of their small home and of Camilla. Mrs. Gregg was an efficient woman, but she had little feeling for children. Camilla had not cared. She had lived a free enough existence, if a lonely one. Her father had seen to her education, and lessons with him had always been a joy.

Camilla remembered him with love and tenderness. Never had she seen a man more handsome, with his poet's brow, his fine dark eyes, and the sensitive modeling of his mouth. When she thought of him now, she pictured him most often in the little room he had used for a study, with his head bent over his books. He had cared for his daughter. Indeed, he had loved her doubly, loving her mother through her. Camilla had been bitterly stricken when he had died four years ago.

The way of her growing up had given her a practical side—someone had to use good sense with a dreamer like her father. And certainly it had given her independence. But there was something of her father in her too, for there were times when her own dreamy, imaginative side took over and made her do strange things.

Now, however, she must accept only the practical in herself, so she laughed at Nettie's lugubrious words and steeled her will against despair. On a gray day like this, when she had just lost a position she needed badly—and lost it because of her very independence—despair seemed ready to seize her if she let down her guard for a moment.

"Never you mind," Nettie said, thrusting back her tears in order to cheer Camilla. "You're the marrying kind, you know. It's a good husband you need, Miss Camilla, and babes of your own."

Again Camilla smiled and did not answer. Sometimes she lingered all too readily over such thoughts, it was true. Pleasant enough dreams in the daytime, but sometimes disturbingly painful during the long hours of the night. Arms were not meant alone for holding tenderly, as one held a child. There was a demand in her for something more gladdening and all-absorbing than seemed to be the lot of the women in whose homes she worked as a governess.

From the window she saw that the hackney cab she had noticed earlier had circled the enclosure of the park twice, as if its fare were not sure of the house he looked for. Now it stopped before the Hodges' door and a man got out, holding his hat against a sudden gust of wind.

"Someone's coming up the steps, Nettie," Camilla said over her shoulder. "There's the bell—you'd better run. And thank you for helping me pack."

Nettie hurried for the stairs and Camilla stood on at the window, trying not to droop with dejection. Tomorrow, she supposed, she would be courageous again, but for the moment it was a temptation to match her spirits to the gray, unsettled afternoon and wonder where she was to turn next, whether she could ever find a position that would give her a lasting home. Or if that was what she really wanted.

If she was pretty, as Nettie said, it was of no special advantage. What good did prettiness do when it brought too easy an interest from men who could never matter to her? At the place before this, the man of the house had been altogether too kind, and had wanted to be kinder. Camilla had spoken her mind and left precipitately. It was unfair that such things should happen when she knew she had done her work well and taken pride in the doing.

Was she pretty? she wondered absently. She put a hand to the dark, glossy waves of hair drawn loosely into a coil at the top of her head and puffed at the sides in the style of this last decade of the century. She knew her skin was as fair in contrast to her black hair as her mother's had been, and that the same pointed widow's peak marked her forehead. Her pink-striped shirtwaist with its bow at the high collar, and her gored gray skirt, flowing into a small train, fitted a well-proportioned figure. And she supposed that wide brown eyes, heavy-lashed, were a good feature. But prettiness—how did one know about oneself? And what did it matter anyway? A governess lived an almost cloistered life, with little opportunity to know other young people—especially young men her own age.

3

She turned from the window and looked at her trunk, ready now to be closed and locked, and at the cheap straw suitcase that stood beside it.

"I'm tired to pieces of this life!" she told them aloud. "I want something better than this!" She would find something better, too. She was not helpless or fearful, as a rule. And she was not without the ingenuity to make something more of her life.

There were her relatives, for one thing—those wealthy, unknown relatives up the Hudson River. She had more family than Nettie guessed, though she never heard from them, or even thought seriously of getting in touch with them. Not after the way her grandfather had treated her mother, or in the face of her father's bitter hatred of him.

John King, in his gentleness, had seldom disliked anyone. But Camilla knew that he blamed Orrin Judd for her mother's death and never forgave him. Exactly what her grandfather's fault had been she did not know, but her father's insistence that she must have nothing to do with her mother's family had made a lasting impression over the years.

Nevertheless, there they were—Orrin Judd and his daughters, in that great house up the Hudson called Thunder Heights. Her mother had told her endless stories about the place as she had known it as a child. Perhaps the day would eventually come when Camilla could face these relatives, if for no other reason than to learn more about her mother. But she would not go as a beggar. Never that!

She heard Nettie breathing heavily as she climbed the stairs, and a moment later the maid was at the door, her eyes wide with excitement.

"It's a caller!" she cried. "A caller for you, Miss Camilla. A dignified gentleman, he seems—and asking for Miss Camilla King. I've put him in the front parlor. Maybe he's come to offer you a new position. Quick now—run down and see what he wants."

Camilla did not run, but she could not help a faint rising of curiosity. No one knew as yet of her need for a new position. Perhaps it was some friend of her father—though she had not imposed her troubles on them.

At the parlor door she paused so that she might enter without unseemly haste. The gentleman sat in a shadowy corner where she could not see him clearly at first. He rose and came toward her—a man in his fifties, bald except for a gray fringe of hair rimming the back of his head, and ending in two clumps above each ear. His skin had the pink, soft

4

look of a baby's, but his eyes were a cool, wary gray. His straight, tight mouth barely smiled as he studied her. There was no approval in him.

"You are Miss Camilla King?" he asked directly. "My name is Pompton. Alexander Pompton. The name will mean nothing to you, I am sure. But I have come to ask a favor of you."

She gestured him to the sofa and sat down opposite, curious and waiting.

"You are a governess here, I believe," he said. "Are you happy in this work? Are your ties in this household very strong?"

The soreness of her last interview with Mr. Hodges was too recent for caution.

"I have no ties here at all," she said quickly. "Or anywhere else, for that matter. I was dismissed from my position this morning."

He considered her admission soberly, as if it further bolstered his conclusions about her, and she wished she had not blurted out the truth so impulsively.

"In that case," he said, "it should be possible for you to take the boat tomorrow afternoon. I have gone to the liberty of procuring your passage to Westcliff in order to make your way easy."

"Easy for what?" she asked, completely at a loss.

He leaned toward her earnestly, dropping all evasion. "I have been Orrin Judd's attorney for many years, I have come here to ask you to go to your grandfather's sickbed at Thunder Heights. He is seriously ill—he may be dying."

She was silent for a moment, startled and dismayed. "But— he disowned my mother long ago. Even when she was alive he would have nothing to do with us."

"That is not quite true," Mr. Pompton corrected her. "Mr. Judd kept good account of every move his daughter Althea made over the years. Had she been in need, he would have stepped in at once, even though he and your father had little liking for each other."

"My father detested him," Camilla said. "He didn't want my mother to return to Thunder Heights when Orrin Judd finally sent for her."

Mr. Pompton sighed and ran a hand over his pink scalp as if he smoothed thick hair. This errand was clearly not to his taste. "What happened was unfortunate, indeed a great trage-dy. But your father was mistaken in blaming Orrin Judd."

Camilla's fingers twisted together in her lap. "They sent for

5

Papa after she died. He went to Thunder Heights for her funeral, and he came home ill with grief. He said her family was wholly to blame for the accident, whatever it was. He would never talk about it at all. He wanted me to remember my mother the way she was, and I've never known how she died. He said I was never under any circumstances to have anything to do with my grandfather or the others at Thunder Heights."

"Your father has been dead for several years," Mr. Pompton reminded her. "You are a grown woman. It is up to you to make your own decisions. When a man is dying there may be many things he regrets. Your mother was Orrin Judd's favorite daughter, and he wishes to see his only grandchild."

Camilla sat very still, her fingers twisted tightly. A queer, unexpected surge of excitement had leaped within her for an instant. The name of Judd was a magic one to be spoken almost in the same breath with such names as Vanderbilt, Astor, or Morgan. Though in later years old Orrin Judd had pulled in his horns and, with the eccentricity in which only the very rich can indulge, had abandoned the lavish mode of living that had once been his custom. The world had nearly forgotten him, as it was never allowed to forget those others who bore great names and increased their progeny.

In none of her positions as a governess had Camilla ever breathed a word of her grandfather's identity. But she remembered once when she had been very young and her mother had pointed out a tall structure that towered over Broadway. "Your grandfather created that building," her mother said with pride in her voice. The small Camilla had envisioned a very old man with a long white beard like the pictures of Moses in the Bible, setting one brick upon another as she herself piled blocks. For a long time it had been a puzzle to her what he had done once the pile rose higher than his head. But the building had always remained for her, "my grandfather's house."

A faint smile curled her lips, and Mr. Pompton did not miss it. "You would need to stay only a day or two at this time," he said hurriedly, pressing what he took to be an advantage. "The boat trip need not interfere with your obtaining a new position in New York, if that is what you wish. I believe it would be wise not to remain longer. You would at least make your grandfather's acquaintance, perhaps bring him a last happiness. I met your mother only once, but I have seen pictures of her. Your resemblance to her is striking."

6

Yes, she knew that. The way she looked had always brought her father both pain and joy. But why did Mr. Pompton stipulate that Orrin's granddaughter should visit him for only a day or two? If her grandfather wanted her enough to send for her . . .

"I must warn you," Mr. Pompton continued in his solemn tone, "that you may not be altogether welcome at Thunder Heights."

Her mother's tales of the family sprang from the past into Camilla's mind. "You mean because of my Aunt Hortense? But if my grandfather wants me—"

"He may not be well enough to prevail. I'm afraid that your aunt never forgave your mother for running away with John King. But no matter—you must go and not let anything she says disturb you."

"Who else lives at Thunder Heights now?" Camilla asked. "I believe Mama said that Letitia was the middle sister. Has she married?"

"No, Miss Letty still lives there. She is a gentle soul, and I'm sure she will welcome your coming. Then of course there is Booth Hendricks, whom your Aunt Hortense adopted many years ago when he was ten. He must be about thirty-six now and he too has never married. There is another young man, as well—an engineer who has been a close and trusted associate of your grandfather for many years. A Mr. Ross Granger. He is now in New York on business. I expect to see him while I am here. Miss Camilla—will you give your grandfather this last pleasure? Believe me, the matter is urgent. He was ill before this heart attack—there may be little time remaining."

For a moment Camilla could not answer. The emptiness of all the years when she had longed for a family crowded back upon her. How many times she had dreamed of such a family in her young girl loneliness, and now one had been presented to her. A family whom she would not have to approach as a beggar because Orrin Judd himself had summoned her. Perhaps there were matters her father had never fully understood. Besides, she had her mother's own actions to guide her. When Orrin Judd had sent for her, Althea had gone, even over the objections of her husband. Could her daughter do less?

She smiled at her visitor in sudden bright acceptance. "There's no reason why I can't catch tomorrow's boat as you suggest."

Mr. Pompton looked more relieved than pleased. He rose at once and put an envelope into Camilla's hands.

"You will find everything in order, I believe. The boat reaches Westcliff in the late afternoon. I will send a wire ahead so that you will be met and driven to Thunder Heights. I plan to return by a later boat when my business in New York is finished."

She saw him to the door and watched him go down the steps and out to his waiting hack. The day was still gray and gusty, but now there seemed an excitement in the blustering wind. She ran upstairs breathlessly to announce the news to Nettie.

"I have a family!" she cried. "I have a family after all!" And she wrapped her arms about herself, as if she hugged the very fact to her. "Perhaps if my grandfather likes me I can stay a while, in spite of my Aunt Hortense."

Nettie had to sit right down and listen to the whole story, and she didn't leave until the Hodges were heard coming home. It wasn't necessary for Camilla to see her erstwhile employers again until she left. She had her supper in her room that night, and she could hardly sleep for thinking about Thunder Heights, trying to remember all the stories her mother had told her about the days when Althea Judd was a little girl in the great house up the river.

As a child, Camilla had pictured in her mind a great castle of a house, built on a high eminence. A house with shining turrets and windows that caught the tints of sunrise across the Hudson. She knew, as though she had stepped into it, the square antehall with marble hands that reached eerily out of the walls, and the great parlor filled with curios. Orrin Judd and his wife had liked to travel, and they had brought home treasures from all over the world. Camilla's grandmother had died while Althea was a little girl, but there had still been days of wonderful travel for her daughters.

There was an octagon staircase, too—Camilla had always loved the sound of that. It ran up two flights, and its panels of carved teakwood had come from Burma. Up on the third floor was the huge nursery, where Althea had played with her two older sisters. Camilla could imagine its cheerful fire and worn, loved furnishings.

Now that she thought of it, Camilla realized that her mother had talked more of the house than of its occupants. There had always been a soreness in Althea King that had turned away from stories of her father or her sisters. But now Camilla could go to Thunder Heights and see the bright turrets, the marble hands, the staircase, for herself.

It was not, however, the house that interested her most. A warm current of eagerness flowed in her veins, an eagerness to please her aunts and her grandfather, to love them and be loved by them. Whatever had happened in the past must be buried by the years that were gone. She was not responsible for any of it, so how could she be blamed for what was none of her doing? She would be as sweet and agreeable as it was in her to be, so that the family would delight in having her there—even Aunt Hortense who held some unaccountable grudge against her own dead sister.

She went to sleep with a smile on her lips and all her dreams were loving.

II

The following afternoon she bade Mrs. Hodges a polite good-by, kissed the weeping children with the pang she always felt on leaving charges she had grown to love, and went out to her cab, carrying her suitcase. The trunk would follow her in a day or two. She *had* to stay at Thunder Heights for a little while at least.

She had never taken a trip up the Hudson River before, yet the river had always been a part of her memory of her mother. Sometimes the two of them had gone by horse car to the lower tip of Manhattan, where the river emptied into the harbor, and stood watching the busy water life. The Hudson had meant home to Althea King, and she had told her small daughter tales of the dreamer, Hendrik Hudson, and his ship the *Half Moon*. Stories too of the Dunderbergs and the Catskills, of Storm King, and Breakneck Ridge, and Anthony's Nose. All history, it seemed, was part of the Hudson, from Indian days to the present. Commerce had followed the vital artery and made a great nation even greater.

But Althea King had seen the river with more personal eyes. She had known the Hudson in its every mood—when its banks glowed brilliant with autumn foliage, when ice encrusted its inlets, when spring laid a tender hand upon its shores and when summer thunderstorms set the cliffs reverberating.

Yet after her marriage her mother had never again set foot on a Hudson River boat until the final summons from her father. "I want to remember," she had said, "but I don't want to turn the knife in my heart." Strange words to a little girl's ears, but her mother's passion for the river had remained, and now Camilla felt eager and alive, ready to fling her arms wide and embrace the new life that must surely lie ahead. That life was her heritage from her mother, and the river was a vibrant part of it.

Nevertheless, the river had taken her mother away, she thought with a twinge of guilt. Althea had never returned from that last journey up Hudson waters to Thunder Heights. Remembering that, she wondered what the river might hold in the future for Althea's daughter.

The boat that awaited Camilla was one of the Hudson's fastest—four decks high and gleaming with white paint and gold trim. The tourist season had not yet begun, but there was a continual flow of traffic between New York and Albany, and passengers were already boarding when she reached the pier.

The day was gray again. This was storm-brewing weather, with an electric quality in the air and a wild wind blowing— weather that carried excitement in every breath. It was cold for the first day of April, and the cutting wind sent most of the passengers scuttling for the comfort of the gold and white salons.

Since the trip would be a short one for Camilla, she had no cabin, but as soon as she had checked her flimsy suitcase, she climbed the grand staircase, her hand on the fine mahogany rail, and went into the main salon where passengers were making themselves comfortable out of the wind. She looked about, wanting nothing so tame as this. She wanted to be outside where everything was happening.

Over her hat she tied a gray veil that matched her gray *tailleur* suit, knotting it in a bow under her chin. Then she went out on deck into the very teeth of the wind. With a great tootling of whistles the boat was drawing away from the pier, turning its back upon the harbor of New York as it began its journey up the Hudson River. The paddle wheels churned a frothing wake, that sent waves rolling away to rock all smaller craft. Gulls soared and dived in the great air drafts, as if they too felt the excitement of the day.

Every manner of river craft—barges, tugs, ferries, sailboats, freighters—steamed or sailed or chugged about their individual business. As Camilla watched, she let the gale whip color into her face, breathing the fresh, tangy odor—the odor of salt air. It was as if she were truly breathing for the first time since her father's death.

Only one other passenger had dared the cold out on deck. Ahead a man leaned against the rail with his back to her, while the prow of the boat cut through choppy gray water like a great white swan among lesser fowl. He wore a sandy tweed jacket and a cap pulled over his forehead. So absorbed was he by the sights of the river that Camilla could watch him curiously without being noticed.

As she stood below him at the rail, a child of no more than four suddenly darted out of a doorway. The little girl was laughing as she ran up the deck, and Camilla, looking about for her mother to follow, saw no one. At once she hurried after the child, lest she come to harm. But the man had heard the sound of small feet running and he turned in time to see the little girl and catch her up in his arms. Then he saw Camilla approaching.

"An open deck is a dangerous place for a child," he said curtly and handed her to Camilla.

His misunderstanding was natural, and she did not take offense, but accepted the child and walked back toward the companionway just as a frantic mother rushed out and looked around in distraction.

"Here she is," Camilla said. The mother thanked her and hurried the little girl back to the shelter of the doorway. When Camilla turned, smiling, she saw that the man in the tweed jacket was watching her.

He took off his cap and the wind ruffled hair that had the glossy sheen of a red-brown chestnut. "I'm sorry," he said. "I thought she was yours, and it's a wonder I didn't read you a lecture. A child was badly hurt the last time I made this trip, and I get impatient with careless mothers."

She nodded in a friendly fashion and went to stand next to him at the rail, watching the steep cliffs of the Palisades rising ahead. She was glad he had spoken to her. Now she might ask him questions about the river. "Do you know the Hudson well?" she began.

He drew the cap down over his eyes again. "Well enough. I've lived along its banks all my life, and I've been up and down its length a few times."

"How wonderful," she said. "It's strange to think that I've lived all my life in New York City and have never sailed up the Hudson River. Today I feel like an explorer. I wish I could go all the way to Albany."

He stared off into the wind without comment, and she

hoped he wasn't shutting her out. In her eagerness and exhilaration she was ready to spill over in conversation with almost anyone, but she contented herself for the moment by studying the strong line of his jaw, his straight nose and jutting brows. It was difficult to judge his age—probably he was in the mid-thirties. There was a certain ruggedness about him, a muscular breadth to his shoulders that marked him for a man of action, rather than, like her father, a man of books. She observed his hand upon the rail, long of finger and wide across the back. A hand that revealed strength and vitality. The sum of all these things interested her, made her a little curious.

"I'm going upriver to Westcliff," she said tentatively.

He looked at her more directly than before, and she saw that his eyes were gray as the river that flowed past the boat, and set widely beneath heavy chestnut brows.

"Westcliff happens to be my destination too," he admitted, but offered her no more in the way of explanation.

The wind had increased its velocity, tearing at her hat as if to snatch it from beneath the enfolding veil, pulling black strands of hair from beneath its brim. Camilla pushed them back breathlessly and laughed into the gale in sheer delight. There was something satisfying about resisting its elementary force. She would choose a storm any day to brooding safely in the shelter of a small gray room whose very walls shut her away from the tempests and clamor of life.

"I'm glad you're going to Westcliff," she told him, speaking her mind without hesitation. "I'll at least have an acquaintance in the vicinity. I don't know a soul where I'm going. Do you know the place called Thunder Heights?"

His face was not one to be easily read, but she sensed that he was startled. The set of his straight mouth was unsmiling, his gray eyes guarded as he looked away.

"Is—is there something wrong with my going to Thunder Heights?" she asked.

He did not meet her look. "Why are you going there? Surely not to look for employment?"

"No," she said. "I work as a governess and I believe there are no children in the house at present." She hesitated because she had never before claimed openly her relationship to the Judds. Then she went on with a faint hint of happy pride in her voice that she could not suppress. "My grandfather is Orrin Judd. My mother, Althea, was the youngest of Orrin Judd's three daughters. I am Camilla King."

He made no move and his expression did not change, yet it

seemed to Camilla that there was a withdrawing, as if something in him moved away from her. He spoke beneath his breath, almost as if to himself.

"Another one," he said, and she sensed hostility in him.

He was judging her in some mistaken way, she was sure, though she did not know what there was in her Judd relationship to misunderstand.

"My grandfather is very ill," she hurried on. "I—I may be going to his deathbed. I believe he had a heart attack a few days ago."

This time she had truly surprised him. "A heart attack?" he repeated unbelievingly. "He has been ailing for some time, but—how do you know this?"

"An attorney of my grandfather's—a Mr. Pompton—came looking for me. He said my grandfather wanted to see me. Mr. Pompton arranged for my passage and I was able to take the boat at once."

He recovered himself to some extent, but she could see that her news had shaken him. He was studying her face now, clearly without liking.

"So you're still more of the family?" he said, and the inflection was not flattering.

His rude rejection both cut and angered her. She drew herself up with the dignity she had learned to adopt in households where she might be treated with less than the respect she wished. But before she could manage a reply, the billowing thunderheads that rode the sky burst and flung a torrent of rain upon them. Her companion would have taken her arm to help her across the deck, but she drew away and fled from him into the warmth and shelter of the main salon. He did not follow her there, but disappeared along the deck to another entrance.

She found an upholstered seat near a window where rain slashed the glass, obscuring all vision, and pretended to peer out into the storm. She felt somehow disappointed beyond reason. She had been ready to like this man and accept him as a new acquaintance who might well become a friend. But the name "Judd" had turned him abruptly from her, and the realization brought with it a vague uneasiness to stem her earlier feeling of joy. She wished now that she had answered him in some way, or at least challenged him to explain the scornful tone of his voice. When she saw him again, she would do just that. If the Judds were held in bad repute, that was unfortunate, but it had nothing to do with her.

She found the remaining time before Westcliff frustrating.

Longing to view the river scenery, she could see nothing for the driving rain, and though she wandered about for a while below decks, she did not see again the man she had spoken to earlier.

Not until late afternoon did the storm roll away so that a glinting of pale sky showed through the veil of gray. The decks were drenched and wet, the wind still cold, but Camilla went outside eagerly to watch the steep shores of the Hudson glide by. The river had curved sharply and seemed now to be enclosed on all sides by rocky cliffs, as if the boat had turned into some great inland lake. This she knew, must be the gateway to the Highlands. She watched, entranced, as the boat glided around the jutting crags, always finding one more opening to let it through.

Ahead on the west bank loomed a great hulking mass of mountain, its stony head cutting a profile into the sky. She could not see beyond its jutting, thickly wooded sides—still covered by the brown woods of winter—but Westcliff must not be too far ahead.

"That is Thunder Mountain," a quiet voice said in her ear.

She turned quickly to find her recent companion beside her. This time she did not wait, or give him a chance to escape again.

"May I ask why you spoke so scornfully of the Judds?" she said.

He did not seem taken aback by her sudden question. A flicker of amusement lifted one corner of his mouth and vanished.

"I should have identified myself," he told her. "My name is Ross Granger. For the last ten years or so I have worked as a close associate of Orrin Judd. Your sudden news about his illness came as a shock, since he seemed no worse than usual when I left him last week."

Her eyes widened in surprise. "Then you must be the person Mr. Pompton wanted to see in New York. You must have missed him."

"That's possible," he said and turned back to watching the river. "You can see the house now," he added. "Up there below the mass of the mountain—there's your Thunder Heights."

The white boat, cutting through choppy gray water, was slipping past the mountain, and Camilla could see that its far slope gentled, opening into a wide, tree-grown level high above the river. She forgot that the rail was sopping wet and clung to it tightly with her gray gloves. Now she could look up and see the house for the first time.

The point of prominence on which it stood commanded an entire sweep of the river, and the structure was as fantastic and impressive as anything in her dreams. Orrin Judd had built to suit himself, as Camilla knew, and he had built with imagination, but little regard for restraint. The house was a conglomeration of wooden towers and gingerbread curlicues, with sloping roofs from which jutted gables and dormer windows. A wide veranda, arched and bracketed beneath its eaves, gave upon the river, and Camilla searched its length eagerly to see if any of the family stood there watching the boat steam past. But the veranda was empty, and so were the grounds. Shutters framed blank windows which stared at her without recognition. Plainly the house did not know her, and was not waiting for her.

The turrets were no longer bright as Althea King had described them. Storms had weathered the house to a dingy gray, left too long unpainted, and the trees crowding about gave it the look of a place uninhabited. It appeared enchanted, spellbound, there on its remote heights. Not a house, but the picture of a house, torn from the pages of fantasy.

"What a strange, wonderful place," Camilla said softly. "I think I'm going to love everything about Thunder Heights."

The man at her side made a faint, derisive sound. "If I were you, I wouldn't approach it with ready-made sentimentality. You're quite likely to be disappointed."

She would not let his words dampen her feeling about the house. Even if the place didn't know her now, it would accept her later. How could it refuse, when she would offer it the love of a granddaughter coming home?

"It's strange to think that my mother grew up there," she murmured.

"How did she escape?" Ross Granger asked dryly.

What an annoying person he was, she thought—without sentiment, or kindly feelings. Why had her grandfather kept him on all these years, if he thought so little of the Judds? Then, because she hated to condemn anyone in this moment of anticipation and eagerness, she relented. Perhaps he did not really know her mother's story.

"My father came to teach in Westcliff," she told him, "and my mother fell in love with him. But Grandfather Orrin had other plans for her. I suppose he didn't think much of a poor schoolteacher as a husband for his daughter. So one night they ran away to New York and were married there. My grandfather never forgave her and she only returned once—just before her death."

"I've heard several versions of that story," he said. "I came to Thunder Heights four or five years after your mother's death, so I never met her. It was always Pompton who had the job of keeping track of her, and later of you. But she must have been a bit frivolous and reckless—your mother."

Once more she sensed disapproval in his tone, and resentment prickled through her.

"I remember her as being gay and happy," she said with dignity.

Ross Granger looked up at the house on the mountain. "Frivolity seems out of place at Thunder Heights. Its gay times are long past, I'd say. You're likely to be frowned upon if you so much as laugh out loud these days. For my taste, I prefer this second house coming up here below the Judd land. That's Blue Beeches, and I can assure you its architecture is more typically Hudson River than Orrin Judd's house."

Blue Beeches, though further upriver, was below the Judd heights and closer to the water. It shone in bright yellow contrast to its more somber neighbor above. Its green shutters looked freshly painted and it stood upon the bank with the foursquare solidity of brick, as if it knew its own sound position as a family house well accepted by the community. Here there were signs of life. A woman sat rocking on the broad veranda, while three children of varying ages ran down to a small landing at the water's edge, waving eagerly as the boat went past. Ross raised an arm and returned their salute, and the children shouted and waved all the harder.

Apparently Ross Granger had friends here, among the children at least. She was puzzling over further questions to ask him, when he drew her hands from the wet rail and turned them over to reveal the gloves soaked and stained.

"Better go change your gloves before we dock. That's Westcliff coming up ahead of us."

It was exasperating to be given directions, as she might have directed a child in her charge. Perhaps he regarded her in that light—as a foolish girl who soiled her gloves and had to be looked after, however reluctantly, because he worked for her grandfather. Her indignation with him increased as she hurried below to put on a fresh pair of gloves from her suitcase. When she carried the bag up on deck, Ross Granger was there ahead of her, his own large suitcase at his feet. The dock was clearly visible now, with the clustered houses and white steepled church of Westcliff behind. On the small dock townspeople had gathered to watch the boat come in. Her companion looked down at them with interest.

"I see you're to be met," he said. "There's your cousin, Booth Hendricks, looking for you."

"Cousin?" she repeated. "Oh, you mean the one Mr. Pompton said was adopted as a child by Aunt Hortense?"

"Yes—he has kept his own name in spite of adoption. He's the tall fellow down there in the gray derby."

Camilla studied the figure of the man Ross Granger indicated. He was lean and dark, with a thin, melancholy face. Even at this distance she could see that he was handsome. He looked rather like an actor her father had once taken her to see play Hamlet at the Garrick Theater in New York. The knot of his cravat, the loop of gold watch chain across his well-cut vest, the gray derby on his head, all were fashionable to a surprising degree. Booth Hendricks would have looked at home on Fifth Avenue in New York. He seemed out of place in Westcliff. Perhaps, like her, he knew himself as an outsider. She felt sympathy quicken for this cousin by adoption, and she went down the gangplank eagerly to meet him.

III

BOOTH HENDRICKS CAME FORWARD TO GREET HER. HE HAD only a careless nod for Ross, but he held out his hand to Camilla and flashed her a quick smile in which a certain astonishment was evident.

"Cousin Camilla!" he said, his dark face glowing with an unexpected warmth. Then he turned coolly to the other man. "So you're back? We thought you might not make it in time. Can we give you a ride out to the house?"

Ross Granger shook his head. "Thanks, no," he said, his tone equally cool. Clearly there was no liking between these two. "I've business in the village first. I'll walk out as usual." He touched his cap casually to Camilla and walked away, to lose himself in the crowd.

Booth stared after him for a moment. "Did Pompton arrange for you to come upriver with Granger?" he asked.

"No," Camilla shook her head. "I met him by chance on the boat. He didn't know Grandfather was ill."

Her cousin seemed to shrug the other man aside. "No matter. The pleasant surprise of your coming is the important thing. Though I may as well warn you that you're going to be something of a shock to the family. We had no preparation before Pompton's wire. My mother says it's history repeating itself. I suppose you know how much you look like your mother?"

The flattery of frank admiration in his eyes was pleasantly soothing after Ross Granger's prickly remarks and critical attitude.

"I'm glad I look like her," she told him warmly.

Booth hailed a rig waiting on the narrow dirt road. The driver flicked a hand to his cap and drew up before them. Booth handed her suitcase up and helped Camilla into the carriage, then climbed in beside her. The driver flapped the reins, and they started off along the main street of the village.

"It's one of our little economies at Thunder Heights to keep no horses." Booth spoke lightly, but there was a sting in his voice. "Westcliff has little choice to offer in the way of hired rigs. I'm afraid you'll find us backward in a good many ways. Hardly like the gay city you've come from."

"I didn't lead a very gay life there," she confessed. "And I'm looking forward to seeing my mother's home. How is Grandfather's health?"

Booth Hendricks shrugged. "My presence at his bedside hasn't been requested. I gather he survives. Amazingly, considering his years. You should be good for him."

"I hope so," Camilla said. She went on a little timidly, longing to put something of her happiness into words. "Two days ago I never dreamed I would be coming here. I've grown up feeling as though I had no real family. But now I can hardly wait to meet my grandfather and my aunts. And to see my mother's home. I want to know everything about her. I want to ask a thousand questions and—"

The man beside her put one gloved hand upon her own, stemming her outburst. "I know how you must feel. But perhaps a word of warning at this point is a good idea. Thunder Heights isn't a particularly happy house. It's a house in which it is better not to ask too many questions. Perhaps that's one reason we are all a little disturbed by your coming. My mother and Aunt Letty won't want old sorrows brought to the surface and made acute again. They've suffered enough. Will you take my advice, Cousin, and move softly?

Don't ask too many questions—at least not in the beginning."

She felt a little dashed, but she could only nod agreement. Once more uneasiness fell upon her as the carriage moved on, and she was silent, watching the road they followed.

A bank sloped toward the river on their left, with wooded hills rising above on their right. Ahead the blunt, rocky top of Thunder Mountain thrust into the sky, but the house on its slope was well hidden by the brown forest that grew all about. Spring seemed far away this chilly April day, with leaf buds still close-furled nubs along dry branches.

The road curved inland around the property of Blue Beeches, and Camilla caught a glimpse of its mansard roof among the trees below. They were climbing now, the horse moving at a walk, the harness creaking with the uphill pull. A thick, untrimmed privet hedge came into view, the leafless broom of its twigs interwoven and untamed until it had grown to a monstrous height, shielding the property behind it from the road. Rain had begun to fall again.

"We're passing the house now, though you can't see it," Booth informed her. "The driveway approaches from the southern exposure."

In a few moments their carriage pulled up before an entrance in the hedge to what had been a wide driveway. The driver got down to open a once handsome iron gate, badly in need of fresh black paint. Stone gateposts rose on either side, and on each crouched a mournful stone lion. One lion had lost the tip of its tail, the other both its ears. Just inside the gate was a large coach house, deserted now, with empty stables below.

The driveway was overrun along the sides with encroaching weeds. All about, the forest crowded in, darkly bare and forbidding, its branches rattling as rain slanted through them. The approach seemed increasingly dismal, and Camilla felt the last of her eagerness melt bleakly away.

"Good luck that we're nearly there," Booth said. "I've no taste for being soaked in a leaky carriage."

The house was upon them now, looming out of the rainy dusk, huge and crouching and gray. The driver pulled up the horse, and Booth sprang down upon the carriage block and held out his hands to Camilla.

"Welcome home," he said dryly, and gestured toward the house behind him. "You'll find it carpenter's gothic at its most fantastic. Orrin had the money to build with brick, but since his beginnings were in lumber, he wanted to show what could be done with wood."

Camilla left the carriage and waited at the foot of the steps, looking up at the house, while Booth paid the driver and took down her suitcase. The structure stood at right angles to the river, with its back to the north, and a single-story wing had been attached on the land side.

Light shone in upstairs windows and through an arched fanlight above the heavy door of glass and wrought iron. But no one came eagerly to greet her, and as the clopping echo of the horse's hoofs disappeared among the trees, she was aware of a vast silence that seemed to engulf river and house and mountain. Accustomed as she was to city noises, the stillness seemed oppressive and a little eerie. She was glad when Booth led her up the steps to the front door. There he took out an enormous key, smiling at its size as he held it out for her to see.

"Always we have to be picturesque here, rather than comfortable. Grandfather Orrin sent clear to New Orleans for this door and it's heavy enough for two to pull."

A grating of metal shattered the silence, and he pushed the heavy door open so that she could walk into an antehall that was much as Camilla had imagined it. The room was large and square, with a light wood floor set in fine parquetry and an ornate plaster ceiling molded in rosettes. Except for a small rug or two, it was completely bare of furnishings, with a door opening on either side, and a wide arch straight ahead. But it was the room's curious lighting fixtures that Camilla noted with recognition. From the walls on either side, and from either side of the arched doorway ahead, marble hands protruded, each grasping a torch whose flame was a burning candle behind a glass shield.

"I see you're to be given a rousing welcome," Booth said to the silence. "Ah well, come along—I've warned you."

The arch of the doorway ahead was marble, and the smaller enclosure beyond contained the octagon staircase, with its panels of intricately carved teakwood. From a tall window behind the stairs, and from some unseen source of illumination above, light fell upon the steps. As Camilla followed Booth, a girl in a maid's uniform came running down, to bob a curtsy to them when she reached the bottom.

"This is Miss Camilla, Grace," Booth said to her. "Will you show her upstairs to her room, please."

Grace bobbed another curtsy. "If you please, mum," she said, gesturing toward the stairs.

Booth gave the girl Camilla's suitcase. "I'll see you at dinner, Cousin Camilla," he said.

She felt a sudden reluctance to leave his company and go off into the unknown reaches of the house. The lack of any welcome from her aunts had quenched her eagerness completely. Booth, at least, had been friendly. But he did not see her perturbation, and when he turned away to a door opening off the antehall, there was nothing to do but follow Grace.

Stairwell and halls were cold and drafty, adding to her feeling of chill. At the second floor Grace waited for her, and as Camilla climbed the stairs she saw that the light from above came from an oil lamp in a carved cinnabar bowl, hung beneath a wooden canopy from the ceiling of the stairwell. The octagon shaft of the stairs was set in the heart of the house, and two halls rayed out from it on each side at the second and third levels. On the second floor Grace led the way toward the river wing of the house.

"Mr. Judd has given orders you're to have Miss Althea's old room," Grace told her in an oddly furtive whisper. Then, apparently regarding Camilla more as a fellow conspirator than superior, she went on. "Miss Hortense don't like that much, but she don't dare say no, when the old—when Mr. Judd, that is, sets his mind on something. It's a real pretty room, mum. Hasn't been opened for years, so we had to rush to get it ready for you today."

She turned a pink-tinted cloisonné doorknob near the end of the hall and opened the door upon a room alive with firelight, gracious and inviting in the cold, rainy dusk. Grace set the suitcase down and ran across the room to brush a wrinkle from the dull gold bedspread, to flick imaginary dust from a two-tiered rosewood dressing table. Then she nodded toward a water pitcher and basin set on a marble-topped stand.

"The water's still hot, mum. I brought it up myself just before you came. Thought you'd want a good wash, after your trip. Dinner is at seven-thirty. Prompt, mum. Miss Hortense don't like to be kept waiting. She gets nervous." The girl watched her, as if waiting for some response to her sly hints.

Camilla paid no attention, longing for her to go. This was her mother's room and she wanted to know it in every detail. But not while a stranger watched her.

"When am I to see my grandfather?" she asked.

Grace shook her head. "Nobody's told me that, mum.

Though I know Mr. Judd has been asking for you. The nurse said so."

The girl gave another uneasy bob of knee and head and went out of the room.

Once she was gone, Camilla could turn slowly and look about the lovely room that once belonged to Althea Judd. The pink marble mantelpiece above the lively fire was carved with a rose leaf design, and a small French clock of gilt and enamel ticked away upon it. The carpet was soft-piled and of a paler gold than the bedspread, the wallpaper light gray with a gold fleur-de-lis pattern. There was a small gray and gilt French desk with a little chair to match—a desk from which her mother, who had loved parties, must have sent out many an invitation. A pink upholstered chaise longue near a French door invited one to comfortable lounging. Heavy gold brocade draperies, faded and a little shabby, had been drawn across the room's tall windows and French doors. The ceiling was enormously high, promising the cool passage of air on summer days, and a handsome plaster medallion marked the center, from which hung a gay little French chandelier, adrip with crystal.

This was her mother's room. She wanted to feel it, to believe in it, to reach across the years to her mother through it. But the room, though charming, remained remote. It was not yet ready to accept her, to speak to her.

She went to one of the doors and opened it upon a small balcony that fronted the river. It was raining harder now, and though wind swept a spatter of drops in upon her, she stood for a moment trying to make out the river, far below this high level on which the house stood. Rain and the failing light obscured her vision, however, and she closed the door, returning quickly to the warmth of the fire. Tomorrow perhaps it would be clear and she could see the view of the Hudson this house must command.

The water was steaming hot in the pitcher, as Grace had promised, with a towel laid across the top to contain the warmth. Camilla gave herself up to the refreshing comfort of bathing. The pale green cake of soap in the rose leaf dish had a delicate scent, and she wondered at such luxury in this remote place. But then, with wealth, anything could be ordered from New York. Or from Paris, or London, for that matter. What a strange economy to keep no carriage, no horses.

When she had put on a clean shirtwaist and changed to a

fresh, though somewhat wrinkled, blue skirt, she lay down on the chaise longue to await the summons of her grandfather.

As she relaxed, savoring the pulsing heat of the fire, she thought of the little she knew about her Aunt Hortense. Hortense was the elder of the three sisters, with Letty the middle one. From her mother, Camilla had received the picture of a woman with an unbridled temper and an enormous vanity. There had been little love lost between older and younger sister. Once, when Camilla had been no more than seven, her mother had said casually that Hortense had suffered from a lifelong unrequited love affair with herself. The words had stayed with her, though they had little meaning then, and she wondered about them now.

A light tap roused her from her musings, and she went quickly to open the door. At a glance she knew that the slight gray figure in the doorway could not be Hortense.

"It's—Aunt Letty, isn't it?" Camilla said.

The woman's face, pale and fine-skinned as eggshell china, seemed to crumple into tiny lines, as if she were about to burst into tears. In her hands she held a small lacquered tray with a teapot and cups upon it. Too moved to speak, she held the tray out wordlessly.

Gently Camilla drew her into the room and closed the door.

IV

MISS LETITIA JUDD WAS SOMEWHAT LESS THAN FIFTY. SHE was of medium height, but she managed to seem tiny because of her small bones and general air of frailty. She wore her gray hair bound about her head in a coronet of braids that gave her a certain dignity and presence, even when she was on the verge of tears. Her long-sleeved dress was of a light gray material that had a tendency to float when she moved, and she wore a coral brooch at the high, boned ruching of the neck. She looked immaculately neat in every detail.

As she entered the room, a small gray tabby cat came with her, padding lightly across the carpet with an air of interest in unfamiliar territory.

"This is my friend, Mignonette," Letty said, and smiled tremulously at Camilla. "See—I've brought you some hot peppermint tea. It's just the thing for heartening one after a long trip."

She set the tray upon a marble-topped table near the fire, and not until she reached out to put it down, did Camilla note that her right arm was twisted and crooked. Her full sleeve, tight at the wrist and edged with lace, hid the deformity to some extent, and it was hardly noticeable except in the fact that she could not straighten the arm.

"My little sister Althea's daughter," she murmured, and turned to look at Camilla. While all else about Letty Judd was pale and softly gray, her eyes were a dark brown, deep and surprisingly intense, with lashes as long and dark as Camilla's own. "You are *so* much like her. Even that black peak of hair on your forehead. And the light way you move. But there, I mustn't welcome you by crying."

She seated herself in the silk-cushioned rocking chair Camilla drew to the fire, her hands clasped in her lap so that the bend of the crooked arm seemed natural. The glow of the fire gave color to her pale, fine skin, but when she held out her left hand to the warming blaze, Camilla saw that her hands were strangely unlike the rest of her. Though small-boned, they were far from fragile. There was a strong, muscular look about them, and the skin was tanned and freckled, as if they had weathered the sun of past years and gone unprotected.

Beneath Letty's tender gaze, the lack of welcome which had been so evident to Camilla in the beginning seemed to lessen in importance. For the first time the fire began to warm away her chill, and the fragrant odor of the tea was tangy and cheering. She sat opposite her aunt while Letty poured a cupful, her crooked arm seeming to hamper her little. The gray tabby padded back across the room and looked up expectantly.

"Not now, dear," Letty said to the cat. "We're only going to stay a minute." She smiled at Camilla, as if apologizing for the bad manners of a child. "Mignonette loves all my herb teas. She joins me by having a saucerful every afternoon." She held out a cup and saucer to Camilla. "There you are—and do flavor it with a bit of clover honey. You'll find it gives you strength and courage."

Camilla spooned a little golden honey into the tea and sipped it gratefully. "How is my grandfather? When will I see him?"

At her words Letty's withheld tears brimmed over, and she

24

drew a lacy bit of handkerchief from her sleeve, leaving a trace of lavender scent in the air about her.

"He is very weak today. Hortense won't let me go near him, for fear I'll upset him." Her dark eyes lifted suddenly to hold Camilla's own with intense pleading.

"What is it, Aunt Letty?" Camilla asked. "If there's anything I can do—"

Letty shook her head. "No, no—nothing. That is, there's nothing you can do now." Her manner became faintly agitated, and her hands clasped and unclasped nervously in her lap. "You must believe that what happened wasn't my fault—you must believe that I didn't intend—"

She was upsetting herself to such an extent that Camilla dropped to a velvet ottoman beside her and took the small, weathered hands into hers, feeling the wiry strength of the fingers. It was natural to adopt a protective role with Aunt Letty. Camilla felt drawn to this frail, somehow proud little woman, and she let the strength of her own youth and returning courage flow into the clasp of her hands. Her aunt looked hopefully into her eyes.

"Perhaps you've come in time. I think Papa is sorry for a good many things. It's wonderful that he has sent for you. You belong here with your family, my dear."

Unexpectedly, tears stung Camilla's eyes. Such words made up a little for the lonely years behind her. Letty saw that she was moved and tried gently to reassure her.

"Booth is delighted with you. He came to tell me how pretty you are and how lucky we are that you've come. Booth is a dear boy. A bit moody perhaps, at times, but brilliant and talented. It will be good for him to have someone young in the house."

She would have gone on, but a peremptory knock sounded at the door and she sat back quickly, withdrawing her hands from Camilla's clasp.

"That's my sister Hortense," she whispered. "It's better not to keep her waiting. She has very little patience."

Camilla went quickly to the door. Next to her grandfather, she sensed that this was the most important meeting of her visit here. More than anyone else it was her difficult Aunt Hortense whom she must please, whom she must win, if she were to become a part of this family. Smiling and eager, she opened the door to the overwhelming presence of the woman who stood there.

Camilla was not sure how she had pictured Hortense in her mind, but certainly her imagination had produced nothing like this tall, handsome, red-haired woman in elaborate dinner dress. She might have been beautiful, had her expression been less petulant and sharp. Certainly her red hair, untarnished by the years, was spectacularly beautiful in its high piled rolls and waves held in place with combs jeweled in jade. Her emerald green dinner gown was perhaps less than the latest fashion, but she wore it like a duchess, as she did the diamonds in her ears. The cut of the gown displayed firm, unwithered flesh and her figure was full and fashionable. Whether her eyes were green or blue or gray, it was difficult to tell, but one had a feeling that there was little their darting gaze missed.

She noted her sister's presence without pleasure, and Letty rose as she came into the room.

"I'll leave you alone," Letty said, and once more Camilla was aware of a certain dignity about her fragile person.

"Thank you for coming, Aunt Letty," Camilla said warmly, and accompanied her to the door. The little cat went with them and darted into the hall. Camilla turned to face Hortense, bracing herself, the eager smile a little stiff on her lips.

Her aunt was moving about the room with an air of interest, as if she had not set foot in it for a long time.

"I hope it has been cleaned satisfactorily," she said. "We had so little warning of your coming. And we don't have the servants we used to have in the old days. There's always trouble getting this spoiled new generation to stay. I never could understand why Papa wanted this room left exactly as it was when Althea was alive. It's a better room than mine—I'd have liked it for myself."

Camilla, still waiting for some greeting, watched her aunt doubtfully, uncertain of how to meet this outburst. Indifferent to her niece's gaze, Hortense paused before the tray with its cups of cooling tea, the color of pale topaz. She sniffed the peppermint odor and wrinkled her nose.

"Don't let my sister dose you with her brews. She uses little sense in such matters and they don't agree with everyone." Then, having apparently satisfied her curiosity about the room, she turned her scrutiny upon Camilla and there was open antipathy in her eyes. "So you are Althea's girl? You'll be a shock to Papa, of course. But it's his own fault for sending for you behind our backs. It has, of course, been a shock to us to learn that you were coming."

Vainly Camilla tried to think of something to say, but any opportunity for amenities of greeting had passed.

"I—I hope you don't mind my coming," she said feebly. "Mr. Pompton—"

"Pompton's an old fool," Hortense said. "Papa did exactly the same thing that time years ago when he took a sudden notion that he was going to die and he had to see your mother at once. It was Althea who died, and he's been hale and hearty all the years since, until now. Let's hope history won't entirely repeat itself."

"About my mother—" Camilla began, seizing the opening.

"The less said about your mother, the better," Hortense told her, making a futile effort to tuck a lock of red hair into the trembling mass of puffs and pompadours. "When she married and left this house, your grandfather gave orders that her name was never to be mentioned to him again. Even after he remanded that order and invited her here, her death upset us all so badly that by mutual agreement we have avoided the subject of Althea King. Of course we speak her name when necessary—but we don't *discuss* her. You understand? The memories are too painful."

Reminding herself that she must please and placate this woman, Camilla suppressed a twinge of indignation. "Yes, of course, Aunt Hortense," she said mildly.

"Good. While you look like your mother, I can only hope that you lack her wild, reckless spirit. Whatever happened to her she brought upon herself. Remember that. Come along now and I'll take you to your grandfather. But don't stay long—his strength is fading."

She swished through the door ahead of Camilla, leaving her niece to trail behind.

She led the way toward the opposite wing of the house, circling the opening of the stairs. Before a door near the corridor's end she paused.

At her knock, a nurse in a blue striped uniform, with a puffy white cap on her head, looked out at them, nodded and led the way into a large, dim bedroom. Here the fire on the hearth had burned to embers and what light there was came from a lamp set on a table near the great, canopied bed. It was a handsome room, Camilla saw as she followed Hortense through the door, with fine mahogany furniture of vast, baronial proportions.

The old man in the bed lay propped against the stack of pillows, his hair and beard grizzled with gray, his eyes, sunken above a great beak of a nose, still vitally alive in his weathered face.

"Your granddaughter Camilla is here, Papa," Hortense

told him. "You mustn't talk to her for long, or you'll tire yourself."

"Get out," said the old man in a surprisingly strong voice.

"Now, now," the nurse said roguishly, "we mustn't excite ourselves. Miss Judd and I will step out in the hall and give you ten minutes with the young lady."

"You'll step out in the hall and stay there until I send for you," said Orrin Judd. "Get out, both of you, so I can have a look at the girl."

Hortense moved with a little toss of her head, and the nurse followed her. Camilla approached the bed and stood within the radius of lamplight. At her grandfather's right lay a huge open Bible on a mahogany stand. He reached out to rest one hand upon it, as if he asked for strength. Then he looked up into her face. For a few moments old man and young woman studied each other gravely.

"You're like your mother as I remember her," he said at last, and now there was a quaver of weakness in his voice. "You're my lovely Althea come back to me when I need her most."

"I'm glad I could come, Grandfather," Camilla said gently.

He sighed long and gustily, as if all the breath left to him had gone from his body. His eyes closed, and she watched him anxiously, wondering if she should call the nurse. But in a moment they opened again—the eyes of a fallen eagle who had not surrendered his freedom—and she felt their hunger searching her face.

"I should have got around to seeing Althea's girl before this. I've let so much go these last years. Too much. The house and the family with it. Bring over a chair and sit where I can look at you. I need to talk to you quickly, before it's too late."

The nearest chair was a massive piece, but she dragged it over to the bed and sat down on its velvet seat. He breathed heavily for a while before he spoke again.

"The vultures out there are waiting for me to die. But it doesn't matter if they hover, now that you're here. Between the two of us we'll fool them all, won't we girl? By the look of you, I know you can be trusted. Because you look like *her*—like my Althea. Sometimes I have the feeling that she's still around here—her spirit anyway—lively and gay, just as she used to be. Will you stay here, Camilla, and help me beat the vultures? We must change things all around, you and I."

"I'll stay if you want me to, Grandfather," she said softly.

He turned in the bed and reached to a table on the far

28

side, groping for something upon it. Camilla would have risen to help him, but he gestured her back.

"I've got it. This is the way we looked in the days before Althea ran off and married that—that schoolteacher." He seemed to have forgotten that the schoolteacher was Camilla's father.

She took the framed oblong of cardboard and held it to the light. Orrin Judd sat in a carved chair in the center of the picture, with his daughters about him. The print was yellowed by the years, but still clear. In those days he must have been a giant of a man, rugged and handsome and forceful. The youngest daughter, Althea, stood straight and lovely within the circle of her father's arm, smiling warmly at the camera. On his other side Hortense leaned against him, a hand upon his shoulder, as if she strove to draw his attention back to herself. Letty stood beside Althea, a thin, frail girl with a smile that was somehow sad. Her right arm hung at her side with no evidence of deformity.

"My three girls," Orrin said. "Their mother and I wanted too much for them. We planned so much. But she wasn't here long enough to see them grown and somehow—it all went wrong."

He was silent for a moment, and then sudden anger stirred in his voice.

"I should have forbidden the house to John King! What could *he* do for Althea—who might have had everything?"

Camilla could not let his words about her father pass. "She had everything she wanted most, Grandfather," she told him gently. "If you had really known my father, you might have loved him."

The old man stared at her unblinkingly for a moment, and she could not tell how deeply she might have angered him with her words. Then he said, "I like spirit, girl. At least you stand up to me honestly. You don't talk simpering nonsense."

He took the picture and laid it upon the open pages of the Bible, and now his gaze seemed suddenly a little vague, as if he had lost the focus of his thoughts.

"Perhaps I'd better let you rest now, Grandfather," Camilla murmured.

At once a look of alarm came into his eyes. "No, no! Don't leave me, girl. There's something I had to tell you. Something that happened—"

He had begun to gasp for breath, but when she would have left his side to call the nurse, he reached out and grasped her hand in a grip that was crushingly strong. Between rasping breaths he tried to force out the words he must speak to her.

"Trouble," he gasped. "Trouble in this house. You must watch for it, girl. There's something wrong afoot. When I'm well I'll get to the bottom of it. But for now—" he struggled hoarsely to speak, "watch—Letty," he managed and could say no more.

"You mustn't excite yourself, Grandfather," she whispered. "Rest now and we'll talk again tomorrow. Then you shall tell me whatever you want me to know."

His grip loosened, fell away. "Tired," he whispered weakly. "Althea's home is your home—you must help me save it. Don't let them—"

"Of course, Grandfather," she assured him hurriedly. "I'll stay for as long as you want me, and I'll help you in every way I can."

He seemed to hear her words and gain reassurance from them. Though he said no more, she sensed the rise of loving kinship between herself and this very old man. The blood line was strong and bright between them. They belonged to each other. She knew he read her look aright and was comforted, and she was assured that they would learn to know and value each other. But now he lay spent, and she went quietly away.

In the hall outside the nurse sat on a carved chest, resting her feet and dozing. Hortense had disappeared.

"You'd better go to him now," Camilla said.

The woman started up and hurried into the room, closing the door behind her.

Camilla followed the empty hall back to her room and sat quietly before the fire, feeling both torn and heartened. She had crossed the years so swiftly to stand at her grandfather's side, and in those few moments of interchange they had given each other their love and trust. Strange that it should be as simple as that. Yet it was a searing thing, too, because of all that troubled him, because of the regrets and sorrows that crowded upon him out of the past. She would do as she had promised. She would stay on in this house as long as he needed her. The antipathy she had seen in the eyes of Hortense Judd troubled her, and she had a sense of failure there. But the most important thing was to help this despairing old man who was her grandfather.

What he had meant in trying to warn her of some sort of trouble, she did not know. It was clear that he was filled with distrust of everyone under this roof, though such a feeling might well be no more than the product of his weakness. She

30

must leap to no conclusions until she had talked to him further, until she knew the family better.

The French clock on the mantel marked the time as nearly seven thirty. She rose to look at herself in the dressing table mirror and smoothed back her dark hair so that the peak came into clear evidence on her forehead. Once her mother's face had been reflected in the depths of this very mirror, and it would be easy to imagine her there again, smiling out of the shadows over her daughter's shoulder. Perhaps there was a fulfilling of destiny in the coming of Camilla King to the house where her mother had grown up, and whose halls must still remember the echo of her footsteps, the sound of her voice.

A thought came to her, and she went to her suitcase and took from it a green velvet jewel case. She had nothing in which to dress for dinner, as Hortense chose to dress, but at least she might wear a bracelet of her mother's. Althea had kept only a few favorite pieces of the jewelry Orrin had given her, and now her daughter had them for her own.

The bangle was made up of gold medallions alternating with carved peach stones. Camilla fastened it about her wrist, feeling that it dressed her up for the occasion and that, wearing it, she would take something of her mother with her downstairs. There was a yearning in her to start anew with this family to which she now belonged. She wanted to free herself of her own early uneasiness and forget the unhappy warnings of an old man who was sick. This time she knew better what to expect, so she would not be surprised, or taken aback. She must show her aunts, her Cousin Booth, how ready she was to like them, how eager for their liking in return.

With something of her first feeling of hope recovered she opened her door just as a deep-voiced Chinese gong sounded from the depths of the house. No one appeared, so perhaps the others were already downstairs. She went down the octagon staircase alone. Not knowing where the dining room lay, she opened a door toward the land side of the house and found that she had guessed right.

The others were not there and Camilla hesitated, looking around the long, wide room. Dark wainscoting ran halfway up the walls and above it pictured wallpaper presented a country scene in raspberry against cream, its busy pattern repeated to a demanding degree. The darker red carpet was figured in a design of yellow roses, faded now, and worn threadbare about the long mahogany table. The sideboard and china closet were of vast proportions to fit the size of the room. The dining table had been set with linen and spode china, with candles alight in the branched silver candelabra at each end.

Booth Hendricks came in first, wearing informal dinner dress. The lapels of his jacket were of satin, his shirt front stiff, with pearl buttons studding it. At sight of Camilla his eyes brightened.

"What a pleasure to see someone young and pretty in this house. Are you rested from your trip, Cousin?"

"I wasn't tired, really," she told him. "I've been too excited to be tired. And now that I've seen Grandfather, I'm not so worried as I was. I didn't know how he would receive me."

"And how did he receive you?" Booth asked dryly.

"With affection," she said, and explained no further.

Letty came in, still wearing the floating gray dress that became her so well, and her eyes turned to Camilla questioningly. Camilla smiled and nodded in reassurance. When Hortense entered the room, Camilla gave her the same warm smile, but her aunt paid little heed to her. All her attention was for Booth. She took his arm and let him lead her to her place at one end of the long table.

"Have you had a good day, dear?" she asked him. "Have you been able to work?"

He seated her with a gallant flourish in which there was a hint of mockery. "What do you mean by a good day, Mother? Can any of us remember such a thing in this house?"

Hortense made the small *moue* of a flirtatious girl. "At least we've been rid of Mr. Granger's dour company for a few days."

Camilla had hardly given Ross Granger a thought since she had entered the house, but now she wondered about his place in this group.

Booth had come to seat Camilla at Hortense's left, while Letty slipped quietly into her own place across the table.

"Granger is back, you know," Booth told his mother. "He came up on the same boat with Cousin Camilla. So now I suppose there'll be the devil to pay." He smiled wryly and shrugged as he sat down at Hortense's right.

Hortense glanced quickly at Camilla. But if she meant to ask a question, she changed her mind. "In any event, since the gong has rung and he's not here, we shan't wait for him."

Tonight, in the candlelight, her hair seemed a softer red, with tints of gold brightening it. But no mellowness of light could change the unhappy drooping of her mouth, or change the hard restlessness in her eyes.

Grace, young and inexpert, brought in a silver soup tureen and placed it before Hortense. Then she scuttled back to the kitchen as though she could hardly wait to escape.

"Grace is new," Hortense informed Camilla. An emerald gleamed on her hand as she began serving soup with a silver ladle. "Our maids are always new. The village girls these days have notions above themselves, and they don't last long with me. One would expect them to be grateful for an opportunity to work for a family of our distinction. But only Toby and Matilda have stayed with us from the old days, and they are both getting old."

The silver, Camilla noted, was monogrammed with an ornate "J," and monograms had been embroidered on each linen napkin. The entire service, indeed the very room, spoke of great days of luxury long past, and the gradual decay of fine possessions. She felt a little saddened by the deterioration that she saw everywhere in the house. How shining and rich everything must have been in the heyday of the past—and could be again, if only someone cared. It was not lack of wealth, but a disintegration of spirit that lay behind the neglect.

"Our mother always preferred dinner at night, instead of at noon," Hortense went on, picking up her soup spoon. "And she liked to dress for dinner, so I try to continue the custom. Such things are proper for a family in our position. Of course, since you have only a suitcase, Camilla, I don't expect you to comply while you're here."

Her aunt's delusion that the Judds were superior in position and worth to everyone else seemed rather pitiful under the circumstances, but Camilla merely thanked her for her consideration and did not mention that her trunk would be arriving soon. It seemed unlikely that Aunt Hortense would be pleased by such news.

The cream of potato soup was good, and she found that she had a healthy appetite. But as she ate she noted that Letty was watching the door and that she only toyed with her spoon.

"How long may we expect to enjoy your company, Cousin Camilla?" Booth asked, and again she sensed the light touch of mockery in his words. Perhaps directed toward those about him, or perhaps himself? She could not tell.

"That depends on Grandfather," Camilla said. "I promised that I would stay as long as he wanted me here."

Letty gasped softly, and Camilla saw that she was staring at the dining room door. Ross Granger stood in the doorway, his expression unsmiling, an angry light in his gray eyes. Hortense and Booth exchanged a quick, understanding glance.

"I see you're back—and late for dinner," Hortense said plaintively. "You know how Papa abhors any lack of punctuality."

Ross did not answer her. His bright chestnut hair shone in the candlelight as he took his place at the table beside Letty, and he thrust a lock of it back with an impatient gesture. Camilla waited for some greeting from him, some sign of recognition, but he gave her none. He seemed lost in a dark anger that set him apart from the others at the table. When Hortense filled his soup plate and passed it to him, he picked up his spoon and began to eat without paying attention to the others.

Letty coughed in gentle embarrassment, with her handkerchief to her lips, and turned to Camilla, seeking to break the uncomfortable silence.

"I've noticed your bracelet, my dear," she said. "How well I remember it."

Camilla held up her wrist, fingering the peach stone medallions. "It was my mother's. I'm very fond of it."

Hortense stared at the bracelet. "I don't know why Althea chose anything so valueless to take with her. She left behind a diamond bracelet that might have kept you all in food and shelter for a long while."

"We were never in want, Aunt Hortense," Camilla said quietly.

"How have you been keeping yourself since your father's death?" Hortense asked.

"I've been working as a governess for the last four years," Camilla told her. "There are always positions of that sort in New York."

"Do you enjoy the work?" Letty asked with interest.

"How could she?" Hortense broke in at once. "A governess is hardly more than a genteel domestic servant waiting on other people's children."

Camilla had come to the table still hoping to win Hortense, to placate her, and, if possible, reach some sort of friendly footing with the family. But the scornful words made her stiffen. Beside her, Booth watched with an amused interest that irked her further. Ross merely stared at his plate, as if he cared nothing about what went on around him.

"That isn't quite true, Aunt Hortense," Camilla said, her tone carefully restrained. "The role of a governess is an important one in any household. If the parents realize it, she can do a great deal for their children. I've always regarded the work as interesting and worthwhile."

It had given her independence too, she realized, enabling her to remain in control of her own life. That was something she would not like to lose.

Ross had been listening after all, and now he surprised her. "Good for you, Miss King!" he said. "Don't let them patronize you. Stand up for yourself."

Camilla said nothing. She was not altogether sure she wanted him on her side if it meant further alienation from the family.

"At least it's a good thing you have some sort of work to return to," Hortense said. "I suppose it's respectable enough work for an impoverished gentlewoman—which seems to be the condition brought upon you by your parents."

Booth flashed his mother a quick, ironic smile. "Oh, come now! Surely Grandfather Orrin will leave her a bit of a legacy? Perhaps she has that small hope to look forward to." He nodded kindly at Camilla. "There is still time for him to include you in his will."

Ross turned grimly to Hortense. "Yes, there's always time to change a will. I suppose that's why you wanted me out of the way for the last few days? So you could keep me from him?"

Hortense turned a furious red, but Booth only smiled. "Do you think, Granger, that we don't know how you've been trying to influence Grandfather lately? Why wouldn't we prefer your absence to your presence when we know how much you disturb him?"

For an instant Camilla thought Ross might rise angrily and leave the table, but he controlled himself and stayed in his place.

Grace cleared away the soup plates and returned with the meat course, while Letty chatted nervously about how much good today's rain had done her garden. No one paid much attention to her, and no one else spoke, but Camilla was aware of a mounting tension beneath the surface affecting everyone at the table. Hortense and Ross had behaved inexcusably, she felt. And Letty was too silent. Only Booth had tried to consider her own comfort and welfare. In any case, she shrank from this discussion of wills while Grandfather might lie dying. She remembered uneasily his warning about "vultures."

When Grace left the room again and Hortense was serving the roast beef, Ross was the first to speak.

"I'd like to know just why you had me sent off on this wild goose chase to New York," he said. "You wanted more than to get me away. What have you been up to in my absence?"

"You are insufferable!" Hortense cried.

Letty put her hands to her temples, rocking her head back and forth as if it hurt her. "Oh, please, please! Let's have peace during dinnertime at least. What is Camilla going to think of us with such talk as this?"

"One might wonder," her sister said tartly, "what she will think of *you*. I am innocent enough."

Letty looked as if she might burst into tears, and Booth turned to her gently and began to speak of the gardens of Thunder Heights in a quiet, relaxed manner. Hortense watched her son, and Ross listened without comment, his eyes upon Camilla.

It was a relief when the floating island was served for dessert and the meal finally ended. By that time, Camilla felt that her nerves were strung on fine wires unbearably tight. The antagonism in the room was almost tangible, and though she was bewildered by it, she was drawn to a high tension herself.

When they rose from the table, she would have liked to excuse herself and go upstairs to the seclusion of her mother's room, but Booth walked beside her, guiding her across the hall to the parlor, and there was no easy way to escape.

V

APPARENTLY IT WAS THE CUSTOM FOR THE FAMILY TO HAVE coffee in the parlor after dinner. Several lamps had been lighted in the great room that ran along the river side of the house, and a wood fire crackled in the grate. The room was crowded with an overabundance of treasures from the Orient. Much of the furniture was of carved black ebony, with cushions of black satin embroidered in gold thread. There were Chinese screens and rich Oriental rugs, and on every table and shelf and whatnot stand were objects of jade or coral or brass, of Satsuma and cloisonné. The ceiling was high and the room's huge windows were oversized, requiring vast quantities of material for the acres of curtains and draperies.

"Cheerful little museum, isn't it?" Booth said to Camilla. "Can you imagine what this stuff might bring at an auction?"

Again he puzzled her. She had a feeling that his seemingly cynical manner, the callous gloss he wore, hid some depth he was not willing to display to the casual observer. He could be lightly mocking, with a certain insouciant charm, yet she sensed a passion in him that might be his real core. What drove this man, what motivated him, she could not tell, but he held her interest.

Young Grace skated in, sliding once or twice on the rugs, and managed to place the coffee service safely on a teakwood table by the fire, before darting away with the air of an escaping doe. Flames danced in miniature across the gleaming silver surface of the coffee pot, as the family drew about in stiff, uncomfortable chairs. Only Ross had absented himself, not joining the family. Mignonette, the cat, awaited them by the fire, moving over just enough to be within reach of Letty's stroking toe.

"The evening ritual," Booth said as he brought Camilla her cup and offered cream and sugar. "For an hour or so every night we sit here enjoying one another's brilliant company and sipping coffee in cups that are exquisite, but too small. Fortunately there are more comfortable rooms in the house where we can withdraw later. So endure, Cousin Camilla, the time will pass."

Hortense laughed uncomfortably, as if she were not always sure how to take this man who was her adopted son. "Booth loves to tease," she said. "You mustn't believe his little jokes. Papa always thought it a good idea to draw the family together here after dinner. He liked this hour when we were girls and we've always kept it up."

Camilla thought of the old man lying helpless upstairs and remembered his sad question, "Where did I go wrong?"

Hortense ran on, as if silence was something never to be suffered for too long. Waving a beringed hand, she pointed out various objects around the room, explaining their significance and relating incidents connected with their purchase when she had gone abroad with her mother and father as a child.

"Did you go with them too on these trips, Aunt Letty?" Camilla asked, when Hortense paused for breath.

About Letty there was still a vague air of listening. Occasionally she cast a furtive glance toward the doorway, as though she did not want to be caught in her watching. She jumped a little when Camilla spoke to her, and stirred Mignonette with her toe. The little cat moved closer to Letty's chair and began a monotone of purring.

"I went to England and Scotland once after I was grown up," Letty said and reached for a basket of crocheting at her side, nervously searching it for her crochet hook. "But I was never strong enough for very much traveling."

"I was always the one with endurance," Hortense said in satisfaction, and went on to describe hardships met aboard that Letty could never have borne.

As they talked, Camilla glanced at Booth, who had taken a chair well back in the shadows. He sat with his long, elegant legs crossed and one slender hand upon the chair arm. Though his face was lost in obscurity, she knew that he too listened to something that was not taking place in this room. When a footstep sounded on the stairs, he leaned forward, his eyes upon the door, and Aunt Letty jumped uneasily, startling the cat.

Ross Granger came into the room with a strong, vigorous step, and once more anger was bright in his eyes as he viewed the group about the fire with clear hostility.

"Mr. Judd was too weak to talk to me," he said. "The nurse tried to shut me out. She told me she had been given orders to keep me out of the room. By whom, may I ask?"

Hortense answered quickly. "Dr. Wheeler said Papa was not to be disturbed or worried in any way. We all know that you irritate him lately. It was I who said you were not to see him until he feels better."

"An order you knew I would disregard. I'm not the one who disturbs him—"

Booth stood up with his usual easy grace and leaned an arm along the mantel, his features somberly handsome in the flickering light.

"Look here, Granger, we know you detest us, and we've stood a good many of your insinuations because of your former usefulness to Grandfather Orrin. But you must admit that you upset him badly the last time you saw him. From what the nurse has told us, we gather that it's you who wants his will changed for some purpose of your own."

Camilla could only admire the control Booth displayed as he spoke so calmly to Ross. The latter was clearly far closer to losing his temper.

Letty's crochet hook moved in and out of her work with

quick silver flashes, and she had stopped watching the door. When she spoke in a small breathless voice, the others looked at her in surprise, as if they had forgotten her presence.

"How can you blame Ross for trying to persuade Papa to change his will? Haven't we all been concerned about the same thing?" she asked.

There was an instant's dismayed silence, and then Ross pounced on her words. "So you *did* want me out of the way, just as I thought. And what was this change to be?"

Hortense said, "It's none of your business. It doesn't concern you, Ross. Indeed, none of the affairs of this family now concern you."

"They concern me," Letty said, and again everyone stared at her. "I'm in perfect agreement with my sister," she hurried on. "What would I do with half my father's fortune, even if it were left to me, as the will reads now? My needs are modest, Ross. I should hate the responsibility of all that money."

"So you'd let your sister sign your birthright away?" Ross said impatiently. "At least I can prevent *that* move—when he's well enough to listen to me. Even if he won't follow a plan I think wiser."

"Even if he won't cut you in as repayment for your years of—ah—faithful service?" Booth asked quietly.

Listening, Camilla shrank again from the scene before her, with its talk of wills while Orrin Judd lay upstairs desperately ill. It seemed callous to a degree that she could not understand. Even Ross, who was an outsider, had been associated with Grandfather Orrin for years and must surely have some liking for the old man. It seemed heartless of all of them to be quarreling over Orrin Judd's wealth. While he still lived, all their thoughts should be for his health and well-being.

Once more Ross managed a semblance of control and addressed himself to Hortense. "I'd like to know exactly what brought on this heart attack. When I left for New York, Mr. Judd was no better or worse than he had been for months. What happened after I left for New York?"

The room was so still that a bit of charred wood falling in the grate made an explosive sound and Mignonette's purr was like a kettle boiling. Booth shrugged and sat down, dropping again into the shadows. Letty's crochet needle paused in mid-air. Hortense clasped her fingers tightly together in her lap. Tension crackled through the room.

"Well?" Ross said. "I gather that something unpleasant did happen. I'd like to know what it was."

Hortense was the first to find her voice. "Why don't you ask Letty? Booth was in the village at the time, and I was in the cellar. Letty was with him. I'm sure we'd all like to know a little more than she has told us about what really happened."

Letty's work dropped into the basket and she covered her face with her hands. "It's true, Ross—I was there. But I didn't intend—I never meant—"

"What was it you said to him, dear?" Hortense pressed her. "Or is it something that you did?"

Letty turned her head a little wildly from side to side. "No—you mustn't ask me. I can't talk about it. You must believe that I meant well."

Ross crossed the room and put a hand forcefully on her shoulder. "Try to tell us, Miss Letty. It may be important for us to know."

But Letty had begun to weep into her lavender-scented handkerchief, and it was Booth who came to her aid.

"Let her alone, Granger. Can't you see how upset she is over her father's illness? What does it matter whether we know exactly what happened? There's no undoing it. And you can't believe Letty meant him any harm. My mother likes to talk. Come along, Aunt Letty—I'll take you up to your room."

Camilla saw affection in the look Letty turned upon her sister's adopted son. His arm about her shoulders supported her, and his every movement was kind as he led her out of the room.

Ross watched them go and then glanced idly at Camilla. "An interesting family you've acquired, isn't it?" he said and went out of the room, leaving Hortense and Camilla there by the fire.

At once Hortense began to rub her brow with her fingers. "Headache," she murmured. "You had no business coming here, of course, and now that you're here ... Most regrettable, I'm sure. If you'll excuse me?" Her words sounded befuddled, as though her thoughts followed a separate road from her tongue.

When she had left the parlor, only Camilla and Mignonette remained. The small gray tabby regarded her distantly and then stretched and yawned mightily, before settling down for another nap while the fire lasted. Camilla sat on for a little while before the orange-red embers, thinking about the tense, uncomfortable scene she had just witnessed, and about the undercurrents of conflict and antagonism that played back

40

and forth between the walls of Thunder Heights. Why had Grandfather said to watch Letty, and what had Letty done that had helped to bring on his illness?

Suddenly she felt overcome by weariness. The long day with its emotional upheavals had left her more drained than she realized. She was eager for her mother's room with its wide, inviting bed and air of peace long undisturbed.

Before she went to her room she paused at her grandfather's door, to see if she might bid him good night, but the nurse said he was sleeping quietly and mustn't be disturbed. She hurried down the long hall to her room, only to find the hearth cold, its comforting warmth dispelled, so that she had to undress shivering, and get quickly into bed.

She fully expected to lie awake for a long while, thinking over the events of the day, wondering about this strange household that lived together in uneasy aversion. But the bed was warm and soft with comforters and her body was utterly weary. She drowsed into sleep before disturbing thoughts could awaken her.

It was the sound of music that roused her sometime in the hours after midnight. Camilla sat up in bed, bundling a comforter around her as she listened. She could not be sure of the direction from which the mournful sound came, but it seemed to drift downward from the floor above. Someone was playing a harp, plucking the strings so that plaintive trills and chords stole through the house like a voice crying. Listening in astonishment, she could make out the strains of "Annie Laurie." Orrin Judd's mother had come from Scotland, Camilla knew, for Althea had always been proud of the Scottish strain in their blood. But how strange to play this Scottish air so late at night.

On Camilla's floor a door opened and closed, and after a little while there was silence. But the music, while it lasted, had made as lonely a sound as Camilla had ever heard. Even after the harp was still, she felt the echo of it along her very nerves, pleading, bewailing. But for what, or for why, she could not tell.

Troubled now, she could not fall asleep again, and after a time she got up and went to the heavy draperies pulled across a French door and drew them back so that she could look out into the darkness. It had stopped raining, but the night was inky black and there were no stars. With the lower mists blown away, she was surprised to see lights far in the distance and wondered about them for a moment, before she realized that they were lights on the opposite bank. That black band between was the river. The far shore seemed another world, with little connection or communication with this one. This, too, was an aspect of the Hudson. It was barrier as well as highway.

The country silence, which had seemed so surprising and all-enveloping to her on her arrival, was not, she discovered, silence at all. She heard the rumbling of a train on the opposite shore, the whistle of a boat on the river, the rustling of trees all about the house. And somewhere not far away, the rushing sound of a brook tumbling down the mountain. Spring peepers were chirping out there in the darkness, keeping up an all-night chorus of their own.

There were sounds, too, within the house. As she drew back from the balcony door, listening now to the house, the very halls seemed to stir and whisper. Someone went past her door and there was the sound of hurrying footsteps on the stairs. Had her grandfather taken a turn for the worse? Camilla wondered.

She drew on a warm flannel wrapper over her long-sleeved white nightgown. When she opened her door, she heard the sound of someone weeping softly. Her own wing of the house was empty, but the lamp still burned above the stairwell and a candle flickered in a holder on the hall table beyond the stairs. It was from that direction the sound of weeping came. Concerned, Camilla followed the cold hall to its far end.

There on the carved chest outside Orrin's door sat the slight figure of Letty Judd, crying bitterly, with her hands over her face. Her sobs had a choked sound, as if they were wrung from her against her will. When Camilla touched her shoulder gently, she looked up with tears streaming down her face.

"Is Grandfather worse?" Camilla asked. "Is there anything I can do, Aunt Letty?"

Letty was still fully dressed, with her long braids bound as neatly about her head as they had been earlier in the day. Clearly she had not gone to bed, and her face looked weary and ravaged. She shook her head at Camilla and glanced sorrowfully toward her father's door.

"He's dying," she said, "and they won't let me in."

Even as she spoke, Hortense came to the door. She too was fully dressed as she had been for dinner. Her face was twisted in a grimace that might, or might not, be that of grief.

"It's over," she said. "Papa is gone."

Camilla heard the words in blank dismay. She had not

expected her grandfather to be gone so quickly—when she had only just found him.

A rising sob choked in Letty's throat. She stood up to face her sister in despair.

"You had no right to shut me out. I should have been with him when he died. It's cruel that you should have kept me away from him in his last moments."

Hortense made a futile effort to thrust back her sliding pompadour. "The sight of you upset him. He didn't want to see you. Besides, he died in his sleep quite peacefully. He saw no one when the last breath went out of him."

"I knew it would come tonight," Letty said dully. "I knew."

"I must call Booth," Hortense murmured. She seemed to waver on her feet, and Camilla moved to her side and took her arm to steady her. Hortense glanced at her in vague surprise, and then seemed to remember who she was. "Your coming disturbed him too much," she said, as if seeking a new scapegoat.

Across the hall a door opened, and Booth came out of his room. He wore a handsome dressing gown of maroon brocade, and he had paused long enough to smooth back his thick dark hair.

"What's happened?" he asked. "Is he worse?"

Hortense's lips quivered and she had difficulty controlling her voice, but again Camilla was not sure that her emotion was one of grief.

"Your—your grandfather is dead, Booth dear," she said. "I was just telling Camilla that I fear her coming—"

"Don't blame Camilla," Booth said. "I'll go downstairs and send Toby for the doctor. Or perhaps I'd better see Grandfather first myself."

With an effort, Hortense seemed to pull herself together. "Please—not now," she said. "Go send Toby for Dr. Wheeler, dear."

For an instant Camilla thought Booth might walk past his mother into the room, but instead he turned and strode toward the stairs. Hortense seemed to sigh in visible relief, and Camilla wondered why.

"Shouldn't someone call Mr. Granger?" she asked.

Hortense paid no attention to her question. "Go to bed." She spoke to Letty, but her look included Camilla. "There's nothing you can do. Miss Morris and I will stay with Papa. You'll do no good here in the cold, Letty. You're likely to be ill tomorrow."

Letty rose stiffly, like a wooden doll. "I want to see him," she told her sister. "Come with me, Camilla."

Reluctantly, Hortense let them by. Within the room the nurse was busying herself about the bed, but she drew down the sheet so that Letty and Camilla could stand beside Orrin Judd and see his face as it had been in the moment of death. To Camilla's eyes he looked younger now and somehow happier—this great fallen eagle of a man.

Letty bent to kiss his cheek, and as she reached out her hand, Camilla again saw the restriction her crooked arm placed upon such a gesture.

"Good-by, Papa," Letty whispered, and went sadly out of the room.

Camilla stood in silence, studying the proud, strong face, as if she might find there the answers to many questions. Only a little while ago he had lived and spoken to her. He had wanted something of her and had said they would talk again, when he was less tired. But now he was beyond reach, and the things he had wanted to say to her, the warning he had tried to make, would never be spoken. A longing seized her to repeat the promise she had made yesterday to help him achieve whatever it was he had wanted. If only she might reassure him again, let him know she was ready to do his bidding. But she had no knowledge of what that bidding was, and without him to instruct her, to stand beside her, there was nothing she could do.

"Good night, Grandfather. Sleep well," she told him softly and turned away from the bed.

An unexpected movement across the room caught her eye, and Ross Granger stepped out of the far shadows. Camilla stared at him in surprise.

"How long have you been here?" she whispered.

He took her arm and led her out of the room. Hortense brushed past them with an indignant glance, returning to her father's side.

"I've been here all night," Ross said flatly.

She knew now why Hortense had not wanted Booth to go into the room. Ross must have been there against her will, and perhaps she had feared a clash if Booth had discovered him there.

"But—why?" Camilla persisted.

"It was the least I could do for him," Ross said. "Though I think he never knew I was there. Get yourself some sleep now. The watch is over."

44

Her throat felt choked with grief, and she could not speak. She nodded and slipped away from him down the hall.

In her room the little clock on the mantel told her, surprisingly, that it was almost five o'clock. Somehow she had thought it was nearer midnight. It seemed all the more strange that someone should have played a harp in this house at such an hour. Had the musician been Aunt Letty? Why had neither she nor Hortense undressed or gone to bed, all this long night through? And why had Ross Granger insisted upon remaining in the same room, even though Orrin Judd was unconscious?

But it was not of these things she wanted to think. Moving automatically, she put paper and wood in the grate, lighted the kindling and watched the newborn flames lick upward, eager and greedy, until the larger sticks crackled with blue and orange light. Then she dropped down upon the hearthrug, warming herself and thinking.

How strange that her grandfather's death should seem so great a blow, when she scarcely knew him. The sense of loss was an aching within her, to which she could not bring the relief of tears. If only she had dreamed that he would welcome her, how gladly she would have come to Thunder Heights long before this. She would not have let her father's prejudice hold her back. Now it was too late, and she could never do for him the things he had wanted to ask of her, because she would never know what they were.

Carefully she went over his words in her mind. He had asked her to stand with him against the "vultures" who were waiting for him to die. He had warned her against them all. He had said she must help him to save his house that Althea had loved. He had spoken of Letty. But in spite of her promise, there were no practical steps she could take.

She held cold hands to the fire, shivering. Now all her own plans must change again. She would stay for her grandfather's funeral and then take quick leave of his family. In spite of Aunt Letty, whom she was ready to love, she could not stay on under the same roof with Hortense. Her aunt did not want her here and would not invite her to stay.

Dawn was brightening the windows when at length she left the fire and went to the French door, opening it once more on the little balcony. The early morning air was clean and fresh with the wet scent of earth and new-growing things. The Hudson had turned from black to pale silver, and the sky above the hills on the far bank was streaked with delicate rose. She stood at the balcony rail, watching the sunrise fling streamers of rose and aquamarine across the sky and reflect its brilliance in the river.

At this quiet moment of dawn she sensed again the changing moods of the Hudson. How still its waters seemed now, as if they scarcely moved. Had her mother stood thus at this very window in some long ago dawn, watching the river she loved come to life with a new day? As Camilla watched, a sailboat moved serenely into view, finding some hint of breeze to puff its sails so that it drifted like a ghost along the smooth water and out of sight beyond the bend. Before the coming of steam those white birds had thronged the river. Her mother had told her of them often and of sailing in them herself. A gull swooped down toward a spit of land that thrust itself into the water just below Thunder Heights, and she heard its shrill cry.

It was as if the river called to her in a voice made up of all these things, setting a spell upon her heart. Yet now she must turn her back on it and go away forever, and she felt suddenly regretful of leaving. She could almost hear her grandfather's voice saying, "Don't run away, girl. Stay and fight."

But what battle was she to fight? And why? Now that he was gone, she would never know.

VI

AFTER AN EARLY BREAKFAST THAT MORNING, CAMILLA PUT on a jacket and went through a door that opened onto the wide veranda. There were steps on the river side, and she walked down them and across wet grass. Once, here on this high ledge, there must have been a pleasant lawn between the tall elms growing on either side. Directly across the river a white-steepled little town hugged a narrow valley, and several small craft were to be seen on the water before it.

What a view there must be from the top of Thunder Mountain. She wondered if there was a way that wound to the crest. But that was no walk for this morning. She turned from house and mountain and followed a narrow brown path that wound down from the heights, crossed railroad tracks that were hidden from the house, and wandered beneath the bare trees that edged the river.

The thought of her mother had been with her often since

she had come here yesterday. But now a sense of her father's presence returned as well. He had lived in Westcliff for a time. He had met Althea while he worked there as a teacher, though his real home was in New York. Where and how had they met? Camilla wondered. Had they walked together along this very path during their secret courtship, with the river flowing calmly beside them as it did now?

By now Thunder Heights was hidden by the trees, and as she walked on, the clamor of bird song rose to full voice on all sides. She came suddenly upon the noisy, tumbling brook she had heard in the night, its waters freshened by spring rains as it rushed toward the river. A little wooden bridge offered a crossing, and she went on along the path.

She followed the curving way only a little further when she came suddenly upon a man sitting on an outcropping of rock above the path. It was Ross Granger, and he was dressed for the outdoors in a corduroy jacket and trousers, his chestnut head bare to the sun.

He had not seen her, and his face in unguarded repose wore a sadness that betrayed his troubled thoughts. Beneath his eyes smudged shadows told of his long night's vigil. For an instant she did not know whether to go or stay, hesitating to break in upon this solitary moment. Then he looked about and saw her.

"You're out early," he said, standing up on the rock.

"I couldn't sleep."

"Nor I," he said.

"Why did you stay all night in my grandfather's room?" she asked him again, feeling that there were matters she must understand before she went away. Otherwise she would ponder them endlessly the rest of her life.

"I didn't want to see him bullied about a new will," he said. "I trust none of them."

"And they don't seem to trust you," she said.

His smile was wry. "Hortense took care of that. She spent the night in the room too, with Letty posted as a watchdog outside, except when she went off to play her harp. But I doubt that he was aware of us at any time."

"It seems to me," Camilla told him frankly, "that it was dreadfully coldblooded for you all to be thinking about wills while Grandfather lay dying."

Ross's expression did not change. "A man is dead for a very long time. The stipulations he leaves behind may affect other lives for generations. This was not a moment to be squeamish about such matters."

A spotted coach dog, young, awkward and big, came bounding suddenly out of the woods and ran to Ross with an air of joyful exuberance. Ross accepted his clumsy greeting, pulling his ears affectionately.

"Champion is from Blue Beeches," he explained. "He's Nora Redfern's dog. Down, fellow, I prefer to wash my own face."

The dog went gamboling off on an exploratory expedition along the edge of the woods, and Ross removed his jacket and spread it on the rock beside him.

"Come sit down a moment," he said. "I want to talk to you."

He offered a hand to pull her up the face of the boulder, and she seated herself on his jacket.

"How much do you know about your grandfather?" he asked when she was comfortable.

"Know about him?" She was not sure what he meant. "Perhaps not a great deal. My father detested everything about Thunder Heights. He never wanted to talk about it. But in spite of the way Grandfather treated my mother, I'm sure she never stopped loving him."

Camilla smiled, remembering, and told him about the building her mother had once taken her to see in New York.

Ross listened gravely until she was through. "Orrin Judd has done great things, big things. It's hard to believe that he had so little in the beginning. He was born in Westcliff, you know. His father was a country doctor. Orrin worked in lumber camps hereabout, but he had a genius for managing men and running large affairs, and he had vision. So before many years were up he owned a lumber business of his own. From that it was only a step into the building trade. Though that's a feeble term for what he wanted to do. He had no training himself as an engineer or an architect, but he learned from the men who worked for him and he was better than any of us. Perhaps he was more an empire builder than a builder of bridges and buildings and roads. He could see the future better than most men. He might have been one of the giants if he hadn't lost heart."

Camilla listened eagerly. These were things she had understood little of as a child, and when she was grown her father never talked about them.

Ross rubbed a hand wearily across his face and went on. "The time is nearly over for giants, I think. Their kingdoms grow too big and they control too many lives. America never suffers kings for long. But even when your grandfather withdrew to Thunder Heights, the world came to him. Not the social world—there's been little of that he cared for in the years I've known him. I mean the business world. He wouldn't go to New York after your mother died, but he made it come to him—often through me."

"I've wondered about your place here," Camilla said.

"Sometimes I've wondered myself. My father was an engineer and his good friend, though many years younger. After he died, Orrin Judd kept an eye on me, sent me to engineering school, since that was what I wanted most. When I graduated, he put me to work on some of his projects. He came to trust me and began to want me near him. Before I knew what had happened I was doing a sort of liaison job for him, instead of following the work I wanted to do. I suppose I've helped him keep the threads in his hands, though I never planned on playing aide-de-camp to a general."

"You've given up years of your life for this?" Camilla said wonderingly.

"I don't count them as lost. He gave me a chance to learn and there were things he intended me to do later. When he felt I was ready. Besides, I loved him."

Off in the brush they could hear the dog chasing some small wild thing. The sound of rushing water, the twitter of birds was all about them. But the two on the boulder were silent.

"Thank you for telling me these things," she said. "I can see how much you've meant to my grandfather. What was the change you wanted to see him make in his will?"

For a few moments he did not speak, but sat watching as the dog bounded onto the path again, following some new and exciting scent. Then he stood up abruptly. His expression had changed, as if he grew angry again.

"My usefulness here has come to an end. The will must stand as he left it. I can't affect that now."

She was puzzled and a little perturbed by his sudden shifting of mood. "But how *would* you change it, if you could?" she asked.

The lines of his face seemed to harden, making him look older than his years. "There's no point in discussing that with you. You're a Judd too, though there's likely to be less of his fortune for you than for the others."

His words carried a deliberate sting, and she stood up beside him indignantly.

"I expect nothing at all from my grandfather," she said.

"It's enough for me that he was kind to me yesterday and wanted me here."

For a moment his expression softened, and she thought he believed her. Then he seemed to think better of such weakening and laughed without sympathy.

"Do you mean that you're willing to go back to being a governess, when if you stay you may get your hands on some of the Judd fortune?"

"There's nothing wrong with being a governess," she returned heatedly. "I like to think I'm a good one. I intend to return to New York right after the funeral. The Judds owe me nothing and I want nothing from them. I came only to see my grandfather."

"Then why didn't you come before this?" he demanded. "Why did you wait till you heard he was dying before you came running to Thunder Heights?"

She felt completely outraged. If this was what he thought of her, then she did not mean to stay in his company another moment.

"Can you tell me if this upper path will take me back to the house?" she asked coldly.

"I'll come with you and show you the way," he offered.

Camilla turned her back on him and managed to get down the steep face of the rock without his help.

"No, thank you. I can find it well enough myself," she said and started up the path.

But he would not let her go alone. He jumped down from the rock and the spotted dog bounded along beside him as they turned uphill and back in the direction of Thunder Heights. Whether she liked it or not, she had to accept their company. She walked quickly, ignoring him, though now and then he pointed out landmarks by which she could find her direction if she chose to come this way again.

For example, he said, there was that weeping beech on ahead, from which she would be within sight of the Judds' house. She could not ignore the tree, for she had never seen one like it. It grew to a considerable height, but unlike other beeches, all its boughs trailed downward toward the earth, making a canopy of blue-black branches around the tree. It was as weird as something out of a witch's tale—a good landmark to remember.

When they reached the tree, her companion whistled for the dog and turned back. "I'll leave you here," he said curtly. "I'm not going in yet. You'll have no trouble by yourself the rest of the way."

He went off without waiting for any thanks she might have offered. For a moment she stood looking after him in a mingling of displeasure and bewilderment. What a strange, unpredictable, maddening person he was. Then she shrugged the thought of him aside and looked more closely about the hillside where she stood. Back a little farther it rose steeply into a cliff overgrown with wild vegetation and scrubby trees. There was a break in the brush at one point, as if a path to the top might open there. She was in no mood for exploration now, however, and hurried down toward Thunder Heights.

She had climbed well above the house, she found as she came out upon a bare, craggy place where she could overlook its gray towers. From this high rocky eminence, she could see a separation in the trees toward the north, and for the first time she had a glimpse of Blue Beeches from the land side.

The sunny yellow of the house looked brighter than ever in the morning sunlight. It shone fresh and clean, where Thunder Heights appeared drab and dingy. Looking at it, she felt an unexpected reluctance to return to the dark Judd household. Blue Beeches seemed far more inviting.

As she watched, she saw the spotted dog bound from the edge of the woods and go loping across a wide lawn. A woman came down the steps, laughing and calling to him. The breeze brought the faint sound of her voice. Camilla could not see her clearly enough to know whether she was plain or pretty, young or old. But it was clear that she had a friendly greeting for Ross Granger as he came more slowly out of the woods and joined her. Linking arms, they went up the steps and into the house.

Wondering, Camilla continued down the hill. The path from the rocky outcropping dipped briefly through the woods again and then came out on a level with the Judd house. Instead of seeking the veranda to make her re-entry the way she had come out, Camilla approached from the rear and saw that here more order and attention had been given to the grounds. A space of earth had been cleared of weeds, and there were paths leading among beds where planting had begun, with a small sundial marking the garden's center. A marble bench near the sundial invited one to rest and contemplation.

Camilla walked along one narrow path, noting bits of green already pushing their way out of the earth. As she neared the house, she looked up at the windows, but saw no

51

sign of life, no face at any pane. Queer how dead the house always looked from the outside, even though she knew there were people within.

Grace opened the back door for her, and Camilla said good morning to Matilda, the cook and housekeeper, as she went inside. Voices reached her from the parlor, and she knew that the sad rites connected with her grandfather's death had already begun. Before she could slip past, a man appeared in the doorway and saw her. It was Mr. Pompton.

He held out his hand to her gravely. "It is sad to meet again under such circumstances, Miss King. But I'm glad you were able to reach your grandfather before his death."

"I think he wanted me here," she said. "Thank you for coming for me."

"That was his wish." His tone was courteous, but his manner seemed no more approving than it had been in New York. It was clear that her coming here was not his desire. "You will be staying on for a time now?" he asked.

She shook her head. "No longer than the funeral. With my grandfather gone, I am not wanted here."

He did not deny this, but made her a stiff bow and returned to the parlor. As she started up the stairs, Booth came out of the library to join her.

"You've been for a walk?" he asked. "Did you get no more sleep at all last night?"

"I didn't feel like sleeping," she said.

His mood seemed kinder and less remote than it had been the night before.

"A sad homecoming for you," he said. "If you stay with us a while, Cousin, perhaps we can make up for it."

She was silent as he climbed the stairs with her, not wishing to point out that his mother had given her little welcome. As they reached the second floor, Hortense came down the hall with a tray in her hands.

She wore voluminous black today, with a fringe of formidable jet twinkling across the bodice. The tray she carried held a tea service, with a quilted English cosy over the teapot, and a glass, medicine bottle, and spoon besides.

"I knew Letty would make herself ill last night," she said impatiently. "And now she has run away to the nursery again. As if I didn't have enough to do!"

Booth took the tray out of her hands. "Let me take it up to her, Mother. Camilla will help me with Aunt Letty. Pompton's downstairs, you know, waiting to see you."

Hortense gave up the tray gladly and made a vague tidying gesture that did her red pompadour no good.

As Camilla followed Booth up the stairs to the third floor, she glanced back and saw that Hortense had not gone down to Mr. Pompton at once, but was gazing after them with an air of uncertainty.

On the third floor, Booth led the way to the door of the old nursery, and Camilla opened it so that he might carry in the tray. The nursery was far from the cheerful room of her mother's stories and her own imagination. It was long and narrow, a bare, cold room. No fire had been lighted in its grate, and on this northern exposure of the house, sunshine had not reached the limply curtained windows. At the far end of the room Letty Judd lay huddled beneath a quilt on a narrow couch. Her face was swollen from crying, and she murmured faint sounds of apology as Booth approached her with the tray.

"You shouldn't bother about me, my dears," she said.

Booth set the tray down on a small table covered by a fringed red velvet cloth. "You know I'll always bother about you, Aunt Letty," he told her cheerfully. "Mother sent you some tea and medicine. We can't have you ill, you know."

At Letty's feet Mignonette lay curled in a warm, tight ball. She stretched herself, yawned widely, and regarded Booth's preparations with interest.

"I'm sorry you're not feeling well, Aunt Letty," Camilla said. "Would you like me to light a fire so it will be warmer up here?"

Booth answered for her. "Don't bother, Cousin. As soon as Aunt Letty drinks some tea and has her medicine, I'm going to take her downstairs."

Letty managed a tremulous smile, and there was affection in the look she gave him. "I like it up here. There are always memories to comfort me. Camilla, your mother used to play with Hortense and me in this very room."

"First your medicine," Booth said, and she swallowed the concoction gratefully.

"Balm and vervain tonic are wonderfully strengthening," she said. "I mixed the elixir myself. What tea did she fix for me, Booth?"

"I've no idea," he said, pouring a cupful with easy grace and bringing it to her. "Your herb mixtures confuse me. At least it's hot and potent."

Letty sniffed the aromatic steam and nodded, smiling. "Mother of thyme with a bit of hyssop. Just the thing. You know what David says in the Bible—'Purge me with hyssop and I shall be clean.' "

She drank deeply, and Mignonette mewed and climbed daintily over the hump of bedding made by Letty's outstretched legs.

"Give her a saucerful, Camilla—there's a dear," Letty said. "She doesn't want to be left out."

Camilla took Letty's saucer and poured tea into it, set it on the floor. Mignonette leaped lightly from the bed and lapped the hot liquid with a greedy pink tongue.

Booth watched, shaking his head. "I've never seen such a cat. Don't those mixtures ever upset her?"

"Of course not!" Letty's tone seemed overly vehement. "They don't upset me, why should they upset her?"

Booth shrugged and turned away to bring a chair for Camilla. Letty watched him unhappily.

"I know what you're thinking," she began.

"I'm not thinking a thing, except that I want to see you strong and well as soon as possible," Booth said. "The funeral is tomorrow and you'll want to be up for that. It's to be a quiet family affair, without an invasion of people from New York."

"I shall be up," Letty said and sipped her tea.

Mignonette licked the saucer and sat back to clean her whiskers tidily.

While Letty finished her tea, Camilla told of her walk that morning and of her glimpse of Blue Beeches and its dog. She said nothing about meeting Ross. She had a feeling that Booth, with good reason, would not approve of that meeting, and she had no wish to displease him.

"I'm glad you've had a look about the place, my dear," Letty said. "But if I were you, I wouldn't go too near Blue Beeches. Not that I have anything against Nora Redfern. As a matter of fact, her mother and yours were good friends in their girlhood. Mrs. Landry, Nora's mother, lives upriver now, and we haven't seen her for years—which is just as well. Nora is a widow with three children. Personally I think she is a young woman of considerable courage, but Hortense doesn't approve of her."

"Or her mother's sharp tongue," Booth added. "If you're through with your tea, I'll carry you downstairs to your room, Aunt Letty. Sad memories won't make you feel any better up here."

"They're not sad memories—they're the happiest of my life," Letty insisted. But she raised her arms to Booth.

He lifted her as if she weighed nothing, and her crooked arm went about his neck as he carried her toward the door. Camilla picked up the tray and followed, with Mignonette springing along at her heels. Just before she reached the door Camilla saw something she had not noticed when she'd entered the room. In a shadowy corner near the door stood a harp. Its cover had been laid aside, and a stool upholstered in needlepoint was drawn before it as if the musician had risen hurriedly from her playing and failed to return. So it was from this room that the harp music had issued in the dead of night.

She hurried down the stairs after Booth and waited until he had carried Letty into her room on the second floor.

"She'll sleep now," he said when he rejoined her. "Grandfather Orrin's death has been a shock to her. A shock to all of us."

"If she blames herself for something in connection with him," Camilla said, "that must upset her more than anything else."

"Aunt Letty is always ready to take on blame of one sort or another," Booth said. "And she has an imagination that gets her into trouble. Don't take her words too seriously, Cousin. I'll go down now and see how Mother is coming out with Mr. Pompton."

He gave her the quick flash of a smile that had surprised her before, always seeming unexpected in his somber face. After Ross's sharp words she warmed to Booth's kinder manner toward her.

As she went to her room she wondered about the circumstances of his adoption. Why had Hortense, who had never married and did not seem a particularly motherly person, chosen to adopt a boy of ten? And how closely was Booth tied to this family? It seemed strange that as a grown man he had been willing to live on in this gloomy household.

Camilla spent the rest of the morning in her room, not knowing what to do with herself. She had an unhappy sense of marking time between the poles of two different lives, belonging at the moment to neither one.

At noontime Letty remained in her room, Booth had gone to the village, and Ross did not appear, so she and Hortense ate alone in the big dining room. Her aunt seemed increasingly keyed up and distraught, and the black jet fringe on her dress quivered and trembled, as if stirred by the agitated beating of her heart. At least she seemed less distant than she had been when Camilla had arrived the day before.

"What will your plans be now, Aunt Hortense?" Camilla asked.

"We'll get rid of the house, of course," Hortense said. "Whether we sell it, give it away, burn it down, doesn't matter. Just so we're rid of it for good!"

"It seems a wonderful place to me," Camilla said gently. "Isn't it rather a shame to let it go out of the family?"

Hortense snorted, her pompadour trembling. "You haven't been tied to it against your will for most of your life. When Mama was alive we had houses everywhere, including a splendid town house in New York. I can still remember the parties and balls, the fun and gaiety, the trips abroad. Even after she died, Papa didn't give up as he did when Althea went away. Life was exciting, with new clothes and gay friends—exactly the sort of existence I like best. But when Althea married, Papa sold all the houses except this one, that was Althea's favorite. He behaved as though she had died and he wouldn't go anywhere, or let us go anywhere. It has been like living in a prison all these years."

Camilla felt moved by a certain pity for her. If a gay social life was what Aunt Hortense had been brought up to expect, it must have seemed a cruelty to have it taken away so arbitrarily.

"How did Aunt Letty feel about such a change?" Camilla asked.

"Letty!" Hortense waved a scornful hand. "She doesn't know what money is for. She can be happy with her harp and her garden and her cat. Given the choice, she'd probably be foolish enough to continue living under this roof in the same horribly dull way. If Papa has left money and property in her hands, she will never know what to do with it. But *I* will know. I have plans for myself and of course for Booth. There's so much I can do for him that Papa would never permit. And now I can laugh at Ross Granger. That young man has been influencing our fortunes for too long a time. The first thing I shall do is discharge him."

She was becoming excited to a disturbing degree and there were spots of high color in either cheek. Camilla sought to distract her.

"Tell me about Booth," she said.

This was a subject to which Hortense could warm. There was no mistaking the doting pride and affection that she lavished upon her adopted son.

"Booth is very talented, you know," Hortense assured her. "He's a really gifted artist. If we could live in New York, he

56

might bring great credit to himself. But what chance has he here? Papa always hated his painting and opposed him at every step. He wanted him to go out and work in some business concern. Imagine! A man of Booth's sensitivity."

"Are any of his paintings hung about the house?" Camilla asked. "I'd like to see them."

"I have one in my room. Hurry and eat your rice pudding, Camilla, and I'll show it to you."

Her fatuous pride in Booth was evident and Camilla felt a little uncomfortable listening to her. Booth, she suspected, was completely indifferent to his adopted mother and she could not help but be sorry for Hortense.

Her aunt's room was on the second floor, across the hall from Camilla's. It was a big, dim room, heavily curtained. Camilla could feel the prickle of dust in her nostrils as she stepped into it. Hortense's love of the sumptuous had been given full play, and she had used a lavish hand when it came to velvet, satin, and brocade—all rich materials in faded yellow, or once brilliant green. Dusty materials, gone too long undisturbed.

Hortense moved about lighting lamps on numerous tables and stands, apparently preferring lamplight to daylight.

"There!" she cried, waving a hand toward the end wall of the room. "What do you think of it?"

The painting was a large one, set handsomely in an ornate gilt frame. It was a picture of two mountain wildcats fighting. Their fiercely struggling bodies verged on the rim of a rocky cliff, with rapids frothing at its foot. A storm was breaking overhead, and the artist had painted in tawny yellows and smoky greens and grays. The result was a wild and disturbing picture.

"Papa detested this painting," Hortense said. "He didn't want to look at it day after day, and he told Booth to get it out of his sight."

Camilla could well understand that her grandfather would not want to live with such a picture confronting him in his own house. She wondered how Hortense could endure its constant violence here in her room. That Booth had painted it was significant. Camilla had sensed a depth of curbed passion in him that he did not reveal to the casual eye. It had spilled out in this picture, betraying him.

Hortense ran on eagerly. "When we sell this house and move to New York, I'll arrange for a showing of his pictures in one of the galleries. I've promised him that for a long time, but Papa would never permit it."

As she left her aunt, Camilla thought that there was far more relief than sorrow in Hortense over her father's death. Indeed, the fact of it seemed to have brought all the suppressed longings that she had stored up over the years seething to the surface. Today she was a woman driven by her rising emotions, ready to let nothing stand in her path.

Letty did not come down to dinner that night, but Hortense said she was feeling better and was sure she would be able to attend the funeral services tomorrow. Ross Granger continued to stay away, and no one seemed to know where he was, or what he was doing.

"He's probably over visiting Mrs. Redfern again," Hortense said.

"Why not?" Booth said carelessly. "Nora Redfern is an attractive woman."

"You know very well how we feel about her," Hortense said. "And why. Ross only does this to spite us. Never mind—he won't be around much longer, I can promise you that."

The meal was a quiet one, and Camilla slipped away when they left the table, avoiding the stiff coffee hour in the overfurnished parlor, and went upstairs to her room. In one sense she could hardly wait to be free of this house and away from it for good. Yet in another she felt that when she left she would be more frighteningly alone than ever before in her life. The thought depressed and saddened her.

She had brought a book by Washington Irving upstairs from the library, but though she got into Althea's comfortable bed and set a lamp nearby on the bedside table, she could not concentrate on the pages before her. Tonight there was no escaping her own life through words in a book.

Loneliness was a specter that sat at the foot of the bed peering at her grimly. In desperation she tried to argue it away. Being alone was no new experience for Camilla King. As a child she had often been lonely, with few children her own age to play with. And since her father's death she had been more solitary than ever. That was one reason she had sought a position as a governess who would live in the midst of someone else's family. With children needing her every moment, she had hoped to lose the feeling of belonging nowhere.

Yet none of her previous experience of loneliness had been as devastating as this. Always before there had been the secret knowledge of her family up the Hudson to dream about—a family to which she belonged through ties of blood.

No matter how stern her grandfather had been to her mother, he was still her grandfather, and she had stored away the reassuring thought that the time would eventually come when she might go to him. Now Grandfather Orrin was dead, and while Letty and Hortense were her blood relatives, the fact gave her little comfort. She was not wanted here by Hortense, and Letty was a vague, sweet dreamer who could not help her. The secret hope which had long supported her was gone, and there was left in its place only a soreness and an aching. Not only must she fail in whatever it was her grandfather had wanted of her, but she must also forsake a comforting hope for the future when she left this house.

She turned out the lamp and lay in the dark, thinking again of the strange things Orrin Judd had said to her. Perhaps he had felt in his last hours that an injustice had been done to Althea and wished that he could make up for it through her daughter. But no legacy could assuage this feeling she was lost to tonight. It was her grandfather's presence she wanted and the developing affection which had been promised between them.

She sighed and turned restlessly in bed. Somehow she must forget the problems of this strange household. But tears came instead of sleep, and she wept bitterly into her pillow. Wept for her grandfather and because of her disappointment in a family that did not want her here—when she had so longed to belong to her own family. Wept too for her father's gentle wisdom which might have guided her now. And most of all she wept for her mother, so tragically, irretrievably lost.

Tonight she could not even summon to mind her mother's gay image to comfort her. In this room she had lost her doubly, for the room was strange and did not know her. With her spirits at the lowest ebb she could remember, she had a gloomy presentiment that she would never know a real home anywhere.

VII

THE SUNLIGHT OF EARLY AFTERNOON RAYED THROUGH THE stained glass window of the little church as the organist played a solemn hymn. The mourners sat with their heads bowed in prayer for the dead, and Letty, in the family pew beside Camilla, pressed her arm gently.

"We used to come here often before my sister Althea died," she whispered. "Papa gave the church that stained glass window behind the altar as a commemoration for Althea, but he stopped coming here when he lost her."

From beyond Camilla, Hortense threw the whisperer a reproving look and Letty fell silent. Booth sat beside his mother, but Ross had not been invited to occupy the family pew. Once when Camilla turned her head, she saw him a row or two back, sitting beside a pretty, brown-eyed woman—probably Nora Redfern.

The minister was a young man, and when he rose to give the eulogy for the dead, Camilla suspected that he could not have known Orrin Judd very well. His words were earnest and well-meaning, but they seemed to have little relation to the man Camilla remembered as her grandfather.

Though the church was well filled, Letty had told her earlier that many would come out of curiosity and perhaps resentment of the Judds, rather than because of any real love for her grandfather. People hereabout considered him a hard man, grown too powerful, so that he had lost his human identification with the humble who had been his friends when he was young.

When the ceremony was over the family followed the casket down the aisle and out of the church. From her place in one of the carriages that would drive them to the cemetery, Camilla looked about for Ross in the crowd, but she did not see him again until they reached her grandfather's grave.

The cemetery lay beneath the sheltering shade of a forest that rimmed its far edge on the upper hillside. Only a few of those at the church had followed the hearse the short distance for the final burial. Letty grew tense now, and as the casket was placed beside the grave, she burst into tears and clung brokenly to Camilla. Hortense bowed her head, the conventional figure of a daughter mourning her father, but Camilla suspected that there were no tears behind her black veil. Booth had been a pallbearer, along with Orrin's doctor, the lawyer Mr. Pompton, and others, and he looked grave, if not deeply grieved. Ross, for all that he had apparently been close to Orrin Judd in life, had not been asked by the family to serve at his funeral.

Camilla saw him standing a little apart, with Mrs. Redfern at his side. His expression was guarded, betraying little, perhaps because he did not want to reveal his feeling. How much did the young widow, Nora Redfern, mean to him, she wondered, that he was with her so often?

The day was gray and cool, with more rain threatening. Camilla stood in silence beside Letty and Hortense and watched gray clouds swirl overhead with the wind at their heels. She felt no surging of grief for her grandfather now. What was being lowered into the ground had little connection with the fierce old man she had known so briefly. The eagle had long since flown its bonds.

When she looked at the earth again, it was to study the names on gravestones nearby. There, with a tall granite shaft guarding it, was her grandmother's grave. Next to that was the headstone for Althea Judd King. It was the first time Camilla had seen her mother's grave, and the tears she could not shed for her grandfather sprang into her eyes. How much her father had wanted to keep his Althea from being buried here. But Orrin Judd had had his way, and she lay in the family plot with others of her kin around her. Now Orrin, who lost her so completely in life, would sleep nearby his dearest daughter in all the time ahead.

Near the cemetery gate, she saw Ross and Mrs. Redfern speaking to Mr. Pompton.

Letty, still weeping gently, put her hand on Camilla's arm. "Pretend not to see her, dear. Just move quickly by. Our families don't speak."

Camilla would have obeyed, but Mrs. Redfern stepped forward and held out her hand in a warm gesture of friendliness.

"I'm Nora Redfern, Miss King. If you are going to be here for a while, do come over to see me. We ought to know each other—our mothers were best friends."

Nora was tall, with soft brown hair curling beneath her tilted hat. She looked like a woman who enjoyed the out-of-doors, and the clasp of her hand was strong and direct.

Camilla thanked her and explained that she would be leaving tomorrow. She could understand why Ross spent so much time with this woman, and she watched with regret as he helped her into her carriage. Hortense had seen the interchange, and her color was high with disapproval. She whispered to Booth and his look followed Mrs. Redfern with a speculative interest. What was wrong here? And how did it happen that Ross associated with Mrs. Redfern, when the rest of the Judd household did not?

When Hortense and Booth and Mr. Pompton were settled in one carriage, and Letty and Camilla in another, Ross came over to join them, a little to Camilla's surprise. Apparently he was coming back to Thunder Heights with them.

Letty still wanted to talk on the drive home, needing to pour out thoughts that were troubling her.

"Papa was always just," she told Camilla. "He always tried to protect me, even if he didn't care much for girls who were sickly."

"He cared about you," Ross assured her gently. "You mustn't doubt that."

"He was unhappy these last years," Letty said. "And that was my fault. So much of it was my fault."

"I think you blame yourself needlessly," Ross told her. "How could you be responsible for his unhappiness?"

Letty shook her head and dabbed at her eyes with a handkerchief. "You don't know," she said darkly. "There are so many things you don't know."

Ross did not seem to take this seriously. "Perhaps it will comfort you a little, Miss Letty, if you realize that nothing could ever have made him happy again. He would never have found a way to start anew."

"That is true," Letty said wonderingly. "His life was really over, no matter what anyone did. In fact, it has been over for a long, long time, hasn't it?"

She seemed to take more cheer from this thought than Ross had expected her to.

"At least," he said, "it will be better if you don't express the way you feel about all this to any reporters who may try to talk to you."

"Reporters?" Letty echoed in dismay.

"Of course. You don't think a man like Orrin Judd can die without causing a stir, do you? There are some newsmen here already. Pompton had some trouble keeping them out of the church, and I know that Toby chucked two of them off Judd grounds this morning before I could stop him. We'll have to talk to them, of course. You'll all fare better with the press if it's done pleasantly."

"Surely no one will want to talk to me," Camilla said in dismay.

"Why not?" Ross sounded unsympathetic. "In fact, you're likely to give them the best copy. Beautiful, disinherited granddaughter! You'd better brace yourself for a siege if they get near you."

When they reached the house, she found that he was right. A group of strange young men in bowler hats had gathered near the front door, and Mr. Pompton left the carriage to speak to them, while Booth and Ross hurried the ladies into the house.

When Camilla would have left the others to go upstairs, Hortense stopped her. "You're to come to the library at once, please. Mr. Pompton wishes to see us all there. He has agreed to read us Papa's will at once."

Such haste seemed to lack decorum, but Camilla followed her aunts across the antehall where marble hands extended from the walls, and through the door of the library. Grace had set a fire burning against the misty chill of the day, and Hortense seated herself in a deep leather sofa placed at right angles to the hearth. Letty chose a small rocking chair and sank into it with a quick, nervous smile that went unanswered by her sister.

Since Camilla felt she had no real part in these proceedings, whatever Mr. Pompton might wish, she took a chair in a far corner, withdrawn from the main family gathering. Ross had come into the room, and he too set himself apart from the others. He walked to one of the bookcases that lined two walls and began to study titles as though he had no other interest there.

The library was heavily paneled in dark walnut that reflected little light and gave a gloomy air to the room. A long walnut table, its legs ornate with carving, occupied the center of the room, and Booth pushed it back a little in order to give them more space about the fire. Above the mantel, commanding the room, hung a portrait of Orrin Judd.

The picture had been painted in his strong middle years, and the eagle look had been in his face even then. But only Camilla seemed to regard the portrait openly, and she had a feeling that it made the family uncomfortable.

Hortense, looking undisguisedly eager now, patted the sofa and beckoned Booth to a place beside her. Mr. Pompton turned his back to the warming fire and spread apart the tails of the dress coat he had worn to the funeral. His scalp glowed rosy in the firelight, and the two clumps of hair above each ear stood up as if they bristled in anticipation of some unpleasantness. He still looked irritated by his encounter with the press.

Watching them all, Camilla felt herself a spectator at a play. In a physical sense she would remain remote and untouched by whatever happened. When the play was over, she could rise and walk out of the theater, with no more involvement with the players.

Mr. Pompton cleared his throat and looked somewhat disapprovingly at Hortense. "You understand, Miss Hortense, that it is only because I wish the whole family to be present that we are moving with such unseemly haste."

"Yes, yes, we understand all that," Hortense said, plucking at a black lace frill on the front of her gown with impatient fingers. "Do get on with it. Then perhaps we can return to our sorrow."

He threw her a suspicious look and explained that one of the firm instructions Mr. Judd had given was to the effect that there was to be no formal mourning period. He had wanted no one to pretend grief, or to dress in black, or avoid social duties.

"As you know," Mr. Pompton continued gruffly, "Mr. Judd sent me to New York a few days ago to find Miss King and ask her to come to Thunder Heights. While I was away on this mission, and without my knowledge or advice, he drew up a new will."

Camilla sensed the quickened attention of the room. Hortense glanced at Booth with an air of triumph.

"He must have listened to me," she whispered.

"Or else to Granger," Booth said, glancing around at the man who stood before the bookshelves.

Ross continued to page through a volume he had taken down, and if the change of wills was news to him, he gave no sign.

"The new will," Mr. Pompton said, "has been legally drawn and witnessed."

He began to read aloud, and Camilla caught the wording of the first bequest.

" 'To my eldest daughter, Hortense Judd, I leave the family Bible, with the hope that she will learn from its wisdom.' "

Hortense sniffed, her impatience growing. "If Papa has doled out everything stick by stick, this is going to take us all day."

"Believe me, madam, it will not take very long," Mr. Pompton said, and continued with the task in hand.

To his second daughter, Letitia Judd, he had left the treasured photograph taken of himself and his three daughters. Letty nodded in pleasure and her tears began to spill again.

"I shall treasure it too," she murmured.

Hortense threw a look of scorn for such simple-minded gratitude.

Several small sums had been left to Toby and Matilda, and to others who had worked for Orrin in the past. His bequest to Ross was a strange one.

" 'In view of the years of trusted service given me, I wish Ross Granger to be permitted the occupancy of the rooms above the coach house for as long as he cares to use them.' "

Ross did not look around, or acknowledge the request in any way. What a strange thing for her grandfather to do, Camilla thought. Surely Ross's quarters in this house must be more comfortable than such an arrangement would be. Besides, if his work for Orrin was finished, he would be leaving soon.

When Mr. Pompton paused, Booth looked quickly at Ross, and Hortense put a hand on her son's arm, as if to restrain him.

Clearing his throat, Mr. Pompton continued. " 'To Camilla King, daughter of my youngest daughter, Althea Judd King, I bequeath this house of Thunder Heights and all the property therein.' "

For an instant the words meant nothing to Camilla. Then, as she began to grasp their meaning, she was so astonished that she did not hear what followed. Mr. Pompton had to repeat the fact that Orrin Judd had left, not only Thunder Heights, but his entire fortune and business holdings to Camilla King, who was herself to be the sole executor of the will.

Camilla's shock and bewilderment were like a mist through which she struggled for some landmark simple enough in its meaning for her to grasp. She was aware of Hortense's gasp and the startled silence of the others. Even Ross had turned and was watching her. With an effort she forced herself to listen and understand the meaning of the stipulations Mr. Pompton was reading.

In order to inherit this house and fortune, Camilla King would have to live at Thunder Heights, preserve it in good state and continue to care for the rest of the family as long as they chose to live in the house. They were to live on the present allowances given them. If any member of the family chose to leave Thunder Heights, he was to receive nothing at all thereafter. Nor was Camilla to receive anything if she chose to leave.

The full meaning of the burden her grandfather had placed upon her was clear now, and Camilla rose uncertainly to her feet.

"I don't understand why Grandfather did this. He must have made this will before I came here—"

"He was insane when he made it!" Hortense cried hoarsely.

Mr. Pompton shook his head. "Madam, Dr. Wheeler would quickly vouch for his sanity. I regret the fact that he did not consult me about this will. Perhaps he would have done so if he had lived. Then I would have warned him that such stipulations were too general and difficult to fulfill. They can be regarded only as Mr. Judd's wishes. I doubt that a court would uphold them."

Hortense recovered herself abruptly. "Why didn't you say so at once? Of course we will fight this in court. The whole thing is preposterous."

"If you will allow me a word—" Mr. Pompton bent his disapproving gaze upon her, "the stipulations could probably not be enforced. But the main body of the will remains sound. Mr. Judd has left everything he owns to Miss King, and I doubt that you could touch that in a court. What she does with it is her own affair. She may go or stay, care for her aunts or not, as she pleases—the inheritance is still hers."

Hortense had begun to breathe deeply, harshly, as if she restrained herself with difficulty. Letty was watching Camilla in bewilderment, as if she did not altogether understand what was going on. The sardonic look was once more in Booth's eyes, though he took no active part in what was happening. Ross was regarding her sharply, his arms folded across his body.

How could she possibly accept this legacy? Camilla thought. A small sum of money she would have received gratefully. But not this, when so clearly the true rights to it lay elsewhere.

"What happens if I refuse the legacy?" Camilla asked.

Mr. Pompton looked faintly skeptical, as if he found it hard to believe that she would do such a thing.

"Since there is no other legatee," he said, "the same thing would happen as would happen in the event of your decease. The money and property would revert to the next of kin."

"To Aunt Hortense and Aunt Letty?" Camilla asked.

"Exactly." Mr. Pompton reached among his papers on the table and drew out an envelope.

"Then I'll refuse it!" Camilla cried. "I have no right to it. And I don't want the burden and responsibility of it."

"Bravo!" Booth cried. "We have a heroine in our midst."

Mr. Pompton wasted not a moment's glance in Booth's direction. He crossed the room to Camilla and held out the envelope. She saw that her name was written upon it in a wavering hand and that it had been sealed with red sealing wax and imprinted with the initialed emblem of a ring.

"This letter is from your grandfather," Mr. Pompton told her. "I do not know its contents. When Toby brought this new will to my office while I was away, he brought the letter also. It was to be given you only in the event of your grandfather's death."

Camilla took the letter almost fearfully, turning it about in her hands.

"The girl has refused the legacy," Hortense said sharply. "Is anything else necessary?"

"I cannot accept a refusal hastily given and without due thought," Mr. Pompton said. "It is my duty to see that some attempt be made to carry out Mr. Judd's wishes. Perhaps you would like to take the letter away and read it, Miss King? It is not necessary to do so here under our eyes."

She accepted the offer quickly. "Yes—yes, please. I'd like to do that. I'll return as soon as I've read it."

She did not look at the others as she left the library and crossed the hall to the parlor. Someone had left a cloak over a chair, and she flung it about her shoulders as she hurried toward a veranda door.

It was not raining now, but the air was heavy with moisture as Camilla leaned upon the railing, looking out over what had once been a fine lawn. Beyond and below lay the river, wreathed in fog, with misty swirls drifting among nearby trees. From the water came the low mooing of a foghorn on a boat.

All these things she was aware of with her senses, without knowing that she was aware. She steadied herself with one hand upon the damp rail, holding in the other the sealed envelope she dreaded to open. How could she follow her grandfather's stipulations and live here, knowing that the family would resent her and want her away, knowing they must hate her because they were tied to her for as long as they chose to accept her charity? Under such circumstances, could she even count on Aunt Letty to befriend her? If she accepted this inheritance she must give up her own freedom and the sense of independence that meant so much to her. She would have to give herself to Thunder Heights. Forever. The prospect was frightening.

She took her wet hand from the rail and looked at it absently. A memory of the river boat and Ross Granger turning her hands palm up swept back. What did he think of this strange turn of events? But what he thought did not matter. She had the feeling that she ought to make up her mind before she read her grandfather's letter. Yet how could she know her own heart and mind so swiftly?

With a resolute gesture she lifted the envelope and broke the seal.

My Dear Granddaughter (the letter began):

You do not know me, which is not your fault. Nor do you know that I have long followed your fortunes and watched you from a distance. I am aware that you have been a loyal daughter to your father, and that since his death you have conducted yourself with good sense and courage. You are able to work with pride for your living, and this is a trait I admire.

I have thought more than once of asking you to come to Thunder Heights for a visit, so that the two of us could become acquainted and so that you might forgive an old man for his sad mistakes of the past. It may already be too late.

Recently I have had a severe shock, and it may be that this time I shall not recover. Those who live under this roof with me I do not trust. I know now that the things I have built and worked for must not go into their hands, to be wasted and flung aside. What I have built is sound and good. I want it to remain with someone of my own blood who will be loyal to me.

You are the only possible answer to this desire of mine. For this reason I am changing my will. Thunder Heights will be yours. Restore it, my dear. Make it what it was in your mother's day. I have no wish to turn my two elder daughters out of this house, so I must ask you to keep them for the rest of their lives. And Hortense's adopted son, Booth, as well, though I have no personal liking for him.

Keep my daughters loyal to this house and to their name. Give neither of them anything if they move away. On this point I am adamant.

The business problems are large ones—I lack the strength to go into them now. We will talk about all these matters, and I will explain my distrust, my hopes, my fears to you. Then you will be armed and guided when the time comes.

By the time you read this, I hope we will have long been good and trusted friends. I will be able to go in peace, knowing that what I leave behind rests in responsible hands. Do not fail me, Granddaughter.

Your loving grandfather,
Orrin Judd

Camilla read with a growing sadness and with an increasing sense of being trapped. The will she might put aside and refuse to consider. This letter—the last wishes of a man whom she had learned, even in so short a time, to love and respect—must be considered solemnly.

Folding the letter, she put it back in its envelope and looked out again upon the swirling mist. The brown grass below the veranda was wet, but she went down the steps and across it with little heed for shoes and skirt hem. She walked between the old elms that bordered each side of the wide lawn, noting that leaf buds were showing along every limb.

She paused at the rim of a steep hill that dropped away in a thick stand of trees, concealing the steel ribbons of railroad track below. Here she turned about so that she could look up at the house and at the dark mountain towering behind. How grim the structure looked—as grim and forbidding as the stony cliff above. The weathered gray of the house seemed dingier than ever with wet mist clinging to its towers. The weed-choked clumps of thin grass added to the picture of woeful neglect.

How could her grandfather, who loved the house, have let it go like this? He must indeed have been driven far along a road of despair and hopelessness. Perhaps in writing his letter he had tried in some degree to retrace his steps, to mend what he himself had broken. If the weeds were destroyed and grass planted, this might again become a beautiful lawn. The house cried for repairs and fresh paint to make it once more a showplace on the Hudson.

An odd, unexpected excitement ran through her—almost a sense of exhilaration. It lay within her power to make such changes if she wished. The realization was sudden and heady. What if she accepted her grandfather's trust? What if she set about bringing the house out of its bad years and back into such glory as it had once known long ago? Might this not be a splendid and satisfying thing to do? Orrin Judd had wanted Althea's daughter to breathe new life and hope into Thunder Heights. He had believed that she could do this very thing.

Could she? Did she dare accept not only the trust, but the challenge?

Someone came out of the house and stood upon the

veranda, watching her. It was Letty Judd. She wore black today, but the material was soft and light, and a silk scarf about her shoulders softened their thin contour. Her injured arm was held tight across her body. Standing there at the head of the veranda steps, she seemed strangely of a piece with the house—a part of all the mystery it stood for. Letty Judd was a woman filled to the brim with secrets.

But though Camilla's sudden vision of her in that moment was clear, she refused to be daunted. She lifted her skirts so they would clear the wet grass and ran back to the steps, her face glowing and eager.

Letty saw the look and held out her hands in pleading. "Don't stay here at Thunder Heights. Let the house go. Let all of us go. That's the only wise choice, the only safe choice."

Camilla hesitated at the foot of the steps as distrust flicked through her mind. If she gave up this fortune and went away, Letty would inherit half, along with her sister Hortense. Yet Letty had disclaimed all interest in the money, and Camilla put the thought away almost as swiftly as it had come. This, she knew, was one of the dangers of accepting such a fortune—that she might become suspicious and distrustful, as her grandfather had been. And she did not want that.

She went up the steps and took Letty's hands in her own. "This is your home, Aunt Letty, and you shall live in it as long as you like, and with everything you need or want. Help me to make something good out of Grandfather's wishes."

Letty regarded her sadly. "You're going to stay, aren't you? I was afraid you might. You have the look of your mother about you—of Althea when she had a notion between her teeth and meant to carry it through, no matter what. No one ever changed her mind when she looked like that. It's a dangerous trait to inherit, my dear. It won't be easy for you to stay here."

Camilla smiled at the thought that she might indeed have a notion between her teeth, and that she might even like it.

"Come back to the library with me," she said, and drew Letty into the house.

No one had stirred in the walnut-dark room. Mr. Pompton stood with his back to the fire, his hands clasped behind him under lifted coat tails. Hortense sat bolt upright on the sofa, her fingers intertwined in her lap. Booth leaned beside her with an air of being faintly amused, as if nothing of consequence hung in the balance. Ross seemed again wholly absorbed in books on a shelf and he did not turn when Camilla entered the room.

She could feel the warmth in her own cheeks, sense the brightness of excitement which must stamp her appearance.

"I've made my decision," she told Mr. Pompton. "I'm ready to accept my grandfather's legacy and his stipulations. I shall remain at Thunder Heights."

VIII

A LOG ON THE FIRE CRUMBLED INTO ASH, THROWING UP sparks as it fell. For a moment there was no other sound in the room.

Then Mr. Pompton began to gather up his papers with a dry rustling that betrayed neither displeasure nor approval.

"Exactly," he said, as if he had expected all along that she would make no other choice.

"My grandfather's letter—" Camilla began, but Hortense interrupted her by standing up. She looked pale and stricken.

"Help me to my room," she said to Booth, and he gave her his arm and led her to Letty, who stood watching in the doorway.

"Aunt Letty will take you upstairs, Mother," he said, and came back into the room.

In the face of Hortense's precipitate exit and Mr. Pompton's remote and impersonal manner, something of Camilla's first exhilaration had begun to fade. But Booth, at least, spoke to her kindly.

"I'll admit that I hadn't expected matters to go in this direction," he said. "Forgive us, Cousin, if we don't seem altogether happy. It's rather a shock to my mother to find herself in the position of being dependent upon a niece she hardly knows. I only hope we can accept Grandfather Orrin's wishes with good grace." He smiled wryly. "As a matter of fact, you'll probably do better justice to the handling of Grandfather's fortune than my mother would. Certainly better than Aunt Letty. Or, for that matter—Booth Hendricks. So, for whatever it's worth, you have my support, Cousin Camilla."

He held out his hand and she put her own into it, touched and surprised. She had not thought that Booth would react like this.

Ross Granger shoved his book back on the shelf and looked around at them. There was nothing of conciliation or acceptance in his face.

"This is all very touching," he said. "But you must admit that the situation could hardly be more ridiculous."

"You might explain that remark, Granger," Booth said.

Ross threw him an irritable look. "Do you mean you don't find it ridiculous that all of this"—he waved a hand to encompass the Judd fortune—"has been left unequivocally in the control of an inexperienced girl of twenty-three?"

"You can always resign, you know," Booth put in, his eyes brightening as though he enjoyed this moment of clash.

For an instant Ross stared at the other man wrathfully. Then Booth shrugged, smiled at Camilla and went out of the room. Before Ross could speak again, Mr. Pompton cleared his throat and addressed Camilla.

"If you are willing, I'll come to see you as soon as I have things somewhat in order. There are various legal matters we must go over together. In the meantime I'll say good day. If you wish, I can make a statement to the press on my way out and take the reporters off your hands."

She thanked him, and when he had gone she looked uncomfortably at Ross. He appeared thoroughly angry, and she had no idea what to say to him, how to deal with him.

"I'll make no pretty speeches," he said curtly. "You have my resignation, of course. I'm sure you'll have other advisers who will work for you more cheerfully than I would. I'll try to be out of your way in a week or two."

His angry disapproval was so unfair that she did not want to let him go out of the room without offering some defense.

"Would you like to read my grandfather's letter?" she asked.

He shook his head. "No, thank you. It's sure to be the letter of a weak, defeated old man—not of the Orrin Judd I knew years ago. Reading it would not change my feelings about what he has done."

"I didn't ask for any of this—" Camilla began, but he would not stay to listen. He walked out of the room as though he dared not trust his temper and closed the door behind him.

Alone, Camilla sat at the library table and looked up at the portrait of her grandfather. She felt sick and shaken. This was going to be far harder than she had expected. Her spirits had plummeted from that moment of high elation when she stood looking up at the house, thinking of the changes she

72

might bring to it. Only Booth had spoken to her gently and tried to hide something of his own disappointment. Letty had advised against acceptance. Hortense was distraught and indignant, and even Ross, who was not one of the family, was angry with her.

She felt helpless and appallingly alone. Tears came before she could find strength to fight them back, and her head went down on her arms.

It was Ross who returned to find her there. He came into the library and stood beside the table while she made futile dabbing gestures at her eyes.

"There's no help for it," he said. "You'll have to talk to the reporters. They're not satisfied with Pompton's dry-as-dust evasions. What's worse—Booth is out there now, antagonizing them further. It's you they want to see, and you can't blame them for trying to do the job they've been sent here to do."

She stared at him, panic rising in her. "But—how would I know what to say? I—I've hardly grasped this myself. And—I must look terrible."

A flicker of amusement showed unexpectedly in his eyes. "You do," he said. "Your nose is red and your eyes are puffy. But you can be forgiven, since you've come from your grandfather's funeral. It's just as well if someone manages to look grief-stricken. Shall I bring them in?"

How hard and insensitive he was. She knew by his face that he would probably call the reporters in, whether she agreed or not. It was difficult to make a request of him, but she could not face them alone.

"Will you stay while I talk to them?" she asked.

"I'll stay," he said. "But you're in charge now, and you'll have to manage this yourself. The sooner you take hold, the better it will be for you."

Her feeling of panic increased, and he must have seen it in her eyes, for he softened a little.

"Look—we'll set the stage, shall we? Sit over here with your back to the light. That will give you an advantage. Take a few deep breaths and just try to be yourself. There's no great damage you can do, really. Most of the damage has been done by the situation itself."

As he went to summon the newsmen, she realized that she was gripping the arms of the chair with all her strength.

She was relieved when Booth returned with Ross and the five or six reporters who accompanied them into the library.

"Why did you agree to this?" Booth whispered, taking his

place beside Camilla's chair. "I'd have got rid of these fellows for you in a few more minutes."

There was no time to answer him. The group of newspapermen had ranged themselves around her, and she saw their curious glances as they took in the room's details and studied her.

"How do you feel about being Orrin Judd's heiress?" one of them asked.

She knew her lips would tremble if she tried to smile, and she answered stiffly. "I can only hope to be worthy of the responsibility."

The questions began to come quickly then. Why had Orrin Judd chosen her, when he had never sent for her before? Was it true that he had long ago disinherited her mother? What did he have against the other members of the family that he had treated them like this? Was it true that she was a governess?

They were not polite questions, and they were not intended to spare her. Once, sensing Booth's indignation, she put a hand on his arm so that he would not burst in angrily. Ross had gone to stand before the fire, as Mr. Pompton had done earlier, taking no part in the proceedings, and making no effort to come to her aid.

When the rapid questions confused her, Camilla put her hands up in protest. "There's so much I don't know. Perhaps it would be better if I tell you the little I do know about how I come to be here."

They listened and scribbled notes as she related simply, sometimes haltingly, what had happened from the moment when Mr. Pompton had come to see her in the house in Gramercy Park. All that she told them was the truth, though there were many omissions. She had no intention of giving any hint of the atmosphere in this house, or of the things her grandfather had said to her. She did not mention his letter. It lay in her lap, and once when she touched it inadvertently, she remembered its contents and felt strengthened. She had her grandfather's words and trust to hold to, though she might have nothing else.

When the reporters asked about her plans for the future and how she meant to run Orrin Judd's enterprises, she managed a rueful smile.

"You must know that is a question I can't answer now," she said. "But at least I have plans closer to home. I want to do this house over completely and make it the wonderful place it must once have been."

74

They liked this and took her ideas down as she talked. There was only one more sharp question near the end of the interview.

"What about your mother's death?" one young man asked. "There was some tragedy here—years ago, wasn't there? She was pretty badly smashed up in an accident, as I recall. Didn't your father—"

Ross broke into the interview smoothly. "You've had the time I promised you, gentlemen, and I think you have your story. Let's not torment the young lady unnecessarily."

His manner was courteous but firm as he saw them to the door and out of the house.

"You were wonderful, Cousin," Booth said, bending over her. "And more sensible than I. It's in my blood, I suppose, to hate reporters, since we've fared badly with them in the past."

Now that the ordeal was over, Camilla felt weak with relief. Her knees were trembling as she stood up. Beyond Booth she saw Aunt Letty in the doorway.

"They've bothered you enough, my dear," Letty said. "Come upstairs now and lie down. No, Booth, not another word."

Gratefully, Camilla went with her. She had nothing to say to either Booth or Ross Granger.

When Letty had gone, Camilla lay on her bed in the darkened room, trying to command her own thoughts, to formulate some sensible plan of action.

These first days would be the most difficult to get through, she assured herself. Once the family grew accustomed to the idea of having her here, once they came to know her and accept her, it should not be so hard. Surely they would be pleased when she made plans for the house. Hortense had longed for a gay life. Why couldn't it be gay enough for her right here at Thunder Heights? If Booth wished it, why couldn't he go to New York and arrange for a showing of his paintings? She could do so much for all of them, once they accepted her and began to trust her.

Her immediate task was to win them, to be patient and never angry, no matter what anyone might say or do. The business affairs she could do nothing about. Mr. Pompton would handle those, and she must trust him as her grandfather had undoubtedly trusted him. In spite of his attitude toward her, she wished that Ross Granger were not going away, because he too had been trusted by her grandfather. She could not, however, ask him to stay.

She had no desire at the moment to go downstairs to face the others, and when Grace came tapping at her door with a supper tray, she was relieved.

"Miss Letty fixed it herself," Grace said, setting the tray on the marble-topped table before the hearth.

When Camilla sat down to the tray, she found a brief note propped against a cup. It was from Letty.

> Don't come down to dinner, dear. Let us talk this out among ourselves. Everything will be better tomorrow.
>> Lovingly,
>> Aunt Letty

She was grateful for the respite and happy to have her meal quietly here in her room. She went to bed early and fell asleep at once, waking now and then to the rumble of a train that seemed to come from the earth beneath the house, or to the whistle of a boat, or foghorns on the river, only to fall quickly asleep again.

In the early morning she came wide awake, to find sunlight glowing beyond window draperies, and she sprang out of bed to let it in. The air was brisk and cool, but there was no sharpness in its touch as she opened the balcony door. She looked out across the river toward the morning sun, feeling rested and no longer fearful.

"This is mine!" she thought. "I need never look for a home again as long as I want to stay here. I belong to this now. I have a family." They might not want her here at first, but she belonged to them and eventually they would accept her.

When she had washed and dressed, she hurried downstairs, hungry for breakfast and eager to begin the day. Yesterday had been sad because of the funeral and frightening because of all the new, strange things that had been hurled at her when she was unprepared. But today she felt strong and unafraid. She would laugh at Ross's scowls and coax Aunt Hortense into good humor. She would find ways to make Aunt Letty happy, and she would show Booth her gratitude for his unexpected kindness.

Once more the dining room was empty, and for the moment she was glad to be alone so that she could marshal her plans before she talked to anyone. She had brought paper and pencil downstairs with her, and she set them beside her plate and began to jot down reminders to herself. Unobtrusively, if possible, she must learn to know the entire house. She must inquire into the possibility of hiring gardeners, carpenters, painters, so that the work might be appraised and started as soon as possible. There must be additional household help. Yet with all these changes she must move quietly and without seeming to jerk the reins from the hands of others. She must remember to consult Aunt Hortense, draw her into her plans, move gently until the others could see that only good would come of having her here.

No one joined her at the table as she finished breakfast, though Grace said Mr. Granger was up early as usual, and had gone over to Blue Beeches. He, at least, she would not have to consult, Camilla thought, and undoubtedly Thunder Heights would enjoy a less ruffled atmosphere when he was gone. Yet when she thought of Ross it was always with a tinge of regret. Under other circumstances they might have been friends, and it was sad to see a possibility of friendship lost.

When she had finished her second cup of coffee, she took her newly jotted list and descended from the kitchen to a landing at the back door. From the landing the stairs dropped in a second steeper flight to the cellar below, and she followed them down.

The main room of the cellar, at the foot of the stairs, was a large one, lighted by high windows that rose aboveground. A huge cookstove indicated that the room had once been the main kitchen of the house. What a busy, exciting place this must have been in the great days of Thunder Heights, before the new wing had been built to accommodate a smaller upstairs kitchen.

Camilla followed a corridor that ran the length of the cellar, looking eagerly into one room after another. There were storerooms of various kinds, and finally a room with high stone walls and an air of chill that indicated a larder.

Its door opened inward and stood ajar. These days butter and cream were kept in the ice chest upstairs, serviced from the village, so another use had apparently been found for this room. Along the wall facing the door were rows of shelves lined with dozens of small glass-stoppered jars and corked bottles. A marble slab had been set into a work shelf below at waist height, and a mortar and pestle rested upon it.

All these things Camilla saw at a glance as she stood sheltered by the door, unaware until she moved into the room that she was not alone. At her right, standing before a further row of shelves, was Aunt Hortense. This morning she wore a voluminous green negligee trimmed with yellowing lace. Her red hair, done up in rag curlers, was hidden by a white cap with coyly placed green velvet bows. She had not heard Camilla's quiet step in the doorway, and as Camilla hesitated, she reached up to a shelf and took down one of the labeled bottles.

"Good morning, Aunt Hortense," Camilla said, and her aunt whirled about, nearly dropping the bottle in her hands.

"Don't startle me like that!" she cried. "I didn't know anyone was about."

"I'm sorry," Camilla said. "I didn't see you till I stepped around the door."

She moved toward the shelves and looked up at them with interest, reading the labels. Here were Letty's herbs. The usual cooking herbs: thyme, chives, basil, marjoram, parsley, summer savory—all dried and pulverized, or left in leaf form, all labeled. On another shelf were the medicinal herbs: angelica, chamomile, hyssop, and many more. There were infusions and elixirs and distillations, as well as the dried herbs. As Camilla studied them, Hortense replaced the labeled bottle of tansy she had taken from its place.

"My sister Letty's hobby," Hortense said, her nose wrinkling a little as if she did not wholly approve. "It gives her something to do. But she indulges in too much experiment. I prefer to pick my own mixtures and avoid hers. I came down for something for my stomach and nerves. I hardly slept a wink all night. Is there anything you're looking for down here?"

In the bright morning light, Hortense's skin looked gray and a little withered. Her eyes that were not altogether green, nor altogether blue, had a look of cold resentment in them as they rested upon Camilla.

"I'm not looking for anything special," Camilla said. "I thought I would start at the cellar and begin to know the house. I hope you don't mind. When you feel up to it, Aunt Hortense, I'd like to consult you about so many things."

Hortense sniffed. "I'm certainly not up to it now. Not after the several shocks I've had to endure in the last few days. And after a miserable night. How did you sleep?"

"Soundly," Camilla said. "I hardly stirred till morning."

"She didn't bother you then? She didn't come to your door and try to get in?"

"What do you mean?" Camilla asked. "No one came to my door."

78

"A good thing. She might have frightened you. I've always wanted to lock her in at night, but Papa wouldn't hear of it."

"What are you talking about?" Camilla asked in bewilderment.

"My sister Letty, naturally. When she is disturbed she often walks in her sleep. And we never know what she may do next. I found her climbing the attic stairs last night and I had a time getting her back to bed."

Hortense reached for a jar of peppermint tea leaves, lifted out the glass stopper and sniffed the fragrance. Then she dropped a spoonful of the leaves into the teapot she had brought downstairs, added another spoonful from a jar of rose hips, and picked up the pot. As she reached the doorway, she paused.

"I should think you would be *afraid* to stay on in this house," she said.

"Afraid? Why should I be afraid?"

Hortense shrugged. "You might ask Letty sometime just what it was she gave Papa to drink the night he had his attack." She walked out of the larder, leaving Camilla to ponder her words in astonishment.

IX

IN THE DAYS THAT FOLLOWED, SPRING BEGAN TO MOVE brightly up the Hudson valley. Forsythia spilled its yellow spray, and enterprising crocuses and jonquils poked their heads through the bare earth of winter, announcing a change of seasons. About the house there were changes as well.

Camilla went vigorously and determinedly to work on her plans for renewal and repair. Booth laughed in good nature at her efforts, though he told her plainly that he could see no point in her desire to refurbish the house. Let it fall to ruin, he said, and then they would be rid of the burden and could live somewhere else in more fashionable style.

Nevertheless, he obligingly helped her find carpenters and set them to work. Old Toby obtained help in the village for work about the grounds and went at it with a will. Toby, at least, was all for restoring Thunder Heights to its former glory, pleased at the notion of lording it over the new help. He became something of a Napoleon in his attacks upon weeds and scrubby undergrowth. He planted with a lavish hand—grass and flower beds and new young trees to replace those that were old and dead.

An extra kitchenmaid was hired as well, leaving Grace free for upstairs work, but Camilla quickly discovered that indoor household help was difficult to find. Thunder Heights had a reputation that would have to be lived down. Thus Hortense, who was in need of a personal lady's maid, had to do without, since Camilla was unable to find anyone to work for her.

With Letty's help, Camilla checked slowly through every room in the house, to make sure of all that must be done. Letty was sweet and co-operative and refused her nothing, but Camilla had the uneasy feeling that she too did not believe in what they were doing. Except when Letty was in her herb room downstairs, or outside in her garden, she worked vaguely, as if with fog that blew through her hands as she measured it and would be nothing when she was finished.

Hortense remained hostile to all plans and would take no part in them. There was, Camilla quickly discovered, a convention to which all those in the house, masters and servants alike, bowed in convincing pretense. The pretense was that Hortense ran the house, gave the orders, made all plans, settled all problems. But it became evident in Camilla's first week that it was Letty who quietly executed these matters behind Hortense's back, even while she too gave lip service to her sister as mistress of the house. Camilla might have found something touching about this little game of pretend in which Letty protected her older sister from realizing the emptiness of her rule, had it not been that this sort of thing got in her way when she wanted to act without bowing to the wishes of Aunt Hortense. Camilla intended to make things happen now, and she found she could not wait until Hortense had been placated and coaxed into the new pattern. She tried not to oppose her openly, but she could not follow the example of the others if real changes were to be made.

One morning when Camilla found Hortense alone at breakfast, she tried to talk to her and draw her into some active role in the new plans for the house. But her aunt remained sharply antagonistic.

"If you had any sense," she said, "you'd let things alone. This house has seen too much of tragedy. Don't tamper with it. Don't wake it up, or you'll bring more down on our heads. There are times when I think it has a malevolent will to destroy us all. I don't want to see it repaired and renewed."

Camilla paid little attention to her words. The problem of Hortense was one she still hoped to solve, but it could be postponed in the face of matters more urgent.

Ross Granger, too, remained remote from all that was going on, though not to the extent of refusing to help if some immediate need arose. More than once he looked over repairs that were being made and made suggestions that saved time and waste. But he acted seldom and with evident reluctance. Often he carried his books and papers over to the comparative quiet of Blue Beeches, where there was less pounding and shouting, and where he was apparently welcome, as he worked to wind up his own part in Orrin Judd's affairs.

Camilla's first consultation with Mr. Pompton took place more than a week after the funeral. On the morning before Ross Granger was scheduled to leave, she received the lawyer in the library with a mingling of hope and hesitation, not sure whether or not he might try to stop her from spending money on the improvements she wanted to make. She was prepared to oppose him firmly if she had to. A sense of confidence was growing in her as she found that her orders were obeyed, her wishes deferred to—at least by those she employed.

Mr. Pompton had other matters on his mind, however. He droned on in monotonous detail about investments, holdings, interest, and other affairs of a similar nature, until Camilla's head spun and she felt increasingly confused. Then he relented and let her know that there was little she need do about any of these matters at present, except to sign a few papers. Mr. Granger, he said, had been Orrin Judd's lieutenant for years and he undoubtedly understood all the larger business affairs, which were not Mr. Pompton's province. Mr. Granger had formed a liaison between Thunder Heights and New York, and she could inform herself about these matters through him.

"But Mr. Granger is leaving tomorrow," she said in surprise that Ross had not let him know.

Mr. Pompton smoothed his pink scalp, unperturbed. "And when will he return, Miss Camilla?"

"He's not coming back," Camilla said. "He resigned from this work right after the funeral."

The attorney stared at her as if he did not believe his ears. Then he got up and strode back and forth across the room several times. When he sat down again, he had clearly made up his mind.

"You must not accept Granger's resignation, Miss Camilla. Later, perhaps, when someone else can take his place. But at the moment you cannot do without him."

As Camilla listened, he made very plain the reasons why she could not let Ross Granger drop her grandfather's affairs. Her first dismay began to fade as she heard him out, and she felt faintly relieved. Even though Ross had avoided her lately, his presence in the house had been reassuring. The fact of his being here had more than once bolstered her courage. She did not know quite why this was so, since she and Ross seemed seldom to be together without conflict or irritation. Nevertheless, at the moment she felt only relieved to hear that his continued presence was necessary.

When Mr. Pompton finished, Camilla rang for Grace and sent her upstairs to summon Mr. Granger from his room. He left his sorting and packing and came down to the library with his bright hair on end and a smudge of dust along one cheekbone.

"Please sit down," she said, and plunged in before she could frighten herself by thinking what might happen if he refused. "Mr. Pompton has just made me understand how indispensable you are in Judd affairs. Must you really leave us, Mr. Granger?"

He did not seem surprised. "Your cousin Booth and your Aunt Hortense don't want me here. And I certainly haven't meant to force my services on you."

Mr. Pompton coughed impatiently. "Stop play-acting, Granger. You know she can't move a finger without you."

Ross's straight mouth relaxed into a smile. "Miss King has been moving very fast in a number of directions without me."

"Women's matters," Mr. Pompton scoffed. "Supervising pots of paint and getting seamstresses in to make new draperies. Planting grass and clipping back the underbrush." He slapped the table before him impatiently. "What does she know about the Judd projects that are now in the making? These can't be dropped in midstream."

"I'd like to learn," Camilla said quickly.

Mr. Pompton and Ross Granger exchanged glances that were clearly despairing.

"You must stay, Granger," Mr. Pompton said. "You owe it to Orrin Judd."

Ross glanced at the portrait over the mantel. "I suppose it's impossible to leave without making some attempt to help. For a time at least."

"Then you will stay?" Camilla asked, and found that her tone sounded meeker than she had intended.

Ross hesitated for a moment longer, before he gave in. "All right—I'll stay. But not under this roof. I'd have moved out long ago, if Mr. Judd hadn't insisted that I be where he could call me the instant he wanted me."

"He left you the use of the rooms over the coach house in his will," Pompton said. "That was a bribe, wasn't it? To give you what you wanted, so you'd stay on and assist Miss Camilla?"

"Perhaps." Ross smiled wryly. "Or else it was meant to infuriate Hendricks."

Camilla looked from one to the other. "I don't understand. Why should it infuriate Booth?"

"Mr. Hendricks has his studio in those rooms," Mr. Pompton said. "He dabbles at his painting there."

So that was where Booth went when he absented himself from the house.

Camilla considered the matter, still at a loss. She did not want to antagonize Booth by putting him out of rooms he liked to work in. At the same time, she did not dare to lose Ross, and he was clearly firm about getting out of this house.

"There's no immediate hurry, is there?" she asked. "If you'll give me a little time, I'll talk to Booth and persuade him to work somewhere else."

Ross quirked a doubtful eyebrow, but did not object to a delay. Mr. Pompton gathered up his papers, found still another for Camilla's signature, and then went off, shaking his head doubtfully.

"I'd better get to my—unpacking," Ross said when Pompton had gone.

On impulse Camilla held out her hand to him. "Thank you for staying. I know you didn't want to."

He took her hand, bowed over it remotely and went out of the room without further comment.

Left alone, Camilla wondered about the best way to approach Booth. Perhaps Letty could help her on this, since she and Booth seemed on affectionate terms.

Camilla found her in the rear garden. Her aunt knelt at her work, the sleeves of her gray dress rolled up and her hands gloveless as she handled the soft brown earth, preparing it for planting. So this was why Letty's hands were not the pale, protected hands of a lady, but had a sturdy look of usefulness about them.

Much of her work seemed to be done with her left hand,

but she brought her right hand frequently into play by bending her body forward to accommodate the stiff arm. Her rolled-up sleeve revealed to a pitiful extent the misshapen right arm, thin and twisted. As she drew near, Camilla saw with a pang of dismay the ugly, welted crescent of a scar on the inner flesh of the arm.

At that moment Letty heard her. The bent head with its silver coronet of braids came up, and at once Letty pulled down her sleeve to cover the scarred and crooked arm. The gesture seemed more automatic than distressed, as if it were something she did out of long habit, to save the sensibilities of others. Her smile of greeting for Camilla was affectionate.

"Spring is the exciting time of year," Letty said, sounding as exuberant as a girl. "There's something about the smell of earth warming in the sun that's full of wonderful promise. I can almost feel things beginning to grow."

"I can at least see them beginning," Camilla laughed, and sat down on a flat rock at the edge of Letty's garden. "There's green everywhere you look today. Are you planting flowers, Aunt Letty?"

"No—herbs. Toby raises a few flowers, and I've planted a white narcissus fringe along the edge of the wood up there. But it's my little friends the herbs I like best. Look at coltsfoot there—already blooming. He's a bold one. That means warm days are on the way. He comes up as quickly as a dandelion, and just as bright and yellow, with his thick leaves close to the ground."

She gestured toward the plant beside her, and Camilla reached out to touch a leaf and turn it over, revealing its white, woolly underside. Watching Aunt Letty, listening to her, Camilla felt once more impatient with Hortense and her unkind insinuations. It was not Letty in this household who was to be distrusted.

"They're all so different, these herb people," Letty went on, more talkative now than Camilla had ever seen her. "Sage has leaves like velvet, while some herbs have leaves shiny as satin, or prickly, or smooth, or tough. Of course they're not much when it comes to flowers, yet the garden can look gay as a carnival when my herbs are in bloom. You'll see, later on."

Her bright, intense gaze, strangely young, lifted to meet Camilla's look frankly.

"I'm glad you're going to stay with us, my dear. At first I thought the only answer for you was to let the house go. But perhaps I was wrong."

"I hope so," Camilla said soberly.

"Of course you mustn't live the way we've lived." Letty prodded the earth with her trowel, continuing her work. "I mean shut in with each other, turning our backs on Westcliff and all our neighbors. Booth has a few friends he meets away from the house, but that's not enough. You could open the house, if you wanted to—make it like it was in the days when we were young and your mother was alive."

Camilla moved on the rock and drew her knees up, clasping her hands about them. "That sounds like fun, but there's so much to be done first, and it's still hard to believe in what has happened to me. I haven't begun to get used to it yet. Yesterday, when I was going through my trunk after it arrived from New York, I found myself wondering how I could remake some of my clothes, so they would last another season."

She laughed out loud, remembering her own foolish behavior. Suddenly, as she puzzled over the problem, it had come to her that she might have all the new clothes she wanted. Whereupon she had rolled up a bundle of her old things, rejoicing in an outburst of reckless abandon, and packed them off for charity. A gesture which left her with hardly a stitch to her back until the matter was corrected.

Letty laughed with her gently, as she told the story. "Perhaps you'll let Hortense help you with your planning of new gowns."

"Of course," Camilla promised readily. "Let's plan a new wardrobe for all three of us."

Letty nodded a little absently and returned to her work.

In a little while, Camilla knew, she must bring up the subject of Booth, but it was so pleasantly peaceful here in the herb garden that she wanted to postpone that problem for the moment. She wondered about Letty as she watched her work. It would be interesting to know what thoughts went on behind her present tranquility. She did not look like a woman who would walk in her sleep, or ever intend the slightest harm to others. Did she ever guess how her sister maligned her?

In the picture Grandfather Orrin had left, Letty's right arm had looked as straight as her left, so the crippling must have occurred after she was grown. What had caused the ugly scar that welted her arm? And why had so sweet a person as Letty never married?

"A normal social life would be good for Hortense, too."

Letty paused, trowel in air. "She has been hungry for gaiety for a long time."

"Yet she doesn't approve of what I'm doing," Camilla pointed out. "She says the house is born to tragedy and we must let it alone, or be destroyed by it."

Letty sat back on her heels to gaze up at the dark towers above them. "I know what she means. Once death has stepped into a house it leaves a shadow."

"Every old house knows death," Camilla protested. "Why should we mind that? Grandfather was an old man and he must have lived a full life. Perhaps we shouldn't grieve too much for his going."

The silver braids about Letty's head shone in the sun as she bent over the bed where she was working, crumbling earth idly in her fingers. Her silence was only a cloak for her thoughts, Camilla knew, and she spoke to her softly.

"You're thinking of my mother, aren't you, Aunt Letty? That she died in this house—died too young. Will you tell me what happened? When those reporters were here, one of them mentioned her. He spoke of her being—smashed up. Why shouldn't I know the truth, whatever it was?"

Letty's brown eyes, so warm and unlike her sister's, rested on Camilla's face for a moment and then flicked away. In that instant Camilla glimpsed in them something of—was it fear? There was a long silence while Letty dropped seeds into the earth and patted them down, moving on along the row, not minding the earth stains on her skirt. A robin, fat and red-breasted, hopped close enough to pull a worm from the far side of the herb bed. There was a warm odor of earth and sun and pine needles in the air, and Camilla thought she had never been in so quiet and peaceful a place. Peaceful except for the glimpse of quickly hidden uneasiness she had seen in Letty's eyes.

While her father had refused to speak of Althea's death because of his own pain, and his desire to keep his daughter from unnecessary hurt, the silence which surrounded Althea's death at Thunder Heights had in it something more. Something that savored of concealment, of a fearful reluctance to have the truth known.

It would be no use, Camilla knew, to repeat her question. The time for the answer to be given her was not yet ripe. In as matter-of-fact tones as she could manage, she began to speak of Booth's studio over the coach house and of the fact that Ross, if he were to stay, must have the use of those rooms.

Letty listened, nodding thoughtfully. "Of course we can't afford to lose Ross Granger if he is willing to stay. Booth will have to give up his studio. But he won't want to, you know. And he can be difficult when he chooses. Perhaps I had better speak to him."

For just a moment Camilla was ready to accept Letty's offer. For all that Booth had been kind, she had a feeling of strangeness about him. He had never shown anger toward her, yet she had a sense of dreading his anger. Nevertheless, she put aside her feeling of readiness to rely on Letty. If she was to make her home at Thunder Heights she could not sidestep the difficult tasks. This was something she must solve herself. She had come to Aunt Letty only for advice.

"I'll speak to him myself," she said.

There was approval in Letty's look. "You're right, of course, dear. Perhaps you might offer him some other place when you tell him about this. Why not—the nursery? It's big enough and the light is good up there. Booth only moved his workroom out of the house because Papa came to dislike the smell of paints and turpentine. But I don't think the rest of us will mind it up at the top of the house."

"Thank you, Aunt Letty," Camilla said. "I'll go talk to him now."

But still she did not spring up at once to go in search of Booth. "I saw your herb collection in the cellar the other day," she went on idly. "You must have given a great deal of study to the subject to put up all those different things."

Letty nodded. "I love to mix my tisanes and infusions. Herbs have so much to give when you understand them. I used to treat most of the villagers in the old days, whenever they got sick. They trusted me more than they did the doctor. There was a friendly rivalry between Dr. Wheeler and me at one time. Of course I don't do that any more."

Camilla studied her aunt's face with its fragile bone structure and hint of inner strength. "Why did you stop, if you helped people and if you enjoyed nursing them?"

Letty did not answer at once. She pressed earth over seeds she had dropped and smiled down at them fondly.

"You have to be careful about planting herbs. They're likely to come up—every one—and grow elbow to elbow like city folk. So we have to give them room in the planting."

Camilla waited, and after a moment Letty went on, not meeting her eyes as she spoke.

"Hortense didn't like what I was doing. She didn't think it was a fitting occupation for a Judd."

"Why not start again, Aunt Letty?" Camilla asked.

"It's too late," Letty admitted sadly. "Too late for so many things." She bent her head, so that only her silvery braids were visible.

There was no point in postponing her unwelcome task any longer and Camilla stood up. "Do you know where Booth is now?"

"I saw him going out toward the coach house this morning," Letty told her. "He's probably still there. If he's angry with you at first, don't mind. I'll get him to come around."

"I'll get him to come around myself," Camilla said with a resolution she did not entirely feel. She walked around the house and took the driveway in the direction of the stable.

X

As she approached, the coach house could be seen ahead near the gate. Here, too, an unconventional imagination had been at work in the design. It looked almost like a miniature of the main house, with its own turrets and gables and the barge-board bracketing that was typically Hudson River.

She found the barnlike lower door ajar and saw that it was somewhat the worse for weathering. More repairs would be needed here, as well as fresh paint. From the open doorway she could see a steep flight of stairs running upward to the floor above. She did not approach them at once, but moved among the dusty stalls and examined the big room where a carriage had once been kept. Dust and cobwebs lay over everything. Only the stairs had been swept clean. An old set of harness hanging from a nail rattled as she struck it in passing and Booth's voice challenged her at once from above.

"Who's down there?"

She went quickly to the foot of the stairs. "It's I—Camilla."

He came to the head of the stairs and looked down at her. "A pleasant surprise! Come up, Cousin Camilla, and see my workshop."

Holding to a rickety handrail, she mounted the stairs and took Booth's extended hand. He drew her up the last step, and she stood blinking in the bright, spacious upper room.

Booth wore a long gray linen duster revealing smudges of

paint, and he held a palette in one hand. An easel had been set up in the center of the room with a nearly finished painting upon it.

"You're just in time for coffee, Cousin," Booth told her. He set the palette down and brought an armchair for her, dusting it before she seated herself. "My housekeeping's not of the best, but I don't like servants moving my stuff around."

When she had taken the chair, he stepped to an alcove, where a coffee pot had just started to bubble on a small stove. The fragrance of coffee was laced by the odors of Booth's paint materials—a combination Camilla did not find unpleasant. While he busied himself with the coffee, she studied the painting on the easel.

Once more she was caught by the violent power of Booth's work. This view was one of the Hudson, with what must surely be an exaggerated Thunder Mountain rising from the bank. Black storm clouds boiled into the sky above, and the whole was a moment held suspended in a flash of lightning. At the foot of the precipice Hudson waters churned to an angry yellow in the sulphurous light, and a tiny boat was caught in the instant of capsizing and spilling its occupants into the water. Booth had endowed the painting with a wild terror that made Camilla's scalp prickle.

"Are your pictures always so violent?" she asked.

Booth set the coffee pot down and came over to her, interested at once in her reaction to his work.

"So you see what I've tried to catch? The moment of danger! The very knife edge of danger, where there is life one moment and possible death the next."

She could see what he meant, and even sense the fascination such a moment might have for him as an artist. But she wondered what might drive a man to preserve such moments repeatedly on canvas. The picture she had seen in his mother's room had portrayed the same "moment of danger."

He saw the question in her eyes. "Can there be any greater excitement in life than the moment just before a man solves the last mystery?"

There seemed a dark elation in him that was disturbing. From the first she had sensed about him a strangeness that she did not understand, and which she remembered when she was away from him. Because it made her uneasy now and a little self-conscious, she left her chair to wander about the room, examining other paintings that leaned against the walls.

"Your mother spoke of arranging a show for you in a New York gallery," she said. "Why don't you go ahead with that now?"

He returned to the stove, filled a cup from the coffee pot and brought it to her. "I suppose I could—if I cared enough. Grandfather Orrin never approved of my painting. He didn't consider it a man's work. Not that I cared. I paint for my own amusement."

Amusement was a strange word for a product so gloomy. She sipped her coffee and moved on about the room, pausing to study the scene of a fierce cockfight, in which the feathers of the birds were bright with blood as they met in deadly combat. The next picture was an unfinished painting of a woman who struggled to hold a rearing horse, its hoofs flailing not far from her head. Her face had not been completed and the background was a vague blur, but the wild eyes of the horse, its distended nostrils and bared teeth, had all been carefully depicted.

Booth noted Camilla's arrested interest and crossed the room to turn the picture against the wall. "I don't put my unfinished work on view," he said.

There was almost a rebuff in his manner, and she glanced at him, puzzled. What haunted this man? What drove him and made him so strange? Darkly strange and strangely fascinating.

She returned to her chair, moving it so that she need not stare at the painting of the capsizing boat with its little human figures flung out over the torrent.

"Your model has courage," she remarked. When he said nothing she went on. "I've always loved to ride. Do you suppose I could buy a horse hereabout and ride again at Thunder Heights?"

Booth sat down upon a high stool, hooking his heels over the rungs. "Why not? Grandfather Orrin's not here to forbid it."

"Why wouldn't he keep horses when he had a coach house built?"

Booth drank a swallow of coffee, hot and black. "We hardly needed them, since we had few places to go. The world came to Orrin Judd when it had to, and it could hire its own hacks."

She knew he was evading her question, but she could not bring herself to challenge him.

"If you're seriously interested, Cousin," he went on, "I'll

keep an eye open for a horse that's been trained to the sidesaddle. I think I can find you a good one."

"I'll appreciate that." She finished her coffee, wondering how to bring up the subject of Ross Granger and these rooms.

He gave her an unexpected opening. "I suppose you'll plan to clean up the stable below and keep your horse here when you get one? There's room for a stableboy beyond that partition."

Camilla forced herself to the topic in hand. "Did you know that Mr. Granger has agreed to stay on for a time? Mr. Pompton says we can't do without him. He has been my grandfather's eyes and ears for so long that there's no one to take his place."

She stole a look at Booth as she spoke and saw that he had stiffened.

"I was afraid we wouldn't be easily rid of him. I suppose you've come to tell me that I'm to move out of these rooms and let Ross Granger take over his—inheritance? Is that it?"

She could feel herself flushing. "Perhaps we could fix up the old nursery as a studio for you. The light there should be better than you have here, and it might be more convenient to do your painting inside the house."

"I suppose this is a plan Aunt Letty has suggested? You were afraid to come here and ask me to move, weren't you, Cousin?"

"I came," she said simply, not caring to admit her reluctance.

"So you did. But what if I tell you I don't choose to move? What if I tell you I don't care for the nursery?"

She looked away from the rising anger in his eyes. "I don't blame you for not wanting to move, when the place has been yours for so long."

"Your sympathy touches me, Cousin," he said, and began stacking his finished paintings against the wall. "All right then—I'll move. But please understand—I'm not doing it to suit Granger's convenience."

She set her cup and saucer aside and went to stand beside him. "You needn't hurry. Mr. Granger can wait. I'm sorry it has to be this way."

His look softened unexpectedly and he smiled. "I believe you mean that, my dear. Don't worry, I'll cause you no embarrassment. But remember that I'm doing this for you, not for Granger."

"Thank you," she said, and turned toward the stairs, retreating instinctively from his gentler mood, lest he ask more of her than she was ready to give.

He did not let her go alone, but came with her toward the house. As they followed the driveway, he slipped her hand into the crook of his arm, as if he wished to reassure her. Camilla was sharply aware of him close at her side, moving with his air of restrained vitality, as though the dark power that flowed through him was held for the moment in leash. What might it be like if he once lifted his self-imposed restraint? An odd sense of excitement stirred her.

As if he knew her reaction to his nearness, he tightened his arm so that her hand was pressed against his side.

"Tell me, Cousin," he said, "how does it happen that a young woman as attractive as you are has gone unmarried in New York?"

"I have never known very many men," she admitted, and tried to quicken her step.

He held her to the slower pace, and she knew he was amused by her quick confusion and the warm color she felt in her cheeks. Booth Hendricks puzzled and dismayed her, and as often as not he filled her with a sense of—was it attraction or alarm? Perhaps a mingling of both, for it might be dangerous to grow too interested in this man.

"We must mend this lack in your life," he said. "Unless you know a variety of men, you're likely to be too vulnerable to attention from almost any man."

He went too far, but she did not know how to reprove him, was not even sure that she wanted to.

When they neared the house the sound of carpenters working on a scaffolding above the front door reached them, and Camilla looked up at the new repairs in satisfaction.

"The house looks better already. I'm eager to see it painted."

Booth's look followed her own with indifference. "I'm afraid I agree with my mother that it's a waste of good money and energy. But if it pleases you, Camilla, if it makes you happy, then I suppose it serves a purpose in our lives."

He released her hand from his arm and left her at the foot of the steps, going off in one of his abrupt withdrawals, so that it seemed all in an instant that he had forgotten her. She went into the house troubled by a curious mixture of emotions. At the moment she was not at all sure how she felt about Booth Hendricks.

Letty met her in the upstairs hall. "Did you see Booth? How did he react when you suggested a change of studios?"

"I know he didn't like it," Camilla told her, "but he tried to be kind. I suspect that he's angry with Ross. I'm relieved to have the interview over."

Letty was studying her with quick understanding. "You look upset, dear. Why don't you lie down in your room for a little while and let me bring you a tisane to make you feel better?"

It was easier to allow Aunt Letty to minister to her, than to resist or refuse to be doctored. But when she was in her room again, she could not lie quietly on a bed. Her visit to Booth's studio had been upsetting in more ways than one. She had sensed in him a bitter anger that might one day explode into the open. When it did, she hoped it would not be directed against herself. Or did she hope for just that? Did she want to be involved with Booth at whatever cost to herself?

She was still walking restlessly about the room when Letty tapped at the door. As Camilla opened it, Mignonette streaked in first, leaving Letty to enter more slowly with a tray in her hands.

"Here you are, dear," Letty said. "There's hot toast in that napkin and a bit of rose petal jam. Let the tea steep a minute, and it will be just right."

"Thank you, Aunt Letty," Camilla said, grateful for her consideration and affection.

Letty patted her arm lovingly and hurried away. For once Mignonette did not follow her mistress. She came to sit before the small table that held the tray, looking up at it expectantly.

Camilla laughed. "You're staying for your saucerful, aren't you?"

The little cat mewed in plaintive agreement.

"All right," Camilla said, "I'll pour some for you, but you'd better be careful—it's scalding hot."

She filled the saucer and set it on a piece of wrapping paper on the hearth. Then she poured a cupful for herself and stirred it, waiting for it to cool, sniffing the sharp aroma that was a little like that of the daisy, and not altogether pleasant. Mignonette was already lapping daintily around the cooling edges of the liquid, and Camilla watched her in amusement. A strange taste for a cat. Letty must have fed her tisanes when she was a kitten, that she had grown up with so odd an appetite.

Feeling that she must drink some of the tea whether she liked it or not, Camilla raised her cup. The cat made a choking sound, and she looked down to see that Mignonette was writhing as if in pain. While Camilla watched, too startled to move, the little cat contorted her body painfully and rid herself of the tea she had just lapped up so greedily.

Camilla set her teacup down and ran to the door to call Letty. It was Hortense, however, who came down the hallway.

"Letty's gone downstairs. What is it?"

"Mignonette is sick. I just gave her a saucer of tea and she's throwing it up."

An odd expression crossed Hortense's face. She cast a single look at the cat and then picked up the untouched cupful of tea. She sniffed it and shook her head.

"I'll take care of this," she said and picked up the teapot as well to carry away.

Camilla poured water into the saucer for Mignonette and began to fold up the paper. In a moment Hortense was back.

"You mustn't let my sister dose you with these things," she said. "She overrates her knowledge of medicinal herbs, and it's best not to give in to her whims. What if you had drunk what was in that cup and hadn't the faculty of getting rid of it as Mignonette did?"

She went off without waiting for an answer, and Camilla regarded the cat doubtfully. Mignonette was trying weakly to clean herself, and she looked up at Camilla with an air that might have been one of entreaty. Camilla picked her up gently and carried her downstairs in search of Letty.

Grace said Miss Letty was in the cellar larder, and Camilla went down the lower stairs. She found Letty at work cleaning shelves, with Booth assisting her in a desultory fashion. They were taking down bottles and jars, wiping them and replacing them in neat order.

Camilla held out the cat. "Mignonette drank some of my tea just now and it made her painfully sick for a few moments. She really frightened me. Though I think she's recovered."

Letty turned and Camilla saw the color drain from her face. She almost snatched the cat from Camilla's hands and held her close, stroking the small body tenderly. Camilla had never seen Letty angry before, but now she fairly bristled with indignation.

"No one gives Mignonette anything without my orders," she cried. "Never, never do such a thing again!"

Camilla heard her in astonishment and found no answer.

"Perhaps," Booth said quietly, "we had better think of Camilla. Did you drink any of the mixture, Cousin?"

"No." Camilla shook her head. "Aunt Hortense came in when I told her the cat was sick, and she took the pot and cup away and emptied them. I hadn't even tasted the tea."

Her words seemed to bring Letty to herself. While she did not release her hold on Mignonette, she gave Camilla a weak and apologetic smile.

"I'm sorry, dear. Mignonette means so much to me that I—I was cross for a moment. It was most inconsiderate of me."

Booth was watching her, his gaze alert and questioning.

"What was in the tea, Aunt Letty?" he asked.

Holding the cat to her shoulder with one hand, Letty hurried to the row of shelves behind the door and took down an empty jar. "Why—it was just my usual marjoram and mint mixture. I used the last of it—see."

Booth took the jar from her hands and removed the cover, sniffing before he gave it back to her. "Are you sure? Sometimes I wonder how you tell all these leaves and powders apart when you're working with so many ingredients."

"It's quite simple," Letty said with dignity. "I know the appearance of each one as well as I know the faces of those about me. And every scent is different too."

She put the empty jar back on the shelf, and Camilla noted idly a vacant place on the same shelf a little farther along, where a bottle had been removed from between two others.

"Tell me, Aunt Letty," Booth said, "did anyone else know you were going to fix this pot of tea for Camilla?"

For just an instant Letty's gaze wavered. It was nothing more than a flicker, yet Camilla sensed in it indecision and hesitation. A shock of distrust that was close to fear flashed through Camilla, leaving her shaken and apprehensive.

Then Letty was herself again, and if she had experienced a moment of doubt in which she had seen a choice of action before her, the fact was quickly concealed by her more usual manner. Had she thought in that instant to conceal blame, or to place the blame elsewhere? In any case, she did neither.

"I'm sure it wasn't my tea that upset Mignonette," she said. "I tell you what—I'll fix you some fresh tea, dear. It won't take a minute."

Camilla started to refuse, but Booth broke in smoothly. "Make some for me too, Aunt Letty. The three of us can have a pot together. I've had a bad morning."

He glanced at Camilla, his look faintly mocking, as if he

dared her to refuse. His mood had lifted strangely into something laced with excitement, and far from reassuring to see.

Letty made the tea, heating water on the stove out in the main room of the cellar, where a fire already burned beneath a simmering mixture. There were several straight chairs about a round table in the big room, and they sat down to drink a mint tea that Letty had flavored with leaves of fragrant balm. Mignonette, apparently none the worse for her experience, trustfully took a saucerful from Letty's hands. But only in the small cat was there any trust, Camilla thought as she sipped the fragrant tea. Letty's eyes did not meet her own, while Booth's gaze met Camilla's all too readily. She felt a little sick with distrust, so that she could hardly swallow.

Before they were through, Hortense came downstairs and regarded them in astonishment.

"Do join us," Letty said almost gaily, but her sister refused.

Booth slanted an oblique look at his mother. "You shouldn't have thrown out that pot of tea so quickly. It might have borne looking into. Could you tell whether anything was wrong?"

"They all smell vile to me," Hortense said. "That cat was at death's door. What affected the cat might have killed Camilla."

Letty busied herself with Mignonette, and one would have thought by her manner that she had heard nothing of the talk going on about her. Yet there was a rigidity in the movement of her head that told Camilla how intently she listened. It seemed as though some duel went on below the surface among these three—as though each knew something Camilla did not know, and each suspected the other two.

Camilla let the rest of the tea cool in her cup. The bitter taste in her mouth gave it a flavor she could not endure.

That afternoon at Ross's request, Camilla had a talk with him in the library. After what had happened to Mignonette, she was in no mood to discuss business matters, but Ross insisted and she lacked the strength to oppose him.

They faced each other beneath Orrin Judd's picture, and Camilla found it difficult to attend to his words. She would have preferred to pour out her own doubts and bewilderment, but Ross, she suspected, would dismiss such notions as feminine nonsense. His own manner was as correct and impersonal as Mr. Pompton's would have been, and such a bearing did not invite confidences.

"Did you have any trouble getting Hendricks to agree to move out of the coach house?" Ross began.

"None at all," Camilla said. It was not to Ross that she would admit her confusion about Booth.

He studied her with a skeptical air, as if he were ready to discount anything she might say. She blinked in the face of such scrutiny, finding him no more an easy person to be with than was Booth. Or did most men leave her ill at ease? she wondered, thinking of Booth's words. Not vulnerable—merely uncomfortable.

She made herself meet Ross's eyes and take the lead. "Why are you so anxious to move out of the house?" she asked.

"Frankly, I don't want to be under the same roof with your Aunt Hortense or her son. I'm sure no love is lost between us and we'll be glad to avoid chance meetings that wear on the nerves when we meet constantly about the house."

"What about mealtime?" Camilla asked. "Won't you be joining us then?"

"Only for dinner," he said. "I can manage the rest myself. The coach house is set up for light housekeeping, and I can work straight through the day out there, with plenty of room for office space. But this isn't why I wanted to see you. If I'm to stay on here for a time, I'll need to know your wishes in various matters."

Camilla nodded. She had no idea what he expected of her.

"If you choose," he went on, "you can make final decisions from here, just as your grandfather used to do. Even though he remained at Thunder Heights, he never let the reins go slack. It's to be hoped that you'll follow in his footsteps."

His face was expressionless, but Camilla could hardly believe that he meant what he was saying.

"How could I possibly—"

He broke in at once. "Or you can go down to New York yourself and meet the directors of his business holdings and discuss problems with them whenever you like."

Now she was sure he was baiting her. "I can't make decisions concerning matters I know nothing of."

"I agree." He nodded as though her answer satisfied him. "A few days ago you said you wanted to learn about your grandfather's affairs. If you like, we can meet for a time every day so that we can go into them together."

She could imagine him as a stern, remote tutor, and herself as his humble student. The prospect did not please her.

"Isn't there another choice? Since you understand all this so well, can't you make the necessary decisions and talk to the businessmen in New York?"

His smile was cool. "You've mistaken my identity," he told her. "I'm Mercury, not Jove. I've played messenger for your grandfather, and on occasion I've advised him on engineering projects. But I've never made final decisions. I doubt that anyone would listen to me."

Camilla gave him a sidelong glance, once more aware of his look of vigor, as if he were made for an outdoor existence and never for the work of a clerk—or a messenger.

"You'd have to begin at the very beginning," she said with a sigh.

"Shall we start tomorrow morning at nine, then?" he said.

When she nodded, he stood up, as if only too eager to escape her presence. Whether she liked it or not, a period of tutelage lay ahead, with Ross Granger as her mentor.

XI

NOW A TIDAL FOAM OF CHERRY, PEAR, AND APPLE BLOSSOMS surged north along the Hudson. This was a joy not to be experienced to any such extent in New York, and Camilla reveled in the pink and white beauty. She found a favorite spot beneath the plumes of a flowering peach where she could often sit overlooking the Hudson, watching the busy river traffic. Here petals drifted on every breeze, settling about her on the young spring grass.

Escaping the house and its submerged antagonisms, she could make herself forget the episode of Mignonette's poisoning. Or at least she could convince herself that in so lovely a world such forebodings as grew out of the incident were foolish. These days she felt an increasing, comforting affinity with the river.

With Ross's occasional help, she was learning to identify by name some of the boats that passed. She knew the cargoes of the flat barges, and the freighters that plied their way up and down the Hudson. She might have preferred her instruction from Booth, but he had little interest in the river.

It was unfortunate that her business conferences with Ross

were less amiable than her river discussions and that the tension between them increased. At first he tried conscientiously to make clear the complicated details on construction that he set before her. But with no background for understanding the vast reaches of the Judd building empire, and no natural flair for the figures and blueprints Ross laid before her, she was soon weltered in confusion and, at length, boredom. When she tried to talk to him about her own eager plans for the house and the grounds, he shrugged them aside as being of no consequence. This, more than anything else, infuriated her. Why should he expect of her talents that she did not have, and ignore the real gifts she felt she was bringing to Thunder Heights?

The outdoor painting was nearly finished, and she could regard the old house with new pride. She had refused to have it painted a frivolous yellow, like Blue Beeches. Silver gray seemed to suit its seasoned quality, and now its turrets gleamed a clean, pale gray against the surrounding green of the woods, with the roofs a dignified darker gray. The house had lost none of its eerie quality in the painting and there was still a somber air about it, but at least it was handsome again, as it had been in its youth. Camilla had already had the satisfaction of seeing passengers on the river boats look up at the house and gesture in admiration.

Yet all this Ross ignored, as though she were a child playing with toys and not to be taken seriously. He thought it a waste of time and money to trouble about the house when there were matters of moment at stake. The real quarrel between them, however, came over the bridge.

Perhaps the matter would not have brought on such a crisis if she and Ross had not been particularly at odds with each other that day. Their disagreement came over the improvements she insisted upon for the coach house. So far Booth had not found a saddle horse for her, but Camilla wanted the stable to be ready for one when it was found. The invasion of his premises with pounding and sawing and the noise of workmen had irritated Ross. The place had been all right, he said—let it alone!

As a consequence he was shorter than usual at their morning sessions in the library, which had become their schoolroom. When he mentioned the bridge out of a clear sky one morning and said they must soon go seriously to work on this as an important future project, she asked flatly why they should consider building a bridge across the Hudson, with all the enormous expense and complications such an undertaking would involve. Mr. Pompton was urging her to sell more and more of her holdings and invest the money in other ways. He thought it foolish of Ross to try to teach her anything of her grandfather's business affairs, and she was ready to agree with Mr. Pompton.

Ross contained himself and tried to be patient about explaining the matter.

"Camilla, you must realize that for miles up and down the river, there is no way for people and commerce to cross, except by ferry. How do you think this country can continue to grow, if those who have the means and the imagination shun their responsibility? Can't you see what such a bridge would mean to the entire Hudson valley? And can't you imagine how it would look?"

His hands moved in a wide gesture, as if he built before her eyes a great span of steel and concrete. He had come to life as she had never seen him do before. She had not thought of him as a man who could dream and the realization surprised her. Nevertheless, she could not go along with so staggering a project.

"Did Grandfather think such a plan practical?" she challenged.

Ross looked thoroughly exasperated. Perhaps all the more so because for a moment he had let down the guard he seemed to hold against her.

"He was certainly for the idea in the beginning. I'll admit he lost interest in a great many things in the last few years, and perhaps he was no longer as pressingly keen on the bridge as he was at the start, but I'm sure he never gave up the idea completely. The legislature in Albany is interested. I've appeared before committees more than once. And we're in a position to underbid the field when the time is ready for action. But a great deal of preparatory work must be done. The location we will recommend must be settled on. Materials must be selected well ahead of time, construction contracts worked out in advance—oh, a thousand details must be taken care of before we can even present our story for a final contract."

He reached into a briefcase and drew out a sheaf of engineering drawings he had brought into the library.

"Here—you might as well see what I'm talking about," and he spread before her the detailed drawings for a suspension bridge across the Hudson.

None of them had any meaning for Camilla, but she could recognize the gigantic nature of the project, and she could

100

well imagine the myriad difficulties it would represent. Perhaps her grandfather would have taken to the task eagerly in his younger days, but she could well imagine his shrinking from its complexities in his last years.

"For one thing," she said, trying to sound reasonable, "I don't see why such a bridge hasn't been built before, if it's really needed. Would it justify the amount of traffic it would handle?"

"With that reasoning," Ross said, "no one would ever try anything that hadn't been done before. But of course we've looked into that very question, and I've been able to convince the authorities that the bridge is needed. However, we'd be building for the future as well. You don't think traffic is going to remain at the horse and wagon stage, or even be confined to trains and boats with the motor car coming into use, do you? Roads and more roads are going to be needed. And bridges to connect them, as we've never needed bridges before!"

He almost fired her with his enthusiasm. She had never seen him so eager and alive and persuasive. The picture he was painting was one to stir the imagination. Yet her grandfather, who knew a great deal about such things, had held back, had not been ready. His reasons had probably been good ones, and not merely the reasons of a man grown fearful and tired. She could not know. And since she didn't know, she could not take so reckless an action as to let Ross go ahead on this.

She rubbed her temples wearily with her fingertips and drew back from the papers Ross laid before her.

"If such a bridge needs to be built, let someone else build it," she said. "With Grandfather gone, it's not for us."

Ross stared at her for a moment. Then he scooped up his papers and went out of the room without another word. Camilla knew how angry he was. For a long while she sat on at the library table wondering despairingly what to do.

Then a slow, resentful anger began to grow in her as well. Somehow Ross Granger always managed to put her in the wrong, and she would not have it. He was not going to involve her in the frightening responsibility of building bridges. Only recently there had been a terrible disaster where a new bridge had collapsed, killing a great many people. Remembering the dreadful stories and drawings in the newspapers, her will to oppose him strengthened. There could be no bridge built under the Judd name unless she gave her consent, and she did not mean to give it.

After that, matters went badly between them. The morning "lessons" became painfully formal, with Ross performing a duty in which he plainly had no interest, until they finally ended altogether. Camilla had a feeling that he might resign again at any moment, and she was resolved to let him go. He, more than anything else, was the fly in her ointment these days. Even Mr. Pompton agreed with her about the bridge, when she told him of it a few days later.

It was a good thing there were other satisfactions for her. Letty had found two skillful seamstresses and Camilla had sent for dress goods and household materials from New York, throwing herself into an orgy of sewing. A whole new wardrobe was being prepared for her, as well as a new wardrobe for the house.

Hortense had been indifferent to an offer of new clothes for herself. In her own eyes she was dressed in the grand styles she had admired as a girl, and she preferred them, she said firmly, to the ridiculous way women dressed today. As for Letty, she was satisfied with her own soft, drifting gowns, and Camilla had to admit that they suited her.

Having new clothes was a pleasure she had never been able to indulge to such an extent before, and she was feminine enough to enjoy it wholeheartedly.

Lately she had caught Booth's eyes upon her admiringly more than once, and she had been pleasantly aware of his approval. Since the day when she had gone out to the coach house to talk to him, she had continued to be drawn to him in an oddly uneasy way. She was not altogether comfortable with him, but she could not help but feel flattered by his admiration.

One late afternoon in May Camilla sat on the marble bench in the rear garden, savoring the fragrant company of Aunt Letty's "herb people." She could always find balm for her spirits here, and things to think about as well. It pleased her that she was learning to identify the herbs and could watch their progress with recognition.

Lungwort had followed coltsfoot, with early blooming flowers of pink and blue. Wild thyme sprouted between the stones around the sundial. The bee balm was growing quickly, and Camilla loved to pinch off a thin green leaf and rub it between her fingers for the lemony scent. Rosemary, Letty said, belonged to warm climates and always faded away in pained surprise at the first touch of winter. But she loved it and planted it anew every spring—so it was up again now,

102

with its narrow leaves breathing more fragrance into the garden.

It was good to sit here and breathe the sweet and tangy perfumes, pleased that she was beginning to separate one scent from another.

She had worked hard inside the house today, helping the seamstress with the rich materials that had come from New York and which were now bringing new life to the dreary interior of the house. Rose damask draperies in the parlor would give the room a softer, more gracious look. The dining room wallpaper was now a cool, pale green that didn't give her indigestion every time she looked at it. The draperies there were to be a rich golden color—luxurious and expensive. She could imagine their folds as they would hang richly at the dining room windows, and satisfaction flowed through her over what she had accomplished and still meant to accomplish.

The feeling swept her weariness away. She mustn't waste what remained of the afternoon light. Her gaze, roving possessively, pridefully over the house, moved to small windows beneath the main roof. So far she had never explored the attic. Why not have a look at it now, while daylight lasted?

After one last breath of the fragrant garden, she went inside and up two flights of the octagon staircase. At one end of the third floor wing, a narrower, enclosed flight led to the attic. She found candles and matches and climbed the final steep steps that ended in the low-ceilinged area above.

Up here the air was dusty and dim, but she lighted two of her candles and set one of the small holders on a shelf, retaining the other to carry about. Beneath the eaves of the house, she was more conscious of the irregularities of the roof than she had been on the floors below. Overhead the ceiling beams slanted upward here, and down there, at sharp angles, with the dormers and gables that cut up the roof plainly evident. A room that must have been a servant's bedroom had two dormers overlooking the front of the house, and along one side of the room, just beneath the ceiling slant, was a long row of clothes hooks. Perhaps some long ago lady's maid, ironing her mistress's starched petticoats and lace-trimmed drawers, had hung them on those hooks as she finished them.

Another room held old trunks, and Camilla raised the lid of one, to be greeted by the pungent odor of lavender buds and other mixtures of herbs in small bags, used against moths. Clothes of a style long past were stored here. Garments which must have belonged to her grandfather and grandmother, and undoubtedly to Letty, Hortense, and Althea as well.

She moved on to a smaller room at the back of the house, carrying both candles now. Here she had to stoop to avoid dusty beams overhead, and a strand of cobwebs brushed across her face. There was another smell here, besides the stuffy odor of dust and the tang of herbal bags—the smell of leather. Holding her candle high, she saw that leather harness of various types had been tossed over the beams. These must have belonged to the day when Thunder Heights had kept its own horses and carriages. She reached up to touch dry leather, cracked and rough beneath her fingers. No care had been given these things in years.

Circling a post in the middle of the room, she came upon a saddle which had been set apart from the rest of the gear. It lay across a slanting beam within easy reach, a single bright stirrup hanging toward the floor. It was, she saw, an elegant sidesaddle with elaborately embossed silver trimmings, and a silver horn for milady to hook her knee over. She had never seen so beautiful a saddle and she held up a candle to examine it more closely.

A thin film of dust lay upon the surface of the leather, but not so thick a layer as covered other objects in the attic. A spider had spun a web in the dangling stirrup, but it was no more than a filament. The dark leather shone richly, reflecting the light of Camilla's candle, and when she touched it she found the surface smooth as satin and uncracked. The silver mountings and the stirrup were faintly tarnished, but not sufficiently so to reveal years of neglect. Someone had been coming up here regularly to care for this particular saddle. She searched further and found the silver-mounted bridle that matched the saddle; it too had been cared for over the years. There were other sidesaddles and bridles, stored carelessly, without attention. Only these things had been treated lovingly.

Camilla took the polished bridle from its hook and held it in her hands, listening to the small chime of dangling metal parts. What fun if Booth could find a horse for her soon and she could use these things herself.

Returning the bridle to its hook, she moved toward the stairs, but on the way a wooden chest caught her eye. It was of a pale, oriental wood, with brass handles and a brass lock. She raised the lid and looked inside. This time the odor that greeted her was the pleasant scent of camphor wood. With a sense of growing excitement, Camilla lifted out a pale gray top hat that a lady might wear while riding. Beneath, carefully wrapped, were a pair of patent leather riding boots. Finally, she drew out the habit itself and held it up with an exclamation of delight.

It was the most beautiful ash-gray riding habit she had ever seen. The style was one of bygone years, but the draping was so graceful, so truly right, that it could surely be worn in any period. Had this habit belonged to her mother? she wondered. Somehow she could not imagine Hortense or Letty wearing it. As she turned it about, she saw that on the right breast a horseshoe had been embroidered in dark gray silk against the pale ash of the material. Within the horseshoe were embroidered the letters *AJ*.

Standing there with the heavy folds of material in her hands, it was as if she had come unexpectedly upon the very person of her mother here in this attic. An old sadness and longing swept through her, and she held the gray habit to her heart as if she clung to a beloved presence. In the swift pain of remembering, she could recall details of her mother's face that she had not thought of in years. She could even catch in memory the faint violet scent that had always clung about her.

She could not bear to leave this habit in the attic. Quickly she bundled it up, then picked up the hat and boots and blew out the candles. Back in her room she laid the garments upon the bed, where she could examine them more carefully.

To her distress, she found that a muddy stain ran down one side of the habit, with a jagged tear in the skirt. How strange that these things had been put away without being mended or cleaned. But she would care for them now. She would clean and repair the habit and try it on. The thought was exciting.

It was almost dinnertime now, however, and for the moment she laid the things aside regretfully. Later she would slip away to her room and put on the habit.

All through dinner she hugged her secret to her and waited impatiently to escape. She paid little attention to the desultory conversation, though when Booth mentioned that he was thinking of a trip to New York, she encouraged him.

"Why not?" she said. "Why don't you take some of your paintings with you and see if there's any possibility of holding a show?"

Booth shrugged the suggestion aside and said he was think-

105

ing in terms of seeing a play and perhaps looking up old friends.

Ross said, "I'll give you a business errand to take care of while you're in town."

Booth agreed indifferently, and after dinner Ross followed him into the parlor to explain what he had in mind. Camilla, glad to be free, left them and hurried upstairs.

A full-length mirror had been set into the door of the French armoire in Althea's bedroom, and when she had put on the habit—even to the boots, which were only a little tight, and the top hat that sat so debonairly on her black hair, she approached the glass with an odd hesitance. Now that she was fully dressed in these things that had belonged to her mother, she was seized by a fear that she would fall too far short of what Althea had been. Perhaps her image would mock her for daring to mimic her mother. She drew a quick breath and faced the mirror.

The girl who looked back at her was someone she had never seen before. The full gray skirt was caught up gracefully to reveal high-heeled patent leather boots, and the ugly tear and stain were lost in the folds. If the leather of the boots had cracked a bit across the instep, that did not matter. The long-sleeved jacket, with its diagonally cut closing, molded her body, outlining the full curve of her breast, the soft rounding of her shoulders, emphasizing her small waist where the jacket came to a point in front. Camilla had tied the darker gray silk stock about her throat and fastened it with a bar pin. The tall hat was pale gray like the habit, and bound with a wide gray veil that hung down in floating streamers behind. If only she had a crop to complete the picture, and more suitable gloves than these of her own, what a dashing figure she would make. But there was more to her appearance than the costume alone.

For the first time she could recognize beauty in her own face. She could not judge for herself whether it was beauty of feature, or simply that of the high color in her cheeks, of the sparkle of bright eyes beneath long-lashed lids, the look of eagerness and anticipation which gave her a new vitality.

She moved before the mirror, stepping and turning lightly, and knew that her movements were lithe and graceful—as they told her Althea's had been. Did she really resemble her mother so very much? Would she light a room when she entered it, as her father had said his Althea could?

A longing to show herself to someone seized her. Perhaps if she went downstairs and walked into the parlor dressed as she was, she might learn the truth about herself in the faces of others, in the look of eyes that would tell her whether or not she was as lovely as her mother had been.

She opened the door of her room and listened. In the distance downstairs she could hear the murmur of voices. They were still in the parlor—an audience waiting for her to astonish them. Even Ross Granger, whom she would love to confound, was still with them. And Booth, of whose disturbing presence she was always aware. Eagerly she ran toward the stairs and paused at the first step to gather up her skirt in graceful folds. Light from the stair lamp in its high canopy above spilled down upon her, and she found it regrettable that no one stood at the foot of the stairs to see her descent.

She ran lightly down and went to the parlor door, stepping into a glow of lamplight. There she waited quietly and a little breathlessly for those in the room to look up and see her.

XII

HORTENSE, THE GREEN JADE STONES IN HER COMBS GLEAM-ing in her red hair, was reading aloud. Letty listened and crocheted, while Booth sat staring at his own long-fingered hands. Ross had spread some papers on a table and was marking them with a pencil. It was he who saw her first and there was no mistaking his astonishment, even his reluctant admiration.

Booth was the next to glance around and see her. He sat quite still, but there was shock in his eyes. The very tension of his body made itself felt in the room, and Letty looked up and rose to her feet with a cry, dropping her crocheting. For a moment she stared at Camilla in something like horror. Then, without warning, she crumpled to the floor. Booth recovered himself and hurried to her side.

Hortense was the last to move. She put down her book and stood up, frowning at Camilla. The frayed ruching of lace upon her bosom moved with her quickened breathing.

"Go upstairs," she ordered, her voice rising. "Go upstairs at once and take off that habit."

Camilla heard her, too surprised to move. She did not in the least understand the consternation she had caused.

Aunt Letty moaned faintly as Booth held Hortense's ever-present smelling salts to her nose.

Hortense threw her sister a scornful look. "Don't be a goose, Letty. It's only Camilla dressed up in Althea's old riding habit." Then she spoke to Camilla. "My sister thought Althea's ghost had walked into this room. You had no business frightening us like that."

Camilla tried to speak, but Booth looked at her and shook his head. It was Ross who got her out of the room. He left his papers, and took her quietly by the arm. She went with him without objection, and he led her across the antehall into the library.

"Sit down and catch your breath," he said. "You look a bit shaken yourself. They probably frightened you as much as you frightened them."

She turned to him in bewilderment. "I don't understand what happened. Why should seeing me in my mother's riding habit upset everyone so much?"

He sat beside her on the long couch, and a frown drew down his brows. "I can't tell you all the details. I came here some years after your mother's death. But I've been able to put together a few of the pieces. I suspect, from the reaction in there tonight, that your mother was wearing this very habit on the night she died. I know she went riding just before dusk, with a storm coming up—which seems a wild sort of thing to do. She rode clear up Thunder Mountain and must have reached the top when the storm broke. The thunder and lightning probably frightened her horse, and it ran away. She was thrown, and the horse came home with an empty saddle."

Camilla reached up with fingers that trembled and drew the pin from her hat. She took off the hat and set it on the couch beside her. Then she pushed her fingers against the place where a throbbing had begun at her temples.

"I didn't know," she said softly. "No one would ever tell me the truth."

Ross went on in the same quiet tone, with none of his usual irritation toward her in evidence. "When your grandfather knew she was missing, he went up the mountain to look for her. He knew that was her favorite ride. He found her there on the rocky crest and brought her home. She was dead when he found her. She must have struck her head against a rock when she was thrown."

Camilla fingered the long tear hidden by the heavy folds of the habit, and tears came into her eyes.

"My father would never talk about what happened. When he came home after her funeral, he was like a different person for a long while. But why should he have blamed Grandfather Orrin for her death?"

"I can't tell you that," Ross said. "There was something queer about her riding out so late that afternoon, with a storm about to break. I don't know any more about it than I've told you."

Camilla sighed unhappily. "I can see what a shock it must have been for Aunt Letty and Aunt Hortense when I walked into the room just now. It was a terrible thing to do. I'll go upstairs and take these things off."

"It wasn't your fault," Ross said, his tone surprisingly gentle. "You couldn't possibly know the effect you'd have on them. Don't worry about it."

His unexpected kindness brought tears, and she covered her face with her hands. She had seemed so close to her mother earlier tonight, and with remembrance all the hurt of losing her had come rushing back, to be painfully increased by what had just happened.

Ross touched her shoulder lightly. "I'm sorry. Perhaps I shouldn't have told you."

"I had to know!" she cried, and looked up at him, her eyes wet.

He rose and moved uncomfortably about the room. Perhaps he was impatient with her tears, she thought, but she could not stem them.

"Look here," he said abruptly, "you need a change from the burdens of this house. You've been taking on too much. Nora Redfern has wanted me to bring you over for tea some afternoon. Will you go with me if she sets a day?"

Camilla looked at him in surprise. This was certainly a change from his recent attitude toward her.

"You n-n-needn't feel sorry for me!" she choked.

There was no mockery in his smile. "Believe me," he said, "I waste no pity on you. But perhaps I sympathize more than I've let you see. You've been without a real friend in this house, and yet you've kept yourself busy and reasonably happy, and you haven't given up trying to crack the guard set up on all sides against you. I may not approve of your actions, but I admire your courage. I don't want to see it broken."

He went to the door and stood listening for a moment. Then he turned back to her.

"They've taken Letty up to her room. Why don't you slip upstairs before Hortense sees you again?"

How unpredictable he was. He opposed her at every turn,

laughed at her plans for the house, scolded her. Yet now he seemed gentle and thoughtful. Almost like a—friend. Tremulously she smiled at him.

"I—I'm very grateful for—" She wanted to say more, but the words would not come, and she moved helplessly toward the door.

When she reached the second floor, Booth came to the door of his room, as if he waited for her. He had changed to a velvet smoking jacket of dark maroon. Cuffs and lapels were of a lighter red satin, and the effect was one of romantic elegance which fitted Booth so well. The look of shock had gone out of his eyes and he studied her coolly, and not without admiration.

"Althea's riding habit becomes you, Cousin. Though I must say you stirred up a nest of old ghosts tonight and startled us all."

She had no answer for that. She did not want to be drawn out of the quiet mood the change in Ross had induced in her.

"How is Aunt Letty?" she managed to ask.

"She'll be all right. Mother is putting her to bed, and she's already sorry she behaved as she did. Though I can understand how she felt. You look even more like your mother than we realized."

When she turned away because he made her uneasy and she had nothing more to say, he stopped her.

"Wait a moment, Cousin. I want to show you something." He gestured to the room behind him. "Will you come in?"

Booth had a small den adjoining his bedroom, and it was into this he invited her. She stepped uncertainly into a room where lamplight shone warmly on brown and gold surfaces, a room attractively furnished with pieces that were genuinely old, and with a touch of Moorish opulence about them. He drew forward a Spanish chair with a velvet seat and leather back, and brought a small carved footstool for her feet. When she was seated, he stood for a moment studying her face with a strange intensity that made her uncomfortable. If he saw the streaking of tear stains he did not mention her weeping.

"It's hard to believe," he said. "You are so much like her."

While she watched him, puzzled, he picked up a picture which had been set with its face against the wall and brought it to her.

"Do you remember this?"

She saw it was the unfinished painting of a girl and a horse that he had taken away from her so abruptly when she had

110

visited his studio. But now she saw something about the picture that she could not have recognized before. The faceless girl who stood struggling with the horse wore a riding habit of ash gray and a high top hat with floating gray streamers of veil.

Camilla looked from the picture to Booth's dark face, and he nodded in response.

"Your mother posed for this when she came back to Thunder Heights before her death. She loved to ride, and she was an expert horsewoman. I didn't want to paint her tamely, without action, and she thought a pose like this exciting. Though of course I had to do the horse from imagination. After what happened, I never finished it."

"I wish you had been able to finish it," Camilla said. "If you'd done her face, it would bring her back to me a little."

He set the picture against a table where he could study it. "Why shouldn't I finish it now? Why shouldn't I give you her face as she was when she was so vitally alive?"

He came to her quickly and put a finger beneath her chin, tilting her head to the light. "From life. Will you pose for me, Cousin?"

The thought gave her an intense pleasure. To help him finish her mother's picture was almost like a fulfillment.

"I'd love to pose for you, Booth," she said. The prospect of working with him so closely left her faintly excited. It was not only because of her mother that she would look forward to posing for him. Perhaps now she would have the opportunity to know him better, to get past the strange mask he so often wore and learn what the man himself was like.

"Good!" He held out his hand, as if to seal a bargain, and she found the touch of his fingers oddly cool and dry. "We'll begin tomorrow, if you're willing. You feel better now, don't you? The tears are over?"

So he had noticed, after all. She nodded. "Ross told me how my mother died. It must have been terrible for you all that night. And for Grandfather especially. You were here then—what happened afterwards?"

"I wasn't in the house when they brought her in," Booth said. "When she didn't come home, I took another horse and followed the path along the river to see if she had chosen that trail. One of the stableboys had already gone after Dr. Wheeler, so he was here when Grandfather carried her in. There was nothing to be done. Grandfather went out and shot the poor beast that had thrown her, and later he got rid of every horse he owned. That's why we've had no carriage, no riding horses for so many years."

Camilla heard him sadly. "As if that would bring her back."

"You won't be afraid to ride, after what happened here?" Booth asked.

"Because my mother met with an accident? Of course not. It would be foolish to give up riding for that reason, when I'd love it so in country like this."

"You'd better break it gently to Mother and Aunt Letty that you mean to buy a horse," he said. "I haven't told them I was looking for one. Grandfather set them both against horses after what happened. They used to ride, too, but they never did again."

He came with her to the door and catching her hand, held her there a moment. "I want very much to paint you, Camilla."

There was a rising excitement in his voice, and she felt again the strength of his dark appeal striking an echo in herself. She turned hurriedly away and went down the hall, hoping he had not read her response.

When she opened the door and looked again at Althea's room, it was to see it with new eyes. In the beginning the room had seemed to reject her, to hold her away as if she did not belong there. But the strangeness was gone, as if the room had warmed to her, as it had not done before.

Had her grandfather carried Althea here to place her upon this very bed? Had she lain here in death, her lovely body still clothed in the very habit her daughter wore tonight? It must have been that way. Perhaps this was why the room seemed different now. She knew its secret, knew its sorrow, and because she knew she belonged to it.

She took off the habit and spread it gently upon the bed. Tomorrow before she posed for Booth, she would clean away the stain as best she could, and mend the rent in the cloth. It was *not knowing* that had troubled her for so long. Now she knew the worst there was to know, and in embracing tragedy and making it part of her own knowledge, it became less instead of greater.

She would not allow her mother's accident to frighten her. As soon as it was possible to find a good horse, she would ride these hills herself. She would mend her mother's riding habit and wear it with love and pride and joy. But first of all, she would wear it in posing for Booth.

After breakfast the following morning she worked for a

while on the habit, then put it on and went upstairs to the nursery. It was fortunate that Ross had given up her education in Orrin Judd's affairs, since this would leave her mornings free to pose for Booth.

He was waiting for her in the big bare room that he had changed very little. He needed only a few essentials for his work, he said, and had added no new furnishings. An old table for his painting equipment was adequate, and he wanted no rugs he might spill paint upon. His easel occupied a place where the light was good, and he posed Camilla facing him.

"We'll leave the face for the last," he said. "I want to get into the mood of the picture again before I touch that. Today I'll pose you standing, so that I can do further work on the color of the habit, and catch the way the folds of material hang."

His mood was bright and incisive this morning, and she felt in him an eagerness to be at work once more on this picture. His hands were light when he touched her, turning her this way and that, seeking to match the pose of the woman in the picture. Though his manner was impersonal, Camilla was sharply aware of him, and the very fact made it difficult for her to assume the pose he wished.

When he got to work at his painting, she was more comfortable because then he seemed to forget her as a woman, so that something of her self-consciousness faded.

The utter quiet of posing for him now opened her mind to a flood of saddening thoughts. Though she could not see the picture from where she stood she could remember it all too well. Fourteen years ago Althea Judd had worn this habit in warm and vital life. She had begun posing for this very picture that Booth would now finish with her daughter for a model. Just such a rearing, fighting beast as Booth had depicted in his picture had flung Althea from her saddle, killing her. Should the picture be finished? Camilla wondered suddenly. Or should it be hidden away and forgotten forever?

"You're tired, aren't you?" Booth said. "I mustn't weary you. Sit down a moment and let yourself go limp."

She realized that her body ached with its effort to hold her pose, and she was glad to relax and pull her thoughts back from their futile path.

He brought a chair for her, and she sat down in it gratefully. Now as he worked on without reference to her as a model, she could watch him as she had seldom had the opportunity to do. His thin, proud nose, his faintly arrogant mouth and gloom-ridden eyes were disturbing in their melancholy. Yet elation had kindled him this morning, and he painted for a while as if his strokes were sure and the picture promised well.

It was a shame, she thought, that a man who was so keenly an artist should be buried in a place like Thunder Heights. What did he ask of the future? Why had he remained here, when there could be so little within these walls to make him happy? She wished she might question him, but she had never quite dared.

"Why don't you plan a trip to New York soon?" she suggested, following the trend of her thoughts along a fairly safe course. "Perhaps you could take Aunt Hortense with you and give her a whirl in the city."

For a few moments he did not look at her, or answer, but worked in concentration with his brush. Then he set his palette down and came to stand before her, studying her intently.

"How eager you are to make us happy, Cousin. And how frustrating you must find us when we resist. I doubt that we're meant to be a happy family, so don't break your heart over us."

"I can't help worrying," she said. "I've come here unasked by any of you, and Grandfather's no longer here to make the rules. I know I've never been welcome as far as your mother is concerned. But isn't there something I can do that would please her?"

"If taking her on a trip to New York will please you, I'll do it, Camilla. You're the one with a capacity for happiness that mustn't be dampened. Who knows, perhaps it really would do her good."

"And you, too," Camilla said.

His laughter had a dry sound. "I'm content with my work. As long as it goes well, there's nothing more I'll ask of you for the moment. Shall we get back to it again? Do you suppose this time you can try for more life in your pose? It's the body beneath the gown that matters. Folds of cloth are lifeless in themselves."

His hands were light on her shoulders again, turning her. He was so close that his touch was almost an embrace, and she had a curious desire to run from it, as if there was a need to save herself in time from the dark forces that drove this man. But she held herself quiet and submissive beneath his hands, allowing him to turn her as he wished.

He stepped back and looked at her, clearly not pleased

114

with the result. "No," he said, and his tone was no longer gentle. "You haven't caught it. You're merely a pretty young woman in a riding habit, posing in a studio. And that's not enough."

There was a sting to his words that brought her head up in an instinctive challenge. At once he stepped toward her and put his fingers at her throat, just under her chin. How cool his touch was. As if all the fire in this man burned at the core and never came to the surface.

"That's it—keep your head high like that. Be angry with me, if you like." The pressure of his fingers was suddenly hard against her flesh. She drew back from his touch in confusion, and he shook his head at her ruefully.

"You must help me in this, Cousin. I want you to be, not merely an attractive girl, but a beautiful, angry, spirited woman, struggling furiously with a horse that must not be allowed to get out of control."

His description made her feel awkward and inadequate. "But you're not painting my face today," she reminded him. "What does my expression matter?"

"I wish I could make you understand," he said more quietly. "Whatever is in your face will be reflected in the lines of your body. As your body comes to life, so will your garments reveal spirit. After all, I want to paint a woman, my dear. The woman you are, if you will let yourself go. You should have seen Althea when she posed for this picture. I was only twenty-one at the time, and she was an inspiration. I'll confess I found her irresistible."

With every word, Camilla felt less spirited and less fascinating. "I'm not my mother," she said defensively. "People are always telling me how exciting she was, but I know I'm not—"

His two hands on her shoulders stopped her as he shook her almost roughly. "You must never talk like that! You have more than your mother had, if you'll only realize it. Your bone structure is better—the planes of your face are finer, keener. There's a fire in you too—I've glimpsed it at times. But you keep it banked. Your mother had a confidence you lack. With confidence, a woman can be anything."

He let her go and turned back to his work table.

"We've done enough this morning," he said. "I've upset you, and I didn't mean to. Let's try again tomorrow."

She did not know what to say to him, how to answer him. How could she be for him what she knew very well she was not?

He looked up from cleaning his brushes and saw her standing there helplessly. The quick flash of a smile lighted his face.

"There," he said, "I've hurt you and I'm sorry. It will go better tomorrow. You'll see. The fault isn't yours, so don't distress yourself. If I can't make you see what I want, if I can't bring you to life for this picture, then the blame is mine. Will you forgive me, Cousin, and let me try again tomorrow?"

She nodded mutely in the face of his kindness and went quickly out of the room and down the stairs, feeling shaken and bewildered. How foolish she had been to think posing for Booth's picture would be a simple and wholly pleasant experience. In a strange, contrary way it had been almost like having him make love to her. The method was indirect and rather exciting, and made her wonder what move he might make next. Made her wonder, too, how she might receive it.

XIII

AS BOOTH PREDICTED, THE POSING WENT BETTER FOR A FEW days after that. But more, Camilla felt, because Booth tried harder to put her at ease, to give her confidence, than because she really rose to the perfection he wanted from her.

Now Letty came in to watch while he worked, and as a result something of the personal climate between artist and model which had come into uneasy existence that first day was lessened. Now Camilla was aware of it only in an occasional look Booth bent upon her, in an occasional touch of his hand.

He made no objection to Letty's presence, and did not seem to mind it. She would sit near a window, crocheting, with Mignonette curled at her feet, seldom speaking, offering little distraction. Once during the morning, she might leave her chair and go to stand behind Booth, studying the picture as he painted. Only then did her presence seem to make him faintly uncomfortable. Once Camilla thought he might speak to her impatiently, but he managed to keep any irritation he felt to himself. After a moment Letty returned quietly to her chair, as if she sensed his mood, and she did not look at the picture again for several days.

116

One morning when Booth stopped the posing session early, Letty invited Camilla to her room.

"If you've nothing pressing to do," she said, "perhaps you'd like to help me with a task that may interest you."

Ever since the day when the saucer of tea had made Mignonette sick, Camilla had experienced a constraint when she was with Letty. She had reproached herself for this feeling, considering it unjustified. She did not want to listen to Hortense's dropping of hints, and yet the actuality of what had happened remained as a bar to the friendship she had previously felt for Letty. There was no reason to avoid her, however, and perhaps it might even be possible to return to more comfortable ground with her aunt, and clear up some of the things that were troublesome, if they could have a good talk.

This was the first time she had been invited into Aunt Letty's private retreat, and she looked about the small room with interest. In one corner a second floor tower bulged into a circular addition to the room, with windows all around and a padded window seat. The wall over the bed sloped beneath a slanting roof, and the entire expanse of the angled wall was covered with pictures of one sort and another, so that only a trace of sand-colored wallpaper showed between them here and there.

While Letty knelt to pull a box from under the bed, Camilla studied the pictures on the slanting wall. Some of them were clearly Hudson River scenes—both sketches and engravings—but there were also scenes from abroad, glimpses of castles and mountains, glens and lochs.

"This looks like Walter Scott country," she said to Letty.

Her aunt was lifting folders and envelopes from the box and piling them on the bed. "It is. Just a few memories of a lovely year I spent in Scotland when I was a young girl."

"And did you meet a young man in the Highlands and give your heart away in the proper romantic fashion?" Camilla asked.

Letty smiled, but there was a flush in her cheeks. "Oh, I met several, and perhaps I did give my heart away for a little while. But Papa didn't approve, and I took it back after a time. It was nothing very serious. Perhaps I always had too many story-book heroes in my mind, to be satisfied with the men I met in real life."

Camilla curled herself up comfortably on Letty's bed, wanting now to pursue this topic.

"What about Aunt Hortense? Why has she never married? Did no young men ever come to Westcliff?"

"Oh, they came," Letty said. "Papa's name was always enough to bring them. But Hortense had an unfortunate faculty for wanting only what someone else had."

"What do you mean?" Camilla asked.

Letty's gaze seemed to turn upon something far away in the past. "There was one man who came to Westcliff—I can remember him as if it were yesterday. He looked as I imagine a poet might look. And he could quote poetry too—in a voice that sounded like one of our mountain streams, sometimes whispering, sometimes thundering."

"My father's voice was like that," Camilla said. "I always loved the way he read poetry."

"Yes, I know." Letty's silver braids bent low over the papers she was sorting.

The tone of her voice startled Camilla. "This was the man Hortense fell in love with?"

There was sad assent in Letty's sigh.

"Was he a schoolteacher?"

"Yes, dear," Letty said. "I see you've guessed. It was your father Hortense loved, and she would have no one else."

"So that's it?" Camilla was thoughtful. "Did my mother know?"

"Hortense took care to let everyone know. She didn't behave very well, I'm afraid. She always claimed that he would have married her, if Althea hadn't stolen him from her. Of course that wasn't true. He never looked at anyone but Althea. She was always the lovely one—the lucky one. They fell in love at their first meeting, and since Papa wanted someone else for Althea, there was nothing to do but run off. Althea told me that night and I helped her get away. Papa never forgave me for that."

There were tears in Letty's eyes.

"I never knew," Camilla said. "Poor Aunt Hortense."

"It has been difficult for her. When she looks at you she sees two people who hurt her, two people she has never forgiven. You must help her to get over that, my dear. Be patient with her."

Camilla leaned back against a poster of the bed. For the first time she was beginning to understand the intensity of disliking she had seen in Hortense's eyes. What insult it must have added to injury when Orrin Judd had left his fortune to the daughter of Althea and John King.

"Was it because Aunt Hortense knew she would never marry that she wanted to adopt a child?" she asked.

Letty's hands moved vaguely among the papers she had heaped on the bed. "That was so long ago. I—I don't remember the details. I suppose she must have felt there would be an emptiness in her life without a child. We needed someone young in this house. I was glad to see Booth come. He was such a solemn, handsome little boy, and so determined about what he wanted."

"Why didn't she adopt a baby?"

Letty shrugged. "I only remember that he was ten when she brought him here, and he was already quite talented as an artist."

"But what an odd thing to do," Camilla said. "Surely if a woman wanted a child, she would want one from babyhood on."

For some reason Letty seemed agitated. Once more she was ready for a flight from the unpleasant. "It all happened so long ago—why trouble about it now?"

"Because of Aunt Hortense," Camilla insisted. "I want to find some way to make her happy here at Thunder Heights, and if I'm to do that, I ought to understand her better than I do."

Letty changed the subject firmly. "There's been enough talk about the past. That isn't why I asked you here. I thought you might like to help me sort my collection of herb receipts. I can't make head or tail of things the way they are."

Letty gathered up a handful of loose sheets on which clippings had been pasted in long yellowing columns, and dropped them in Camilla's lap.

"What I'd like to do is to separate the medicinal information from the cooking receipts and catalogue them both. And I'd like to sort the receipts into categories so that when I want one for mint jelly, I don't have to hunt through a mixture like this."

Knowing other topics were closed for the moment, Camilla set to work with interest. Now that she was acquainted with the herbs in Letty's garden, the next step to their use was fascinating. She read through a receipt for Turkish rose petal jam, and one for marigold custard. There were directions for making saffron cake, for rose and caraway cookies, and tansy pudding. Sometimes Aunt Letty had written her own pertinent comments in the margins, or her own suggestions for changes in the ingredients.

"I should think," Camilla said, her interest growing, "that you should have enough material here for a book about herbs. You've grown them and worked with them for years and you're a real authority. Other people should be interested in what you have to say."

"Do you really think I might do something with all this?" Letty's eyes brightened.

"Oh, I do!" Camilla warmed to the idea. "All you need is to sort it out and make a plan for presenting it. I'll help you and—"

There was a knock at the door and Grace looked into the room. "If you please, mum, there's a note for you," she said and handed a blue envelope to Camilla.

When she had gone, Camilla opened it and read the note. It was from Nora Redfern. Would Miss King permit Mr. Granger to bring her to tea at Blue Beeches one afternoon next week? Nora was looking forward to knowing her better.

Camilla held out the note to Letty. "How very nice—I'd love to go."

Letty read the note doubtfully. "I don't know. We haven't been on speaking terms with Blue Beeches for a long while, you know."

"What is the trouble between the two families?" Camilla asked.

"Mrs. Landry, Nora's mother, and your grandfather had a quarrel years ago. Naturally we took Papa's side and we haven't been friendly with her since."

"But all that can't be Nora's fault. Ross seems to like her." Sometimes, indeed, Camilla had wondered just how much Ross liked the attractive young widow.

"We've all regretted that," Letty said. "Papa never approved of the way Ross made friends with the Redferns. Under the circumstances, it was inexcusable."

Never before had Camilla heard Letty sound so uncharitable. Her attitude seemed more like what might be expected from Hortense.

"I'll be sorry to go against your wishes," Camilla said gently, "but I'd like very much to accept this invitation."

For a moment Letty looked as though she might offer further objection. Then she sighed and began to gather up her papers and notes and thrust them back into their box.

"Wait," Camilla said, "—we must talk about your book."

Letty shook her head. "I'm not in the mood now, dear. Some other time, perhaps." She looked sad again and increasingly troubled.

120

"A few moments ago you thought the idea a good one," Camilla said. "Why have you changed your mind. Surely not because I'm going to see Nora Redfern?"

Letty pushed the last batch of clippings into the box and fastened the lid. Then she looked up at Camilla.

"You know what they whisper about me, don't you? They say I've tried to poison people. If I were to do a book on the subject of herbs, all the whispers would spring up again."

She looked so forlorn that for the moment pity thrust doubt from Camilla's mind. Aunt Letty had burden enough to carry with her crippled arm.

"I think we must pay no attention to such gossip," she said. "It's too ridiculous to heed."

Letty's smile was tremulous. "Thank you, my dear." But she pushed the box resolutely into place under her bed, and Camilla knew that for the moment at least the subject was closed.

When she returned to her room, she sat down at her mother's desk to answer Nora Redfern's note. But her thoughts would not at once relinquish the thought of Letty. One part of her—more heart than mind—wanted to trust in her wholeheartedly. That day when Camilla had talked to her grandfather he had said, "Watch Letty." Surely he had meant to take care of Letty, to watch out for her. But something more questioning in Camilla held back and reserved judgment.

Resolutely she put these disturbing thoughts aside and picked up her pen to write an answer to Nora Redfern. She wrote her note rapidly, accepting the invitation. It would be good to escape from Thunder Heights and visit Blue Beeches next week.

That evening Booth told her that it was hopeless to continue with his painting. Something had thrown him off his course and it would be better to stop for a while. If Camilla were still agreeable, he would accept her offer of a trip to New York for himself and his mother, and they would leave as soon as Hortense could get ready. It was a plan Camilla readily encouraged.

A day later, on the morning they were to leave, Grace tapped on Camilla's door. Mr. Booth, she said, requested a moment of her time in the library.

Camilla hurried downstairs and found him pacing restlessly about the room. He turned with something like relief when she entered.

"Good! I wanted to see you for a moment, Cousin, before Mother comes down."

He stepped to the door and closed it after her. Camilla watched him, puzzled. He looked handsomer than ever this morning, and more than ever the gentleman of fashion. He wore a black coat, gray checked trousers, and gray spats. His gray gloves and top hat lay upon the table.

"We'll get to work on the picture again as soon as I return," he said. "It isn't just because I'm out of the mood for painting that I'm making this trip. It's because of my mother."

"I hope the change will do her good," Camilla said politely, still wondering what lay behind his words.

"She's not going to New York for the change," Booth said. "She's going for the sole purpose of trying to upset Grandfather Orrin's will. I thought you ought to know. She means to see a lawyer of greater eminence than Mr. Pompton and learn what steps she might be able to take."

Camilla nodded gravely. "She's entirely within her rights, of course. I really can't blame her."

"You're more than generous, Camilla. I hope you know that this is none of my doing. Frankly, I think she has no chance of success, and I've urged against the step. But she won't listen to me."

"Thank you for telling me," Camilla said.

He held out his hand, and when she put her own into it, he did not release her at once. It was a relief when Hortense came sailing into the room, flinging the door open with an air of indignation at finding it closed.

She was elaborately gowned for travel. Her skirt was of mauve broadcloth, and she wore an elbow-length cape of black broadcloth, with a high, satin-trimmed collar and huge buttons. The straw hat that tilted over her forehead was wreathed in violets and bound in violet ribbon that clashed with her red hair. An exotic Parisian perfume floated generously about her person.

"I hope you'll have a fine time in New York," Camilla told the impressive figure.

From high piled violets to mauve skirt hem, Hortense seemed aquiver with energy this morning. She ignored Camilla's good wishes and nodded to Booth.

"The carriage has just pulled up to the door. We'd better be going if we're not to miss the boat."

Booth picked up his hat and gloves, but Hortense did not move at once from the doorway.

"I know this is the opportunity you've been waiting for," she said to Camilla. "You may as well make good use of your time while I'm away."

"I'm afraid I don't know what you mean," Camilla said.

"I mean that this is your chance to prove what a housekeeper you are. Matilda and Toby are going upriver to visit Matilda's sister. The scullery maid has the day off, and Letty is turning out the linen shelves upstairs, with Grace's help. So you may do exactly what you like with the rest of the house."

Hortense spoke with the air of a great lady conferring a favor, but Camilla could only stare at her in bewilderment. As she well knew, it was Letty who quietly kept things running, in spite of Hortense's high-handed gestures. Certainly she had no intention of trying to take these duties out of Letty's competent hands.

"I don't want to interfere with the regular routine," she said mildly.

"I've thought from the first that your education has been neglected in household matters," Hortense said, sniffing a little. "I doubt if you can so much as bake a decent loaf of bread. However, the house is yours for the moment—if you choose to take advantage of the opportunity."

"Thank you, Aunt Hortense," Camilla said and suppressed a desire to smile.

Her aunt swept toward the door. Booth arched a dark eyebrow at Camilla and followed his mother without comment. Camilla went to the door and watched him help his mother into the rig.

"Have a pleasant trip," she called as the carriage pulled away.

Hortense said nothing, but Booth turned his head and waved. Camilla stood for a moment looking thoughtfully after them. It was a little ironic that she was paying for this trip to New York so that they might seek legal advice on taking everything away from her. Not that the fact disturbed her. If she lost all this, she would only be back where she was before she came here. She would have lost nothing. There was a twinge of bitterness in the thought.

She walked a few steps across the drive and looked up at the front of the house. It stood gray and strong against the mountain. There was no sign of dilapidation now, no worn, unpainted surfaces, no broken shutters. It was still a house of secrets, a brooding house, but this was part of its character.

There was an impressive grandeur about it, now that it was no longer falling into disrepair and apologetic in its ruin.

Was it true that she would not mind if Thunder Heights were taken from her?

She went up the steps and into the antehall. As usual the marble hands reached out to her, but now their gesture seemed almost a welcome. It was as if the house was ready at last to give itself into her hands.

The malevolent influence, whatever it was, had been lifted. With only Letty upstairs, there seemed no longer any resistance to her presence. When Hortense had said the house could be Camilla's for a time, she had spoken more truly than she knew.

A sudden feeling of release and freedom swept through her. Today was truly her own to use as she pleased. There would be no suspicious eyes watching her, no hand turned against her, whatever she chose to do. Why shouldn't she pick up Hortense's challenge and prove that she could bake a loaf as well as the next woman?

The bread box was nearly empty—she had noticed it this morning. By now she had watched Matilda several times at her baking, and she believed she had the hang of it. It would be fun to fill that box and fling Hortense's words back at her.

She went to get the starter dough from the ice chest. Then she collected her ingredients, and the bowls and utensils she would need. She would not, she decided, work in the kitchen. She liked the larder downstairs where Letty often worked. It was a cool, pleasant room, and there was a ledge with a marble slab that made a good working surface. She went downstairs with a feeling that this was a morning to sing at whatever she did.

Yesterday Aunt Letty had been down here making the green herbal soap that Camilla had found such a luxury in her room, but now everything was neat as a whistle, the way Letty always left it. Camilla set out her things and started happily to work. Into the bowl went her lump of starter dough, sifted flour, and milk. When she had stirred the whole sufficiently with a long-handled wooden spoon, she covered the yellow crockery bowl with a cloth, as she had seen Matilda do. Now it must rise before she could have the fun of kneading it.

Feeling pleased and successful, she wandered idly about the room, studying the neat labels Letty had lettered so carefully, sometimes taking down a bottle to sniff the contents and replace it. On the shelf that stretched behind the door, she saw that the jar which had contained a mixture of marjoram and mint leaves had been refilled, and she took it down to smell the pleasant minty scent. Further along the shelf there had been an empty space the other day, and it had now been filled by a bottle containing a pale liquid of some sort.

The label on the bottle read *Tansy Juice*—a name that had a pleasantly old-fashioned ring. Perhaps she had read about tansy in a book, Camilla thought. She took down the bottle and removed the stopper. The odor was sharp, with a faintly resinous quality and at once she was reminded of the odor of the tea Letty had brought her a few days ago. She would not forget that odor readily—it had reminded her of daisies, as this odor did too. Perhaps Letty had added tansy to the tea that day, since she liked to experiment with unusual flavors.

Camilla put the bottle back and wandered upstairs to see how the linen-sorting was progressing. Grace was standing on a stepladder, while Aunt Letty handed stacks of pillowslips up to her to be set on a high shelf. She looked at Camilla and smiled.

"Did Hortense and Booth get off all right?"

Camilla nodded. "Booth told me the real purpose of their trip to New York."

Letty glanced at Grace. "I know. But don't worry, dear. I doubt that a thing can be done. I tried to argue against it, but I'm afraid my sister seldom listens to me. What are you doing with yourself today?"

Camilla did not want to admit to her breadmaking until she had something to show for it.

"I've been wandering around. I was down looking at your herbs for a while. What is tansy used for, Aunt Letty?"

"I have a wonderful receipe for tansy pudding," Letty said. "I believe you were looking at it the other day."

"I noticed a bottle of liquid labeled 'tansy,'" Camilla said, "and I was curious."

"Yes. I crush a few leaves for juice now and then. When the oils are used for perfume, the leaves have to be distilled, but for cooking we just use their juice. Or sometimes the dried leaves."

A remembrance of that faintly unpleasant scent had stayed with Camilla. "Is tansy anything you might use in a tea mixture?"

"Yes." Letty nodded. "I often put in a pinch of leaves, or a few drops of the juice."

Camilla watched the work for a little while, but another

125

pair of hands was not needed, and she wandered downstairs and outside to the river front. Across the river a train rumbled along the water's edge and she watched it out of sight around a bend up the Hudson.

It was a shame both sides of the river had been scarred by steel rails. How pleasant it must have been when everything was open country, or dreamy little towns, and all the transport followed the water itself.

Thinking of transport made her think of Ross and his notions about a bridge. More than once lately he had returned to the subject, and it had become a sore point between them. A bridge, she thought, her eyes upon the river, would not leave the scar of a railroad track. A bridge might be a thing of beauty, as a railroad bed could never be. Nevertheless, she would not give in to him. She would not become involved.

At the foot of the hill, beyond the tracks, a spit of land cut out into the river. It, at least, had the edge of the water to itself. She had never been down there, and she began a descent of the steep bank, digging her heels in, so that she wouldn't slip in loose earth and dry leaves, holding onto branches to let herself down slowly. In a few moments she had reached the tracks and was out of sight of the house. The shining rails stretched away toward Westcliff in one direction, and out of sight around the foot of Thunder Mountain in the other. She crossed the ties and in a moment was in the stiff grass of the lower spit of land. Here she could walk out beneath a huge willow tree to a place where at high tide Hudson waters lapped a small stony beach. Here there was the ruin of an old wooden dock, and a small boathouse, its roof long ago caved in. The salty smell of the mud flats when the tide was out reached her on the breeze from the river.

She scrambled onto the broken dock and then skirted the crumbling boathouse, exploring. Down here shrubbery grew thick to the very edge of a narrow, pebbled beach, and the wild growth had almost engulfed what men had built upon the river's edge.

Her foot slipped in a muddy spot, and she caught at a thick bush to keep herself from sliding. As she pulled herself to dryer ground, her eye was caught by an object deep in the forked branches of brush. Curiously, she pushed the scrub aside and reached in. To her surprise she pulled out a flexible stick a foot or so in length with a blackened silver head attached to it.

Though the silver was tarnished and dented, she could make out an embossing in the form of tiny chrysanthemums. The wood of the stick was black and strong, and propped there above the earth, it had resisted the effects of rot, though it had been scratched and scarred by long weathering. A leather thong, rotted through, hung from one end.

She realized suddenly that the sorry object she held in her hands was a woman's riding crop. To whom had it belonged, and how had it been lost in so odd a place? At any rate, she would carry her find home, clean it up and polish the silver. Then if it didn't look too bad perhaps she could carry it when she went riding. Undoubtedly someone at the house would know to whom it had belonged. Her mother, perhaps? She could imagine Althea carrying such a crop when it had been polished and beautiful.

XIV

AFTER SHE HAD TAKEN THE CROP TO HER ROOM AND TUCKED it into a drawer, she went downstairs to the larder. Removing the cloth, she looked at the dough and found it a sodden, inert mass in the bottom of the bowl. By now it should have puffed considerably, but it had not risen at all. In fact, it looked sticky and wet and incapable of rising. Probably it needed more flour. She scooped it out on the marble slab and added flour, kneading it in. But now the mass turned dry and crumbly, so she dribbled in a little water and kneaded again. There seemed no way to get it right.

Her hands were sticky with wet flour, and her confidence began to ebb. She had the horrid presentiment that this lump of grayish dough was never going to rise at all. Her dream of triumphantly producing a delectable loaf at dinner was just that—a dream, and discouragement seized her. There was more to breadmaking than met the eye, and undoubtedly Hortense Judd was right about her household talents.

The cellar seemed suddenly a lonely and depressing place. How still it was down here. How empty. She could hear no fall of footsteps from upstairs, no sound of voices, and the chill of stone walls seemed more damp than pleasantly cool. Before her in the bowl lay the grayish lump—and for all that it had not risen, there was a great deal more of it than she had intended in the beginning.

What on earth was she to do with this mess? She could imagine Matilda's annoyance if she found that her kitchen had been invaded and perfectly good ingredients wasted—to this end. Undoubtedly she would report the matter to Aunt Hortense, and Camilla could imagine Hortense's scorn and Booth's amusement. There was nothing to do but dispose of her clandestine efforts where they would not be discovered.

Quickly she transferred the inert weight of dough to the cloth with which she had covered the bowl, and turned up the corners, wrapping it well. Then she took one of Aunt Letty's garden trowels from the tool room and marched resolutely up the stairs and outside.

Through the herb garden she ran toward the woods, where Aunt Letty had planted white narcissus in a winding border at the edge of the trees. She followed the path she had taken back from Blue Beeches that first day when she had met Ross Granger and he had come home with her. Now she knew the perfect hiding place for her unpleasant burden. When she had climbed the rocky eminence and reached the weeping beech tree, she found she was still within sight of the house, but she knew the thick, drooping branches would hide her from view. Smiling, she slipped between them into the shadowy seclusion of the open space around the blue-black trunk of the tree.

The shelter was like a child's secret playhouse. Had her mother played here as a little girl? Camilla wondered. The big dark leaves and thick branches shielded her all around and she was completely hidden. She knelt on brown earth, softened now by spring rains, and began to dig with her trowel. It would take a fairly large hole, she discovered, to hide all evidence of her culinary crime. So absorbed was she in her digging that the sudden crackling of branches being parted came as a startling sound. She looked up in dismay to see Ross Granger peering at her through the wall of her shelter.

"What's wrong?" he asked. "I saw you scurrying up here like a fugitive. Are you digging for buried treasure?"

What she was doing seemed suddenly ridiculous and childish—not at all a role becoming to the mistress of Thunder Heights. She regarded him uncomfortably, unable to think of a reasonable explanation for her actions, fighting an impulse to laugh out loud and further label herself a child.

He glanced from the hole to the covered bundle and the smile left his face. "Oh? That's not Mignonette, is it?"

This was too much. She covered her face with her hands

128

to stifle her laughter and sat helplessly back on her heels. At once he picked up the trowel and knelt beside her.

"Don't worry—let me take care of it. You turn your back, and I'll have it buried in no time at all. If it's the cat, this will devastate Letty. What happened anyway?"

She lowered her hands, and when he saw she was not crying, but laughing, he dropped the trowel and stood up, clearly annoyed.

"The—the only thing that—that died," she choked, "was—oh, look for yourself!"

He stirred the bundle doubtfully with his toe and the cloth fell back to expose the lumpish gray contents. "What is it?" he asked.

She wiped her eyes with a handkerchief and thrust back her tendency to hysterical giggles. "You looked so funny and sympathetic! And now you look so suspicious! I—I was just trying to make bread. Aunt Hortense and Booth left for New York right after breakfast. Everyone's gone from the house except Aunt Letty and Grace, who are working upstairs. Before she left, Aunt Hortense said I couldn't even bake a decent loaf of bread. So I wanted to prove her wrong and confound her with my skill when she came home. But the only one I've confounded so far is myself."

He started to grin, then to laugh out loud, and the tendency to giggle left her abruptly. It wasn't that funny. His amusement was altogether too unrestrained, and she did not like being the butt of his laughter.

He caught her eye and sobered. "Now you're angry with me. But you thought the situation funny yourself until I laughed. If you'll stop scowling at me, I'll help you out."

"Help me out?"

He picked up the trowel again and quickly enlarged the hole. Then he dumped the sodden dough into the grave and covered it, stamping down the earth.

"I don't suppose you want a headstone?" he said.

Camilla had gained time to recover a semblance of poise and she stood up and held out her hand for the trowel. "Thank you, Mr. Granger. Though I really could have managed by myself."

"Oh, we're not through," he said cheerfully.

She looked at him in bewilderment, and once more the amusement in his eyes faded. He was regarding her with an odd tenderness that was almost like a caress. His tone softened.

"Don't think I don't know what a hard time you've had in

129

that house. You've had everyone fighting you, including me, and giving you very little help in your effort to do something to save the old place. To say nothing of the people in it. Orrin Judd would have been proud of you, Camilla. I think you're wasting your time on the unimportant and on what can't be changed. Which makes me very sorry—because I like to see the young and brave and—and foolish—succeed."

The climate between them had changed in some subtle way. There was a long breathless moment while she looked into his eyes and time hung queerly suspended. She was aware only of their closeness in this tiny space, hidden from the world by branches all about, aware only of him, as he was of her. *This is what I want,* she thought. Something in her had known from the first moment she had spoken to him on the river boat that someday it would be like this, and that when the moment came she would not retreat. She had fought him and resented him, and raged within herself because of him. But now nothing mattered except that his strong fine head with the bright chestnut hair was bending close, and there was a question in his eyes.

She raised her own head without hesitation and went quite simply into his arms. He was not gentle now. His mouth was hard upon her lips so that they felt bruised beneath its touch. Her body ached under the pressure of his arms, but she did not want the pain lessened. When he raised his head she would have put her arms about his neck and risen on her toes to rest her cheek against his own, admitting everything—all the wild feeling that surged through her, all the wanting so long held in check because there was no one to want. Her movements were those of one spellbound, as though she had no will of her own, and could bow only to his. But he took her by the shoulders and held her suddenly away, his eyes grave, his mouth unsmiling.

"You *are* something of a surprise," he said.

The words were like an unexpected slap, and the blood rose in her cheeks as though the blow had been a physical one. There was a moment of consternation while she stared at him in helpless dismay. Then she turned and would have run straight away from him, but this time he caught her hand.

"Come along," he said as calmly as though nothing had happened between them. "I told you we weren't through. We've work to do."

Brooking no resistance, he led her down the path toward Thunder Heights. She could not struggle against him without indignity, so she went with him, shocked and angry and confused. When they reached the back door, he did not release her hand, but came with her up the steps and into the kitchen. There he looked about confidently, while she watched him, completely at a loss.

"With your permission, I'll wash my hands," he said. "You still want to bake bread, don't you?"

To Camilla's astonishment, that was exactly what they did. Spellbound once more, she obeyed him, afraid to wake up and face what had happened, afraid to acknowledge the emotion that had swept through her there beneath the beech tree. Under his skillful instruction, she began the process of breadmaking all over again, and he was as matter-of-fact when he asked her to scald the milk as though that exultant moment between them, with the shock of its aftermath, had never been.

"To be good," he told her, "a batch of bread should be made with a large portion of love and cheer mixed in. At least that's what my Aunt Otis always used to say. She had the cheeriest kitchen I've ever seen. There were always yellow curtains and yellow tea towels all around, so that if the sun wasn't really shining, it would seem to be in her kitchen. Aunt Otis raised me, and she used to say there was no reason why a man shouldn't know how to bake bread, when breadbaking was good for the soul. She was right too."

Camilla listened in wonder, her sense of shock lulled for the moment by his words and his companionable presence. She did as he told her, and the dough seemed to come to life under her hands.

"Where is your home?" she asked him, curious now to know all there was to know about this man.

"It's on the river—but down along the Jersey bank," he said.

It was easy now to ask him questions. "Did you grow up there? What of your mother and father?"

"My mother died when I was born, and my father was mostly away in his work as an engineer. As I've told you, he was Orrin Judd's good friend and worked on many a project for him. But Aunt Otis had me in hand while I was growing up."

Looking at the breadth of him, at his bright hair and the mouth that was smiling now, but which she had seen looking firm and stern, Camilla thought silently that his Aunt Otis must have done a very good job indeed. A shiver like a warning sped along her nerves, but she did not heed it.

Whether he regretted kissing her or not, she wanted to be with him, to be near him, and that in itself was something new and frightening.

"Now," he said, "you'll need to put this in a warm place to rise, leave it alone for a couple of hours and—"

She clapped a hand to her mouth. "That's it! I left it to rise in the cellar where it's cool. Of course the yeast never started to grow."

He nodded at her, grinning. "Think you can carry on successfully now? You can knead it after it rises—that's for better texture—and let it rise again. Another kneading and it's ready for baking. Can you fire the stove all right?"

"If I can't, I'll get Grace to help me," she said.

Plainly he was going to leave her now, with so much that was still unexplained between them. Yet she could ask him no further questions. You could not say to a man, "Why did you kiss me, if you didn't mean it? Why did you invite me into your arms if you didn't want me there?"

"I'll go back to my work now," he told her, "and you needn't admit you've had any help. After all, you did the whole thing yourself, so you're entitled to the credit."

Her mouth felt stiff and her lips would not smile easily. She could only nod in silence. He put out a hand and touched her shoulder lightly. Then he was gone by way of the back door.

She could hear him whistling as he rounded the house, returning to the rooms he preferred to keep so far from the house. The sound was a cheerful one, but she did not know whether to laugh or to weep.

A little to Camilla's relief, Ross did not appear at dinner that night, but sent word that he was going to the village, so Camilla and Letty dined alone. With Hortense's restraining presence removed, Letty was ready to chatter, but Camilla felt subdued and pensive, and she listened in a silence that was only half attentive.

There were a few moments of excitement over the bread she had baked. Matilda, coming home from her visit, had found the fresh loaves and admired them generously. Letty said this was the best bread she had tasted in a long while, and Camilla must certainly show Hortense what she could do when she returned from her trip.

Camilla accepted their compliments in her preoccupied state and kept her secret. The thought of Ross was never far away, and she did not want to be alone lest she give herself wholly to dreaming about what had happened.

After dinner, they avoided the parlor ritual, and Camilla followed Letty and Mignonette upstairs.

"Something's troubling you, isn't it, dear?" Letty said when they reached the door of her room. "Would you like to come in and keep me company for a while?"

Grateful for the invitation, Camilla seated herself on a window cushion in the circular tower that made an addition to Letty's small room. Sitting there, high among green branches that pressed against the windows, she felt like a bird suspended in a swinging cage. She could glimpse the river shining far below in the twilight. It was a peaceful spot, and she tried to let her mind go blank, let her feelings wash away in the quiet green light.

Letty made no attempt to question her, or draw her out, but went contentedly to work on her collection of receipts.

"I've decided to think about your suggestion for a book after all," she said. "Whether I try to have it published or not, it will give me satisfaction to compile it."

"I'm glad," Camilla told her, pleased to see her aunt busy and interested. It was a shame that the shadow of such a lie should be allowed to hang over her head. Mignonette sprang onto the window seat and began washing her face with an energetic paw. Camilla pushed her over idly, to pick up a book the cat was sitting on. It was a fat volume and seemed to be a medical dictionary of herbs. The pages fell open and she read at random, her interest only half upon the words.

Sage tea was good for sore throats, it appeared. Summer savory might be used to cure intestinal disorders. Sesame was a mild laxative and could be soothing when applied externally. The action of thyme was antiseptic and antispasmodic. Tansy ... her interest quickened at the name. Tansy could be rubbed over raw meat to keep the flies away, and its leaves were useful in destroying fleas and ants. It was a violent irritant to the stomach, and many deaths had been caused by it.

Camilla looked up from the pages, watching Letty in silence for a few moments as she worked with her papers.

"You said the other day that you used tansy in puddings," she said at length, "and sometimes in tea. But this book says that it's poisonous."

Letty did not look up from her sorting. "It is if one uses too much of it. The Pennsylvania Dutch make poultices of the sap, and they used the leaves in tea in treatments for the stomach. It's all in the quantity used."

The bottle of tansy juice had been there on the shelf and available, Camilla thought, and a jar with tansy leaves. There had been a strong scent of daisies about the tea that had made Mignonette ill. Though of course Aunt Letty had admitted to a touch of tansy in the mixture. She wanted to ask more questions, but she could not in the face of the suspicion Hortense had tried to cast upon Letty. She could not look at Letty and believe her guilty. If anyone was to be blamed for that tea, it was probably Hortense. Had Booth known what his mother had tried to do? she wondered, remembering the look she had caught between them that morning in the cellar.

Letty spoke evenly, quietly, still not looking up. "It's very easy to pick up a few facts and put them together in the wrong pattern. I never let myself do that if I can avoid it, my dear. Too much harm may be caused by a mistaken interpretation."

Camilla glanced at her, startled. "Sometimes I think you're a little fey. Sometimes you almost read my mind."

"It's my Scottish blood, I suppose," Letty said without smiling. "Sometimes I have a queer feeling of knowing when something is about to happen. As I did the night Papa died. And there have been other occasions too. The night your mother rode out to her death was one—" She stopped and shook her head. "I mustn't think about these things. They give me an uncomfortable feeling. I don't want to be queer and—and fey."

Camilla left her window seat and went to sit beside her.

"If there's anything queer about you, Aunt Letty, then it's a nice sort of queerness to have," she assured her aunt.

She began to help Letty with her sorting, and the green light faded at the windows as night came down. The sky to the west might still be bright, but the shadow of Thunder Mountain had fallen upon the house, and here night had already begun.

As the evening wore quietly on, Camilla began to feel lulled and peaceful. Letty was right—she mustn't allow groundless suspicion to grow in her mind. She must live in this house and accept the people in it. She could not afford to question what lay behind every action, or she would find no peace here at all.

She did not remember the little riding crop she had found

until she returned to her room. Then she got it out and carried it back to Letty.

"Look what I found in the shrubbery today," she said, and held out the black crop with its tarnished silver head for Letty to see.

Letty stared at it without recognition for a moment. Then she rose from her work and came to take it from Camilla's hand. The color went out of her face, and she sat down abruptly.

"Where did you find this?" she demanded.

Camilla explained how she had climbed down the bank and walked out upon the spit of land that extended into the river. How she had seen something odd caught in the brush and had found the riding crop.

Letty brushed at her face as though cobwebs clung to it. "No," she said. "No!"

"Do you know whom the crop belonged to?" Camilla asked.

"Of course," Letty said. "It belonged to my sister Althea. Papa had it made for her when she first started riding."

"I saw the saddle with the silver mountings in the attic," Camilla said. "Was that hers too?"

"Yes. Papa brought the saddle and bridle from Mexico."

"Someone has been going up to the attic to care for the leather and polish the silver," Camilla said.

"Papa did that." Letty spoke in a low voice. "After Althea ran away and he was so angry with her, he used to go upstairs sometimes to sit with those riding things she loved. Once when I went looking for him, I heard him talking to them as if she had been there. He was questioning and scolding—all in the manner of a man who couldn't understand what had been done to him. He wouldn't let us mention her name, but he used to steal up there and take care of her things, so that the leather wouldn't dry out, or the silver tarnish. Even after her death, he went right on caring for them. I think it brought him some sort of comfort."

Camilla could imagine her grandfather climbing the attic stairs with his head bowed, going to his sorrowful task. Perhaps in some strange way he had recovered his daughter in love and pain as he worked over her things. The picture was sadly touching.

"Perhaps I can bring my mother's saddle down from the attic and use it again," Camilla said. "Perhaps she would like to have me wear her habit and use her things."

Letty started to speak and then fell silent.

"Why were you startled when I showed you the crop, Aunt Letty?" Camilla asked. "Was my mother carrying it that evening when she went out to ride for the last time?"

Letty rose and went to the window of the little tower room to look out toward the river, shining now in the pale light of a rising moon.

"I don't remember," she said. "I'm not sure."

"No, of course she couldn't have carried it," Camilla mused. "Not if she rode up Thunder Mountain. Not when I've just found the crop down near the water's edge. Even if she dropped it, it could never fly so far out in the river."

Letty nodded as if relieved. "You're right, naturally." She seemed to brighten a little. "I can't imagine how it ever got there. It's very strange. But probably not important."

Camilla took the crop back to her room, but she felt restless and not at all ready for sleep. The moment she settled down and was still, all the thoughts she wanted to put away from her would come rushing back. Perhaps a walk would quiet her, still her thoughts. Softly she slipped through the hall and down the stairs, finding her way in the light from the canopied lamp above.

The servants were in their quarters in the kitchen wing by now, and the house seemed lonely and empty. She opened the heavy door with its iron grillwork, and went outside. The night was soft and cool, and moonlight flooded the world, though the park expanse before the house was dark with the thickness of trees.

Silently she drifted across the grass, not following the drive, but running straight through the park in the direction of the gate. Her urge to run in the moonlight, in the cool night air, was without conscious purpose, and she did not pause until she saw the lights of Ross's rooms above the stable. Then she came to a breathless halt, shrinking back into the deep shadow of an oak tree, watching the patches of light.

Memory swept back on a flood of warmth, to engulf her being. She could hold her thoughts at bay no longer. In memory she could feel Ross's arms about her, she could raise her head and feel his kiss hard upon her mouth. He would be part of her dreams tonight, and she knew no way to rid herself of the thought of him. That he had chosen to put her so quickly aside, that his impersonal manner had told her how much he regretted his impulsive act, seared as though it had just happened.

A shadow moved across a square of light, and Camilla

136

came to herself abruptly. What foolish thing was she doing here—spying upon him out of the shadows! Eager as a schoolgirl for the sight of her love.

Her love.

She did not want it. She had not asked to love this man, but there it was—hurtful and real and not to be lightly dismissed. She turned and ran back through the trees, letting herself quietly into the house, scurrying upstairs to the retreat of her own room.

There was once more an exultation in her, and a torment as well.

XV

IN THE MORNING THE EXULTANCE WAS GONE. CAMILLA awakened feeling as tired as though she had not slept, but her eyes were clear, her thoughts brittle and sharp with self-judgment.

How could she have been so trapped by gentle dreams last night? In the morning light she could look at herself and remember something she had told Booth. She had not known many men. It was true that she was easily vulnerable. Whether it was Ross or Booth, the warm longings that were part of her youth reached out toward a male counterpart in an instinctive answering. Love? How could she have been so foolish? What could she know of love? If she were honest with herself, she must admit that there were times when she had been equally attracted to Booth.

Today there were other things to think of. Regardless of Letty's remark about misinterpretation, she must face the possibility that someone in this house had added a poisonous potion to Letty's tea. Since it was hardly likely to be one of the servants, nor could it be Ross, who was an outsider, the tamperer must be one of the three within this house: Hortense, Letty, or Booth. This morning, with her mood so newly cool and hard, she could even regard Letty with serious doubt, though Hortense was to be more easily suspected.

At any rate, she must get to the bottom of what had happened and discover whether someone had tried deliberately to harm her. If one attempt had been made, there might well be others. By daylight she could be brave and strong. But she knew the shadow of fear that night could bring, and she did not want to live her life in such a shadow.

Yet when she met Letty that day, she could find no means of taking hold of the problem. The moment she moved toward it, Letty seemed to slip mistily away from her probing, and she could not bring herself to question her directly.

She dreaded her first meeting with Ross. If he showed amusement toward her, if he referred in any way to what had happened between them, she would not know how to meet him with her pride intact. Her fears were unfounded, however. He was courteous, though distant, and it was hard to remember that he had worked so cheerfully beside her in a kitchen yesterday. She could not help a certain anger, but she told herself that it came more from hurt pride than from any real emotion on her part.

In the days before Hortense and Booth came home, Ross was completely matter-of-fact toward her. He placed business matters before her as usual, and did not hesitate to show his disapproval when she seemed unenthusiastic about projects that absorbed his attention.

On the afternoon when Hortense and Booth were to return, Ross reminded her of the invitation to tea at Nora Redfern's tomorrow. But she had a feeling that he regretted his original impulse in urging such a visit.

If it had not been for the fact that Camilla longed to make Nora's acquaintance, she might have pleaded some excuse to escape the invitation. But she found that she was looking forward to the occasion more than she had expected to. She would have an opportunity to wear one of her enchanting new afternoon frocks. She would look her very best, and be serenely remote and indifferent to either criticism or approval on the part of Ross Granger.

It was with a sense of regret that she heard the sound of the carriage bringing Booth and his mother back to Thunder Heights. Now the quiet, friendly hours she had spent with Letty would come to an end, and disquieting influences would be at work in the house again.

Nevertheless, she went to the door to greet them, and her first look at the travelers told her that as far as Aunt Hortense was concerned, the trip had been a failure. Booth appeared to have enjoyed himself thoroughly and was ready to talk about what he had seen and done in New York. Hortense was clearly angry and frustrated, impatient even with Booth, and hardly civil to Letty and Camilla.

The next morning Booth was ready to take up his painting again, and this time all went well.

As he worked, Letty came in to join them again and sat down nearby to watch. Once Booth paused to ask a direct question of Camilla.

"What has happened to you, Cousin, since I've been away?"

Camilla was startled. "Happened? Why, nothing much. I've baked bread and helped Aunty Letty with her receipts. The new draperies are up in the parlor. Nothing much else."

For a few moments Booth worked intently on the face of the girl in the picture. Then he flashed the smile that always seemed so unexpected in his dark, sardonic face.

"It was none of those things I meant, Camilla. Even though you're very quiet today, there's something that was lacking before. I can see more than Althea in you this morning."

"I don't know what you mean," she told him, and had nothing more to say.

Letty looked up from her work to glance at her in mild surprise, and Camilla was suddenly afraid that her aunt might add some comment of her own.

"Why don't you play for us while I'm posing, Aunt Letty?" she said hurriedly. "I've never really heard you play your harp."

Perhaps Letty sensed a plea behind her words, for she put her work aside. "Very well—if Booth doesn't mind."

"I've always enjoyed your playing, Aunt Letty," he said gallantly, but his eyes were still on his model, and Camilla sensed a quickened interest and curiosity in his look.

Letty went to the harp and drew off its cover. The fingers of her left hand moved easily on the strings, but she had to bend her body forward to reach them with her crooked right arm. After a few chords she began to play, and the music was nothing Camilla had ever heard before. It had a wailing, melancholy sound, as if the contented, busy Letty Judd of everyday vanished when she sat down to her harp. In her place was a woman lost and tragic. The music seemed to sing of longing and of wasted, empty years with an intensity that was frightening.

Booth looked up from his painting somberly. "You're hearing the music of Thunder Heights, Cousin. It speaks for us all, doesn't it? Trapped and damned and without hope. That's why Mother hates to hear Aunt Letty play. The music tells too much about the things we try to hide from one another."

Letty's fingers were still on the strings. She rose to cover the instrument without a word and slip quietly from the room.

Booth worked in silence for a time, and when he spoke again, it was of another matter. "As you've probably guessed, my mother found no encouragement on her mission to New York. It's possible that the will might be broken. At least the lawyer she consulted didn't try to discourage her as a client. But it seems that it would cost a fine penny—and where is the money to come from? She can hardly ask you to finance her effort to take a fortune away from you, can she, Cousin? It makes for a difficult situation."

Camilla watched him guardedly. "You don't sound as if you minded."

"Why should I mind?" He shrugged graceful shoulders. "I live a more comfortable life under the new regime. While I'll admit that the money would be easier come by in my mother's hands than in yours, Cousin, I've suffered very little."

He worked on for a while longer and then laid aside his brush.

"That's enough for today. It's going well. A change of scene has done me good. And the change in you is stimulating. I shan't give up wondering what caused it. Camilla, I haven't forgotten your wish to find a good saddle horse. I shopped around a bit in New York. But so far I haven't found what I think you might like."

She was relieved to have him speak of horses. "I don't know that I'm that particular. I'd love to buy a horse and go riding soon."

"Trust me a little longer, will you?" he said. "You deserve the best."

Again the faint note of mockery was back in his voice, but she ignored it. She was glad when the posing was over. On and off during the last half hour she had been thinking about the tea at Blue Beeches this afternoon, and she was eager to get away and look through the frocks she might wear.

Somehow it grew increasingly important that she seem beautiful and remote and self-contained to Ross Granger. He must be made to forget that Camilla King had ever moved in so headlong a fashion into his arms. Today she would be out of reach and yet—delectable.

There was still a hurt in her that wanted to pay him back.

The dress she decided upon was of pale blue Chinese silk, trimmed with touches of ivory lace. It was a thin, delicate

140

dress, and she found it satisfying to appear in something that was far from serviceable, and not at all suited to a governess. When she had put on her mother's bracelet of medallions and peach stones and turned before the armoire mirror a few times, she was ready.

Letty came in to admire her just before she went downstairs, and her aunt was warm in her praise.

"I haven't seen anyone looking so pretty and appealing since Althea lived in this house. You'll do us credit, my dear."

Camilla gave her a quick, loving hug, wondering at the perversity of her own thoughts that could at times hold anyone as endearing and guileless as Aunt Letty under suspicion.

As she ran down the octagon staircase, she listened pleasurably to her own silken froufrou, and sniffed the aura of light apple blossom scent with which she had surrounded herself. How lovely it was to feel young and unexplainably happy. Though there was danger in this, lest she forget how out-of-reach she meant to be with Ross.

She was smiling as she stepped into the antehall and was faintly disconcerted to find Booth watching her from the library door.

"Charming!" he said. "And surprising to find a lady of fashion at Thunder Heights."

She could not resist turning about before him, displaying her new frock at its most fetching angles. There was an eagerness in her, a hunger for approval—and masculine eyes were more satisfactory in meeting that need than feminine.

"Your escort is waiting for you outside," Booth said. "I'm sorry I'm not the one who's taking you to visit Nora."

She smiled at him, warming toward everyone today, and went outside. Ross stood at the foot of the steps, and as she came out he turned and stared at her, his startled look gratifying. He would find in her today neither the little governess he had met on the river boat, nor the stubborn heiress who quarreled with him so often. Nor would he find the ingenuous girl of the beech tree. Today she meant to be—Althea's daughter.

Ross recovered from his surprise all too quickly and made no comment on her appearance. She found, however, that he could play the gentleman as smoothly as Booth when he chose. They followed the path that led to the lower level, and crossed the railroad tracks to walk along the bank just above the river. Ross held branches back from brushing her, and helped her up and down steep places in the path as if she were really as fragile as she wanted to believe herself today. Sometimes she wondered if he were laughing at her, just a little, behind his rather elaborate gestures, but she was too happy and confident to mind.

Once they stopped to watch a fleet of little sailboats gliding past on the surface of the smooth blue Hudson, and Camilla followed them out of sight, feeling that they added to the carefree aspect of the day.

The first glimpse of Blue Beeches was always reassuring. It sat foursquare upon its high basement, its generous veranda open toward the river. On a slope of lawn at one side of the house Nora's two older children were playing a game of croquet, while their nurse sat with the youngest, watching. The spotted dog, Champion, saw the visitors and came bounding across the grass toward them. Ross accepted his effusive greeting with affection and held him away from Camilla.

"He misses his master," Ross said. "As we all do. Nora's husband died just over a year ago. Ted Redfern was one of my good friends. I've been trying to help Nora with some of her business problems ever since. She has a lot of courage. I hope you'll be friends."

There was a note of tender affection in his tone that made Camilla glance at him quickly. Was his feeling for Ted Redfern's wife more than that of a friend? She did not like the pang that stabbed through her at his words. It bore too close a resemblance to an emotion that went by an uglier name. She would not be jealous of Nora Redfern!

A maid showed them into a huge parlor with moss green wallpaper and softly cushioned furniture. Everything looked a little frayed and worn, as if the room had never been closed to the children. Over the mantel, seemingly cut through the huge chimney above the fireplace, was a circular window. Blue sky and fleeting clouds could be seen through its high double glass, while the interior flues separated to circle round it.

Nora joined them after a brief interval, flushed and a little breathless. Her brown hair had been swept back from her forehead without any vestige of a pompadour, and tied with a black velvet ribbon at the nape of her neck. The marks of a hasty brush were still upon it. She wore a frock of dark silk that suited her in its simplicity.

"Do forgive me for keeping you waiting," she said, holding out a hand first to Camilla and then to Ross. "I had Diamond out for a ride and I lost track of time. Not that forgetting about time is anything new for me. Ted used to say it was never any use buying me watches because I'd always forget to look at them."

She noted Camilla's interest in the unusual window and smiled.

"My grandfather designed that window when he built the house. In his day there was always a stuffed bird kept between those double panes of glass. But I like to see the sky."

Nora had an engagingly friendly manner, and under other circumstances Camilla would have been drawn to her warmly. But now she found herself a little watchful, a little too much aware, for her own comfort, of every glance that passed between Nora and Ross. She did not want it to be like that—it simply was.

The maid brought tea in a handsome Sèvres service, with watercress sandwiches and frosted cakes on a three-tiered stand, and Nora settled down comfortably for conversation.

"I remember your mother well," she told Camilla. "When I was quite small she used to come here often to visit my mother. Mama lives upriver now. I wrote her that I was going to invite you over, and she wants me to tell her all about you. By the way, when are you going to open up the house again?"

"Open it up?" said Camilla. "I'm not sure I know what you mean."

"Only that when you have it fully refurbished, you must give a party and bring back the old days. How gay it used to be! I can remember coming home from across the river late one night with my parents and seeing Thunder Heights lighted from top to bottom, with Japanese lanterns strung across the veranda and all about that high lawn above the river. We could hear the music clear from the other side. Often here at Blue Beeches there were nights when we could catch the sound of music and laughter."

Letty too had urged her to open up the house, Camilla remembered. "I'd like to give a party," she said, her interest rising. "Perhaps we could invite people from up and down the river who used to know the family. Would you come, Mrs. Redfern? And perhaps your mother?"

Nora hesitated. "Mother would come in a moment— though I'm not sure that would be a good idea. She is pretty outspoken, you know, and there's no telling her what not to say. Besides, your aunts would be angry if you invited her."

"But why?" Camilla asked. "What happened to break up the friendship your mother had with my family at Thunder Heights?"

"Let's not spoil the afternoon with old quarrels," Nora said. "Perhaps your coming will make the difference and we can all be friends again."

"If we give a party, we'll want you both," Camilla insisted. "I should think Aunt Hortense would love the excitement of a party. And I know Aunt Letty would like to see the house opened up for the sake of the rest of us, though I'm not sure she would really enjoy it herself."

"I'm afraid she gave up that sort of thing after her arm was so badly injured," Nora said. "She wouldn't wear evening dress after that, and for a long while she was terribly self-conscious."

"No one ever mentions her injury," Camilla puzzled. "When was she hurt? What happened?"

"She was thrown from a horse," Ross said. "Just as your mother was. It occurred before I came to live at Thunder Heights."

Nora nodded. "It was after Althea had married and gone away. Hortense and Letty used to ride a good deal in those days. Orrin gave Letty a mare that had a maverick streak they weren't aware of. Letty was thrown and dragged. The mare went half crazy, and in her kicking and stamping Letty's arm was stepped on and broken. She might have been killed if Hortense hadn't been riding with her that day. Hortense rescued her and got her home. But the arm never set properly, and the mark of the hoof left a scar she has carried ever since."

"The Judds have had bad luck with horses," Ross said. "With two such accidents, it was no wonder that Mr. Judd would have no horses on the place."

Nora looked quickly at Camilla, almost with a question in her eyes. But before she could put it into words, one of her children came running in. He was a sturdy little boy, with his hair on end, and his face dirty.

"I won! I won!" he shrieked, and flung himself in triumph upon his mother, croquet mallet and all.

When she had applauded him, wiped his face, and sent him back to play, she did not return to the subject of Letty's accident.

"Where do you go riding?" Camilla asked as Nora refilled her teacup.

"Today I followed the river," Nora said. "But my favorite

144

rides are back in the hills. I think I'm happiest when I can ride up through the woods and come out on top of Thunder Mountain."

"I've been thinking of getting a horse," Camilla told her. "I loved riding as a child in the parks in New York. And it would be so much better here."

"In spite of the Thunder Heights jinx when it comes to horses?" Nora asked.

"I don't believe in jinxes," Camilla said quickly.

"In that case, you needn't wait until you buy a horse. Borrow one of mine. I'd be glad to loan you Diamond. He was Ted's horse, really, but I've trained him to the sidesaddle. You may have him tomorrow, if you like. I'm leaving with the children to visit my mother upriver for a few days. Ross can take one of the other horses and go with you. I often loan him a horse when he wants to ride."

Unable to hide her sudden pleasure at the thought of riding with Ross, Camilla glanced at him quickly and saw clear reluctance in his eyes. She rushed into words to hide her hurt.

"Surely it's not necessary for me to have an escort!"

"Indeed it is," Nora assured her. "We can't have you going out in the hills alone until you know your way. It's all wooded mountains back there, with trails crisscrossing. You can lose yourself easily when you get away from the river. You'll take her, won't you, Ross?"

"I'm going down to New York in a day or two," he said. "But perhaps I could manage it tomorrow."

His lack of enthusiasm was obvious, and Camilla would have refused his company if Nora had not settled the matter with the quiet assurance of a woman who knew that what she asked of a man would not be refused.

She felt only relief when the tea hour passed and she could rise to go. She did not want to remain in Ross's company a moment longer than she had to, now that she felt sure where his interest really lay. All her earlier happiness in the day, all her confidence in herself, was evaporating. She had not, after all, proved herself Althea's daughter. Althea had been irresistible.

On the way back to Thunder Heights, Ross continued to be silent and preoccupied. It was almost as if he had forgotten her presence, and she felt further piqued into calling him back.

"Did you know," she asked, "that Aunt Hortense's purpose

in going to New York was to try to break Grandfather's will?"

"I'm not surprised," Ross said. "It was to be expected that she'd try. If I were you, I'd break it myself and pack Hortense and Booth out of the house straight off."

She brushed indignantly ahead of him, heedless of a briar that caught at her dress. "Even if no one else cares, I feel bound by what Grandfather wanted me to do. I'm not free to dispose of his property in any way I might wish."

"You're being sentimental," Ross said. "Why not give those two the money and let them go? You'd be better off in the long run. Orrin Judd was trying to bring back the past. He was trying to undo old mistakes and revenge himself on those he distrusted at the same time. You must live in the present—the future. Don't be a fool."

They were nearing the house now and she began to hurry. "If I'm a fool, I'll be one in my own way. At least my conscience is my own. And—you needn't trouble to ride with me tomorrow. Perhaps I can ask Booth—"

He surprised her by reaching out to catch her by the wrist. She felt the medallions of her bracelet press into her flesh with the strength of his grasp.

"I'll ride with you," he said, his gray eyes angry. "Don't try to change your plans now." Then he dropped her hand abruptly and strode away from her toward the house.

What was the matter with him? She could not altogether suppress a sense of satisfaction that she had at least stirred him to anger.

Very well, she *would* ride with him tomorrow. But she would go as the mistress of Thunder Heights, and she would keep him strictly in his place. She would show him, once and for all, how little he meant to her. Today she had not succeeded very well.

When she went up to her room, she was shaken by a queer sort of fury in which disgust with herself mingled with her anger against Ross. Who was she? What was she? Today she had flung herself through a ridiculous gamut of emotions, from high hope and elation to a disappointment that was out of all proportion to the cause. Why? Because she cared more about Ross Granger than she was willing to admit, even to herself? And because she was beginning to feel that his affections were well occupied elsewhere?

She sat down at Althea's dressing table and looked into Althea's mirror. A black-haired girl with dark eyes that were

146

angry, and a soft mouth that was all too tremulous, looked back at her.

"What would *you* have done?" she whispered, and her question was directed not to herself, but to a long ago image that had appeared in this mirror. But if the shadowy face of her mother looked over her shoulder, it did not speak, or counsel her. Only Nora's words sounded again in her mind. "Why don't you open up the house?"

Perhaps she would do just that. Fling open the windows and doors, open them wide to a more normal life in which gaiety had some part. A life that would bring new faces, new friends to Thunder Heights. She would tell the others about her plan right after dinner tonight.

XVI

WHEN DINNER WAS OVER THAT NIGHT AND ROSS HAD GONE back to his rooms above the coach house, the family gathered on the veranda to enjoy the evening air after a warm day. Behind them the parlor glowed with light, but here on the veranda they could sit in the semidarkness—a quiet, not very companionable group. Into the separate silences Camilla dropped her suggestion.

"Let's give a party," she said.

Letty looked surprised, but said nothing. Hortense murmured, "What for?" and Booth said, "Why not?" in lazy amusement.

Camilla went on in a little rush, speaking more to Hortense than to the others. "Today Nora Redfern was telling me about the way it used to be at Thunder Heights. About the parties Grandfather used to give when you and Aunt Letty were young. We could at least make a beginning and wake the house up. This veranda must be big enough for dancing—"

"It is," Letty said quickly. "Many's the time we used to dance out here in the summertime. Do you remember, Hortense?"

"I want to forget," Hortense said.

"But I'll need your help," Camilla pointed out. "Don't you think a party would be fun on a lovely summer evening?"

"My mother adores parties," Booth said dryly. "She's told

147

me a good many times how she used to shine at them. And how much she missed them."

Hortense gave him a look that was just a shade less doting than usual, but offered no objection.

Camilla talked on about how they could set tables on the lawn, and hang Japanese lanterns—just as they'd done in the old days. And surely friends of the family, people who had known her mother and Letty and Hortense when they were young, could be invited, along with their grownup children. Thunder Heights was beginning to look so beautiful—they must show it off, gain it a new reputation for gaiety and hospitality.

Someone came around the end of the house as she spoke, a dark shadow among the trees. As he reached the veranda steps, Camilla saw that it was Ross. He spoke to her directly.

"What time do you wish to go riding tomorrow? I forgot to ask."

The silence that fell upon the veranda was like that of a breath being held. Camilla was aware of Letty's faint gasp, of Hortense's stillness, of Booth's quick, intent look.

"Will nine o'clock in the morning be convenient for you?" Camilla asked stiffly.

"I'll have the horses here at nine," Ross said, and went away as he had come, through the grove of elms.

"What horses?" Hortense demanded when he had gone.

"Nora Redfern offered me a saddle horse to ride tomorrow, and Ross is going with me to show me some of the trails."

"Nora Redfern!" Hortense cried. "Have you no sense of propriety that you must strike up a friendship with this woman? How can you—"

Letty slipped out of her chair and drifted across the veranda to Camilla's side. "I know you said you wanted to wear Althea's things, but I didn't think you really meant it. Don't go riding, dear. Please don't go riding."

Camilla smiled at her reassuringly. "Aunt Letty, I know how you must feel about horses, but I think I'm a fairly good rider and I want to be a better one. Booth has promised to find me a saddle horse, and then I mean to go riding every day when the weather allows. And as for Nora Redfern, I enjoyed my visit with her this afternoon, and I hope we'll be friends. I see no reason why I shouldn't borrow one of her horses until I have my own."

Letty rested a hand that trembled on Camilla's shoulder. "You don't understand, dear. Papa said there was never to be

148

a horse at Thunder Heights again. He made us all promise that we would give up riding forever."

She unhooked her right sleeve at the wrist and started to roll it up, but Camilla caught her hand, stopping her. "Don't, Aunt Letty. I know. But just because there have been accidents before, doesn't mean there will be another one. I love to ride, and it would be foolish not to enjoy it again."

"Bravo!" Booth applauded, clapping his hands together lightly. "I have no use for faint hearts. The riding habit suits you, Cousin. I say wear it and go riding tomorrow. And give your party. A little excitement about this place will be welcome. If we don't have it, we may well—explode."

Letty went back to her chair and sat down without a sound. Camilla could not see her face in the dim light, but there was something unnerving about her stillness, as if she held some rush of shattering emotion in check. Hortense stood up and walked to one of the parlor doors.

"Ride, then," she said listlessly and went into the house.

Booth yawned and held the back of his hand over his mouth. "These emotional scenes are wearing. That is, when the emotion is suppressed. I'd rather see tears, an outburst of temper, some flinging about in good feminine fashion."

Letty's silence remained complete, her face expressionless.

"At least, Cousin, you've won your point," Booth said. "No one will lift a finger when you go riding tomorrow. I must say I find it generous of Mrs. Redfern to loan you her horse and even suggest that Granger go riding with you. She must be very sure of herself."

His meaning was clear. "A remark like that is uncalled for!" Camilla said sharply.

"Is it?" The mockery had gone out of him. "Perhaps I want to see your eyes opened in time, Camilla."

"Mrs. Redfern's husband has been dead hardly more than a year," Camilla reminded him. "And Ross was his very good friend."

"All the more reason for what is happening," Booth said. "A lonely, saddened woman, and a man who had a great affection for the man she loved. I don't blame them. It's natural enough. But I would hate to see you grow too interested in Granger."

"I can take care of myself," Camilla said stiffly.

Letty coughed gently, but said nothing, still lost in her remoteness. When Camilla rose to go inside, Booth stopped her, his hand light upon her arm, his voice unexpectedly tender.

"I'm not sure you can take care of yourself, Cousin. But I'd like you to know that you can count me your friend."

She was moved in spite of her hurt, and she gave him an uncertain smile as she went into the house.

That night Letty played her harp again.

Camilla heard the eerie music stealing through the house as it had done on the night when Grandfather Orrin had died. Was this music perhaps the emotional release Letty needed—something to keep her from going to pieces when some inner strain became too great for her?

Tonight no door opened, no footsteps sounded in the hall, no one stole upstairs to silence the music. After a time Camilla fell asleep, and when she wakened some hours later, the house was as still and hushed as if no mournful harp music had ever drifted through its corridors. But now, in spite of the silence, she had the feeling that something had changed in the very climate of the house. The harp music had saddened her, but there had been nothing truly frightening about it. In the hush that now lay upon the house—as if the very walls held themselves still to listen—there was something new, something fearful. Into this silence stirred a whisper of sound, as if someone moved in the hall nearby.

Camilla sat up and reached for the matches and candle beside her bed. The candle flared and smoked in a draft from the balcony's open door, then settled to a pale, steady flame. Her attention was fixed upon the corridor door to her room. With a cold washing of fear through her body, she wondered if she had really locked that door tonight.

As she watched, she saw the cloisonné doorknob move almost imperceptibly. An unseen hand turned it softly and carefully as far as it would go, but the lock held and the door did not open. Slowly, softly, as Camilla stared in fascination, it turned back to its original position. The faintest sound of a sigh reached her from outside the door, followed by silence.

Camilla slipped out of bed and into a wrapper. For a long moment she stood with her ear against the panel, listening with all her being, but there was no sound of a footfall to disturb the stillness of the house. Whoever had turned the knob might well be standing just outside the door, waiting. If she opened it, the unseen intruder might spring quickly inside.

But the silence seemed not to be a breathing silence. She had the feeling that whoever had stood there had moved so stealthily away that the hall carpet had hidden any retreat.

Her own fingers could not move so secretly. There was a click as she unlocked the door and pulled it open a crack.

No one stood in the hall outside her room, but now she heard the sound of a creaking step on the stairs above. She looked boldly into the hall and was in time to see the white of a flounced nightgown moved out of sight up the stairway.

She did not hesitate, but ran barefooted toward the stairs and up them to the floor above. Letty was there, drifting smoothly ahead of her down the corridor toward the attic stairs. In one hand she carried a candle, and as Camilla watched she opened the door to the stairs and vanished up them.

Troubled, Camilla hurried after. Aunt Letty was not to be feared, and clearly she was sleepwalking again. She must be stopped and brought back to her own bed, but she must not be startled awake. This must be done gently.

Letty had climbed to the attic by now, and she did not turn as Camilla came up the stairs behind her. She seemed to know exactly what she wanted here, and went at once to the small rear room where Althea's saddle rested over a beam. There she set the candleholder upon a shelf and took the shining stirrup into her hands. Though her eyes were wide open, Letty felt blindly along the stirrup leather until she came to the saddle itself, and her hands followed it to the jutting silver horn. She seemed to be touching all these things, searching them out, as if her hands found some reassurance in contact with them.

Camilla stood silently watching her, wondering what she must do. She wished now that she had called Hortense, who knew how to handle these sleepwalking spells. Before she could decide whether to speak to her aunt, or touch her arm to lead her back to bed, Letty picked up her candle again, went past Camilla without seeing her, and started downstairs.

Softly Camilla followed, and Letty returned to her own room without further exploration and closed her door. In all probability she had gone safely back to bed. Shaken and mystified, Camilla went to her room, and when she had locked the door, she stepped out upon the balcony. The night air was cool and fresh to her hot cheeks, and there was no tinge of horror there.

What hidden thoughts and sorrows roused Letty to make her walk in her sleep? And why would she go to the attic and seek out Althea's saddle? A remembrance of Grandfather Orrin's words once more returned sharply to her mind. "Watch Letty," he had said.

Below the balcony Camilla heard the rustling sound of something moving. Was there someone else abroad on this strange night? But the sound, she decided, was no more than an elm branch brushing the side of the house. Starlight dusted a silver patina over Thunder Heights and shimmered on the surface of the river.

The thought of her ride tomorrow returned, and with it all the things she wanted to shut away. In particular the words Booth had spoken about Nora and Ross. She had been angry with him at first, but his words had only strengthened her own conviction of the affection that lay between those two.

Booth had been right—she must not let herself be hurt. Her wayward feelings must be turned back from the path of disaster.

She went to bed and lay awake for a long while.

In spite of her disturbed night, she was awake early the next morning. The sun, rising brightly in a golden sky across the Hudson, carried out the prophecy of the night. It was a beautiful morning for riding, and she felt eager to be away from the house and out in the hills.

A little to her surprise, Aunt Letty came down for breakfast, looking somewhat subdued.

"I'm sorry you were upset about my riding," Camilla said.

Letty smiled at her with forced brightness. "You mustn't let my foolish fears spoil your plans. This will be a good day for riding—a safe day." She paused to tell Grace she would have just a little toast and a cup of coffee.

"What do you mean—a safe day?" Camilla asked.

"It's not storming," Letty said. "You must never go riding in a storm."

Clearly she was thinking of the horse that had thrown her sister—the horse that had been afraid of thunderstorms. If the idea had become an obsession with Letty, there was no point in trying to argue her out of the notion.

"I love storms," Camilla said. "I even like to be out in them. But I don't think I'd deliberately go riding in a thunderstorm, if that's what you mean."

Letty was staring at her with a wide, misty gaze. "You're so much like your mother. I hope you haven't an affinity for thunderstorms, as your mother had."

The fey quality was evident in Letty again this morning. Her delicate, fine-skinned face had a faraway look about it, as if she moved in wreaths of mist in spite of the sunlight. It might be just as well to call her back to more earthly considerations, Camilla thought, and asked about her garden.

152

"The nasturtiums are thriving this year," Letty said, rising readily to the bait. "Perhaps they're not really herbs, but I love the way they brighten the garden all summer long. In the fall I can use the seeds for pickling. And have you seen my honeywort? The yellow buds are already blooming, though they never really open, you know. Not that it matters, when the leaves are so shining and beautiful."

When she walked about her garden, she was shining and beautiful herself, Camilla thought. One forgot the twisted arm, the ugly scar hidden by her sleeve.

When breakfast was over, Camilla went upstairs to dress for her ride. She put on her mother's habit and boots. The gray top hat with its floating streamers of veiling was as fetching as ever, and she liked the look of it on her dark hair. When she was ready, she opened a drawer and took out the little black riding crop, with its polished silver head. This would make the final perfect touch. Today she would carry it when she went riding, just as her mother had once done.

She went into the hall, to find Hortense at the top of the stairs, filling the cinnabar stair lamp with oil. She had drawn the great bowl down on its pulley, and Camilla waited until the lamp had been filled and returned to place beneath the carved canopy high over the stairwell. Hortense heard her and turned, her greenish eyes venomous this morning.

When Camilla would have passed her to go downstairs, Hortense put out an arresting hand. "I suppose you heard Letty playing her harp last night?" she asked in a whisper.

"I heard her," Camilla said.

"Hush! She's waiting for you at the foot of the stairs. I don't want her to hear. I hope you realize that the harp playing was your fault. She only plays at night when she's unhappy and upset. You've treated her with a complete lack of consideration."

Hortense was hardly the one to accuse others of a lack of consideration, but Camilla did not point out the fact as she started downstairs. And this was not the time to mention the sleepwalking.

"Aunt Letty and I had breakfast together," Camilla said. "She seemed quite all right then."

"We can expect more sleepwalking," Hortense persisted. "That will be your doing too."

"I'm sorry," Camilla said and would have continued on her way, if Hortense had not suddenly seen the riding crop in her hands.

"Where did you get that?" she demanded.

Before Camilla could answer, or knew what she intended, Hortense snatched at the crop. She only succeeded in knocking it out of Camilla's hand, and it went over the banister to fall with a clatter to the floor below. Hortense looked after it in dismay for a moment, then shrugged and went back to her own room.

Camilla ran down the stairs to find that Letty had picked up the crop and was holding it as she watched Camilla descend. She stood tapping the ragged end of the leather thong across her palm in a nervous gesture.

"You look lovely," she said. "Have a wonderful ride, dear. I'm sure everything will be fine this morning."

"Thank you, Aunt Letty," Camilla said, and held out her hand for the crop.

Letty did not give it up. "Will you leave this with me, please? I'd rather you didn't carry it, dear."

"But—why not?" Camilla asked.

"Perhaps—" Letty hesitated, "—perhaps I'm more sentimental about this little riding crop than I am about the other things. Leave it with me, Camilla."

Puzzled though she was, Camilla gave in. Letty held the door open, and Camilla went out into the bright morning.

"Have a nice ride," Letty repeated softly, and closed the door behind her.

Moved by an increasing sense of uneasiness, Camilla stood on the steps, waiting for Ross. She heard the neighing of a horse, and a moment later he appeared, coming up from the river path and around the house, riding a roan mare and leading Diamond, saddled and bridled. Nora's favorite mount was a dappled gray—a handsome, high-stepping creature, with a white diamond blaze on his forehead.

"I hope you can manage this fellow," Ross said. "Grays are supposed to be unsuitable mounts for ladies because their dispositions are unstable. Though I'm not sure I hold with the legend. Nora handles him beautifully."

His words sounded like a challenge, and Camilla felt quite willing to pick it up. She fed Diamond a lump of sugar, stroked his nose and talked to him for a few moments. He seemed to accept her readily enough, and from the mounting block she put her left foot into the stirrup, turning her body so that she went lightly up to hook her right knee over the horn of the sidesaddle. Diamond took a skittish step or two and then, sensing firmness in her hands, did as she wished him to. She smiled at Ross from the saddle, feeling pleased and triumphant.

"Where would you like to ride, Miss King?" he inquired formally, holding to the role of one who had been given a task to perform and meant to carry it out correctly to the letter.

Camilla turned Diamond away from the river, her smile stiffening. "Let's go up Thunder Mountain. I've been wanting to get to the top. Do you know the way?"

"Of course." He went ahead along the drive toward the road, accepting the suggestion as an order which gave him no choice.

She touched Diamond with her heel to catch up, and they rode out side by side between the stone lions that marked the gate in the great privet hedge.

The air was brilliantly clear, with a bright blue sky overhead, but not too warm for comfort. Camilla loved being on a horse again. This high seat above the world, with the feeling of Diamond's smooth-flowing strength beneath her, gave her a heady sense of power.

They overtook an elderly farmer driving a cartload of vegetables to market, and he looked up at them. For an instant he gave Camilla a shocked stare and then touched a finger to his forelock in recognition. Camilla almost laughed out loud in delight as they rode past. Surely he remembered Althea Judd, and he must have been carried back through the years at the sight of her daughter.

She urged Diamond into a canter, and Ross kept pace with her, though now he rode a tail's length behind, still acting the role of groom. He did not take the lead again until they neared the opening to a narrow road up the mountain, when he called to her and trotted ahead.

XVII

THEY WENT SINGLE FILE BENEATH THE TREES, WINDING upward at a gradual pace. Riding along with branches interlacing just above her head, and the river, blue as the sky, sometimes glimpsed below, she could almost forget Ross in sheer physical happiness.

Once he turned his head and spoke to her over his shoulder. "Here's something for you to see."

She followed him into the wide scar of an open place which had once been cleared through the woods. It dropped away in a steep slope of mountain to a rushing stream below. The stretch was overgrown with scrub now, and along the edges of the scar mountain laurel glowed in the bright pink and white blooming of spring.

Ross reined in the mare as Camilla drew up beside him. "When your grandfather was young and worked in lumber, this was a pitching place," he said.

"Pitching place?" Camilla repeated the unfamiliar term.

"They used to snake the logs down the old road and get them started on this slope, where they could pitch them to the stream below and send them down to the river."

Camilla sat very still in the saddle, breathing the spicy scent of the woods about her, listening to the noisy voice of the stream. She could almost see Orrin Judd as he must have been in the strength of his youth—a young man who belonged to the forests and the hills, reveling in this outdoor work.

"Let's go on," Ross said abruptly.

The path wound back into the woods behind the rocky eminence of the mountain, and the climb grew steeper. When they emerged suddenly upon an open space at the top, Camilla had not realized they were so high. She rode eagerly toward the stony head of the mountain, where it towered above the river, dropping steeply away in a face of rocky cliff.

Ross put a hand on Diamond's bridle. "Not too near the edge," he warned. "Sometimes he takes notions into his head."

"I want to stand near the edge," Camilla said, and she slipped out of the saddle without waiting for Ross's help, and let him take the reins from her. While he walked the horses back toward the trees to tether them, she climbed a slope of rock and sat down on a boulder near the very lip of the cliff.

Up here the wind blew strong and free, whipping out the streamers of her gray veil. Below and a little to the north lay the village, its white church steeple like a toy tower on a child's house of blocks. Across the river the unknown town opposite seemed a world away and beyond it rolled the hills clear to the blue haze of New England mountains. When she turned toward the north she could see the outline of the Catskills far away on her left. At her feet the sheer face of the cliff dropped toward the river.

"Can we see Thunder Heights from here?" she asked Ross as he came to the foot of the rocky incline where she stood.

He shook his head. "Not from this spot. Only the face of

the cliff can be seen from below. The trees jut out lower down to hide everything else."

"It must have been near here that my mother was thrown from her horse," Camilla said softly.

"This was the place," Ross admitted, and said nothing more.

He climbed up to stand at the edge of the precipice, looking over the dizzy drop to the river. She could study him now, as she had done that day on the river boat, before she had ever spoken to him. He had seemed less remote from her then than he did today.

Suddenly he pointed. "Do you see the long white boat coming down from Albany? That's the *Mary Powell*. She's not young any more, but she's still queen of the river boats. Listen—you can hear her whistle."

A clear, silvery sound reached them from the river, and Camilla watched the white boat move past their prominence, gliding smoothly as a queen of swans.

"I worked aboard her once when I was a boy," Ross said. "She always seems like a member of my family. It will be a sad day when they take her off the river."

"You love the river, don't you?" Camilla watched his face, forgetting the boat.

"I belong to the river," he said simply. His eyes followed the *Mary Powell* as she disappeared around a bend. "Do you see the place downriver where opposite banks seem to reach out to each other?"

Camilla looked in the direction of his pointing finger. "Yes, I see it."

"That's where your grandfather meant to build his bridge," Ross said. "When he was keen about it in the beginning."

The bridge again. As always it stood between them, as if it were indeed a steel barrier already built. But she did not want to bicker today.

"Why do you care so much about that bridge?" she asked.

He did not answer her directly. "When I was a little boy my father took me on a trip to see Niagara Falls. But it wasn't the falls I looked at, once I was there. It was the railroad bridge John Roebling had built across the gorge. I thought it the most miraculous and beautiful thing I'd ever seen. While I stood there staring with all my eyes, a locomotive pulled a train of freight cars across the span and it stood under all the immense weight without a quiver. And yet to me it looked as fine as though it were strung of cobwebs, instead of great suspension wires. I fell in love with a bridge that day, and it's a love I've never gotten over. I suppose that's something no woman could ever understand."

She was beginning to understand a little as she listened to him and watched the light that had come into his face. She had not dreamed that he felt like this.

"I grew up knowing I would build bridges someday," he went on. "Little bridges, at first—and one day a big one. With a design and innovations of my own. Of course John Roebling made it easier for all bridge engineers when he invented the wire rope that strings the great suspension bridges. He did what had never been done before, and we've been using his method of making wire cables ever since. His methods of anchorage too. He did a lot for bridge-building long before he designed his masterpiece—the Brooklyn Bridge."

"My grandfather knew how you felt about all this?" Camilla asked.

"Of course. That's why I care so much about a bridge here across the Hudson—because he meant to give me the job of building it. When I was ready. He set me at smaller projects in the meantime—I've one good-sized bridge to my credit upstate, but it's not across the Hudson. With this bridge behind me, I'd be ready to build bridges anywhere. I've even built a working model here in these hills. You'll see it in the woods up there if you go back a little way. I've tried some innovations of my own there. With workmen to help me, of course. It's a real bridge, though small."

Camilla listened in growing surprise. Why hadn't he told her these things in the beginning? Why had he always presented the project of the bridge as a business proposition alone?

"Those designs you showed me," she said, "—are they of your making?"

"They are," he answered curtly. "But I shouldn't have expected you to understand them, or have the vision your grandfather had."

"Tell me something else," she went on. "In what way did you want Grandfather to change his will? What was the thing you wanted in opposition to what Hortense wanted?"

His tone was cool as he answered her. "I wanted to see everything left in a trust, where the family couldn't get their hands on the money and tear down everything he'd built."

"With you as executor?"

Anger flashed in his eyes. "That wouldn't be a job to my taste. There were men in New York he could have chosen.

That way perhaps the building of the bridge would have been assured, and the continuation of the construction empire he had built. When he wanted to leave something to me, I told him I'd not accept it. I wanted only this, and I might have won him over if he hadn't begun to think sentimentally of his lost granddaughter."

"I see," she said soberly. "I won't oppose you any longer. Build your bridge. Do as you like about it."

He stepped down from the rock with a violent movement, as if he wanted solid ground beneath his feet. Anger blazed through him.

"Do you know why I'm going down to New York as soon as possible?"

She could only stare at him, seeing no reason for this sudden anger.

"I'm going to find a job of the sort that I can stomach," he told her. "I've had enough of Thunder Heights and working for women. I'll be back to wind up my work here. Then I want to get away."

She scrambled down from the rock a little awkwardly in her boots. "But why do you want to leave when I've just said you can build your bridge? Build a dozen bridges, if you like!"

He looked as if he wanted to shake her. "Do you think the building of bridges is something you can toss out as a sort of largess? 'Build a bridge, if you like. Build a dozen bridges!' Because *you* have the money to pay for them? As if a bridge were a toy! As if you could buy me with a bridge. Because I was foolish enough to—" He broke off and walked back to the horses with a long angry stride, leaving her to follow if she pleased.

What had he been going to say? Because he had been foolish enough to kiss her? She was suddenly angry herself. When he cupped his hands to help her into the saddle, she accepted his touch icily, but she liked it no better than he liked touching her.

Diamond started at the flick of her heel and took off in a dash for the woods. She turned him in the direction of home as they reached the path, but she did not look back to see whether or not Ross Granger was following. She could give Diamond his head now, since he knew the way, and she kept well in advance of her companion. Sometimes she heard the mare's hoofs on the trail just behind, but not once did she turn her head.

Diamond disliked taking the turn to the Judd house, and

Ross went past her on the driveway. He dismounted first and came to help her from the saddle. She dropped down into his arms, and for an instant she was as close to him as she had been that day beneath the beech tree. Her heart thudded wildly, but he let her go and stepped back as if he disliked all contact with her. She ran up the steps and beat a tattoo with the knocker on the front door. He was gone before Grace came to let her in, and Camilla walked into the house feeling keyed to a furious pitch.

Hortense came out of her room as she climbed the stairs.

"I see you've broken no bones," she said.

Camilla went by her without a word, not wanting to betray the intensity of feeling that shook her.

Hortense spoke to her retreating back. "I was in the village this morning, and Mr. Berton at the livery stable tells me he has a bay mare for sale."

Camilla paused and turned around. "Yes?" she said.

"What on earth has upset you?" Hortense asked. "You look mad enough to sour cream."

"What about a bay mare?" Camilla demanded.

"Only that she's been trained to the sidesaddle, and I thought you might be interested—since you're set on having a horse. I told him to send her over this afternoon for you to see."

"Thank you," Camilla said stiffly. "I'll look at her."

She hurried on to her own room, got out of her riding things and flung herself upon the bed. Already her muscles were feeling the effect of this first ride, and she knew she would be stiff and sore tomorrow. But it was not the soreness of her body that troubled her now.

Why must her feelings toward Ross Granger always kindle her to anger? Why must she be furious with him, when all the while—she pulled her thoughts back from the path of danger. This was a road she would not follow!

Before long he would leave Thunder Heights for good. He would no longer be here to sting her with his scorn and criticism. Never again would she ride with him up the mountain trail, or slip from a saddle into his arms. He would build his bridges and he would do it without her help. So why was she not pleased at the prospect?

She turned her cheek and found the pillow wet with tears. That wouldn't do at all. She got up and bathed her eyes, put on a fresh frock and went downstairs to join the family for the noonday meal. She was finishing her dessert, when one of Mr. Berton's stableboys arrived with the mare Hortense had

160

mentioned. Grace came in to say that he was holding her for Miss Camilla's inspection at the coach house.

Glad of something new to occupy her attention, Camilla took some lumps of sugar from a bowl on the table and turned to Booth.

"Will you look at this horse with me?" she said.

Booth had watched her curiously throughout the meal, and she knew he saw more than she wanted him to. But while his eyes were bright with speculative interest, he kept his manner matter-of-fact.

"I'm no expert, Cousin," he said. "But for whatever it's worth, I'll give you my opinion."

When they went out the front door, Letty followed them down the steps and called Camilla back.

"Don't buy this horse, dear," she said.

Camilla felt in no mood to listen to Letty's whims at the moment, but she made an effort to be patient. "Why don't you think I should buy her?"

Aunt Letty put a hand to her breast. "I—I have a feeling about this horse. I can't explain it sensibly. I just know that she's wrong for you."

Letty, undoubtedly, would have premonitions about any horse that might be brought to Thunder Heights, but Camilla was unwilling to listen.

"I'll look at her, and perhaps try her out. If she suits me, I'll buy her, Aunt Letty," she said.

She did not wait for further words from Letty, but went quickly to join Booth and walked with him toward the stable.

"So the Judd temper is up," he said softly. "That means trouble is brewing. There'll be a storm at Thunder Heights, or I miss my guess."

Camilla kept her face averted and walked on without answering him.

When they reached the stable, she saw Ross in the doorway, looking on idly, as Berton's stableboy walked the mare up and down the drive. She did not want him there, watching, but there was nothing to be done about it.

The mare was a dainty, flirtatious creature—a smooth bay in color, with one white sock. Her name was Firefly.

Booth looked her over carefully, approving her lines and good health, but he shook his head over the white sock. "White feet on a lady's horse are a bit fast, you know," he told her. "Though I suppose since it's only one foot—"

"I shan't be stopped by that," Camilla said tartly. Indeed, she would *like* to be thought fast. She would like to be thought anything but what Ross Granger seemed to see when he turned his gaze upon her. He believed her simple and foolish, and he had said as much.

She approached the mare and held out a lump of sugar on her palm. Firefly looked at her askance for a moment, and then thought better of her hesitation. She snuffled up the sugar with velvety lips and no unladylike snorting and blowing. Ross watched, and Camilla, for all that she was sharply aware of him, did not glance his way.

"I still think I can do better if you'll wait awhile," Booth said. "But if you're anxious, this horse will do well enough."

"I'll try her out," Camilla decided. Toby had come over to watch, and she sent him for the silver-mounted sidesaddle in the attic.

While they waited, she turned from the others and walked Firefly along the drive, gentling her and talking to her in a low voice. The little mare seemed to respond, and by the time saddle and bridle had been brought and she was ready, Camilla felt that they were becoming friends.

Her stiffening muscles rebelled a little as Booth helped her into the saddle, but she did not permit herself to wince. She rode the mare around the drive, trying out her paces and her response to the rein. She seemed an altogether feminine creature, confident of her own charms. For all her delicate, ladylike ways, she was not above taking a few skittish steps now and then, as if to assert her independence and attract attention. She would, Camilla felt, be perfect in every way—spirited enough, but obedient to the touch, and ready to be friendly.

When they rode back toward the stable, she found Ross waiting for her in the driveway. He put a hand upon Firefly's bridle and halted her.

"I wouldn't buy her," he said. There was no anger in his voice now, no emotion of any kind. He had simply put himself once more in the position of her adviser—and she would not have him there.

"I like her very much," she told him. "Why shouldn't I buy her?"

"I'm not exactly sure," Ross said. "There's something about the way she rolls her eyes—I don't think she's to be trusted."

At another time she might have listened to him. But Ross had hurt her too often. He had laughed at her offer to let him build his bridge, and had even grown angry at her words. All the hurt he had done her rose to oppose anything he might advise. But before she could speak, Booth came over and took the bridle from Ross's grasp. A certain excitement had come into his face.

"Miss King is capable of making up her own mind, Granger," Booth said. "I think it's time your interference around this place came to an end."

Ross relinquished the bridle at once, but he stood his ground without so much as glancing at Booth.

"Don't buy her, Camilla," he repeated.

The way he spoke her name was unsettling but she did not mean to hear the plea in his voice.

"You sound as fearful as Aunt Letty," she told him lightly. "I really don't believe Firefly is as frightening as all that."

Booth laughed. "There you have it, Granger. And, after all, your advice hasn't been asked."

The antagonism between the two men was close to flaring into the open. But Ross turned his back on Booth and looked up at Camilla.

"I'm leaving for New York by the late afternoon boat. Is there anything you'd like me to do for you in the city?"

She shook her head mutely, and Ross turned his back on them and went into the stable.

"It's easy to judge the caliber of his courage," Booth said, his words carrying after Ross's retreating figure.

"I think there's nothing wrong with his courage," Camilla said, her tone unexpectedly sharp. "You had no business behaving in so outrageous a way."

She slid out of the saddle without Booth's help and spoke to the boy from the stable. "Will you ask Mr. Berton to come to see me, please. I will probably buy the mare. Leave her here for the time being—the stable is ready. And do you suppose you could find me a boy in the village to take care of her?"

His eyes still round with excitement over what had happened, the stableboy agreed to try, and set off for Westcliff. Camilla led Firefly into the stable herself, soothing her when she stepped uneasily among strange surroundings. Booth took off the saddle and put her into her stall. There was amusement in his eyes when he turned back to Camilla.

"So that's the way the wind blows?" he said oddly as they started back to the house.

Before Ross left for New York that afternoon, the purchase of the mare had been transacted. The price was surprisingly moderate, though Camilla had been prepared to pay more. A boy was hired, and the lower part of the coach house once more became a stable. This was a beginning, Camilla thought. Later, when Letty and Hortense were once more accustomed to a horse at Thunder Heights, perhaps she would buy a carriage, and carriage horses as well.

She did not see Ross again, except briefly, just as he was leaving. He passed her on the stairs after he had come in to bid Letty good-by. He was courteous enough, but distant, and she had a sudden impulse to plead with him not to go. If he stayed, she knew she would again be angry with him, and he with her, but she had a feeling that without him there would be no one here upon whom she could wholly depend.

But she could not put any of this into words. "Have a good trip," she told him, and held out her hand.

He took it briefly and thanked her. In a moment he would be gone.

"Will—will you be back in time for our lawn party at Thunder Heights?" she asked in an unexpected little rush of words.

"I hadn't thought about it," he admitted. "Nora is coming, isn't she?"

Camilla could only nod. If he came only because of Nora . . .

"I'm not sure I'll be there," he said, and she could not bring herself to urge him.

He went quickly down the stairs and out the front door.

The next morning, disregarding her stiffness, Camilla went for her first real ride on Firefly. The little mare was a delight, and Camilla took her up the mountain trail again, feeling it familiar now.

The air was calm today, and even up on the rocky top of Thunder Mountain, there was no wind to tear at her hat and veil. She drew rein on the wide treeless plain of the bald top, and sat quietly for a while, to give Firefly a breather and look out over the tremendous view. But somehow the place was filled with memories of Ross, and in a little while she turned back to the trail. This time she followed it on along the side of an incurving hill to see where it might lead. As long as she avoided the back trails that wound inland, she could easily keep from getting lost.

Today she had no sense of buoyancy as she rode, no feeling that she might shed the dark influences of Thunder Heights up here in the hills. All the worries and problems of the house seemed to ride with her. There were so many small things to add up disturbingly by now. There had been the matter of the tea, to which she had found no answer. There

164

were the hints that something untoward had brought on her grandfather's heart attack. There was Letty's odd behavior about the riding crop, Hortense's open dislike of Althea's daughter, to say nothing of Booth's strange attitudes which Camilla did not understand at all. Each segment of the puzzle, however, remained just that—a segment. She could not glimpse the pattern which made up the whole, and of which all strangeness at Thunder Heights was surely a part.

The trail wound inward through a thick stand of pines, and then emerged beyond in the open. Now she could look across the intervening cove of blue water far below, with the railroad trestle cutting across it, to the hill on the opposite side. Surprised by what she saw, she reined Firefly in.

There, crowning the opposite hill—a less impressive prominence than Thunder Mountain—rose what looked strangely like the ruins of an ancient castle. There was the castle tower, crenelated at the top, with a stretch of broken wall falling away behind. The stones looked weathered and old, as if they had withstood wind and storm for hundreds of years. But this was the Hudson valley, and not a countryside given to age-old castles.

She wanted to ride on along the hill and examine the ruins at close hand, but the stiffness from yesterday's ride still troubled her and a glance at her watch, fastened to the breast of her habit by its fleur-de-lis pin, told her it was nearly time for the noon meal at Thunder Heights.

Firefly was willing enough to head for her new home, and they followed the mild incline that led back beneath the trees until a path forked suddenly ahead of them. Camilla could not resist the invitation to explore.

"We'll just follow it a little way," Camilla told the mare. "Just to see what direction it takes."

The new fork dipped toward a stream that she could hear not far away, and when the woods opened to a small clearance, Camilla reined Firefly in. The path went down an incline to the place where a small bridge hung above the stream, leading across to the other side.

But this, as Camilla recognized at once, was no ordinary woodland bridge. It was as beautiful a little suspension bridge as she had ever seen, and she knew at once that it was the model Ross had told her about. Though it was only a miniature compared to a bridge that would cross a river, the cables dipped from the posts that anchored them on either side into gleaming crescents spanning the stream, with other supports dropping in thin strands to hold the planked path of the bridge in immobility. Camilla rode the little mare across its length and back again, and the bridge did not sway or jolt beneath Firefly's dainty hoofs.

She knew she had glimpsed a bit of Ross's dream—a glimpse that was far more vivid to her than any number of diagrams on paper. It gave her, too, a clearer picture of the man. A picture that twisted at her heart. Ross had rejected her from the first, and she must not think of him.

She turned back toward Thunder Heights, knowing she must put this vision of his, this dream of his bridge, away from her, and forget it, as she must forget the man.

XVIII

A WEEK LATER HORTENSE WENT OFF ON ANOTHER TRIP. This time she went alone and not very far. She mentioned her intention casually—that she was going across the river to visit friends, and that she would stay overnight. No one objected, or even commented, and she left for the ferry from Westcliff early in the day.

Letty spent the morning in the downstairs larder, boiling freshly picked horehound plants to make the juice for horehound candy—useful for colds and coughs through the winter. While the horehound mixture simmered, she prepared marigold petals to be mixed with other herbs for seasoning. Leaves of mint, tansy, and thyme had been set out for drying, to find their way eventually into small bags to be used for scenting linens and blankets, and for keeping insects away. Camilla worked with her, helping where she could, learning under Letty's skillful instruction.

It seemed to her that Letty looked a little wan today, but that was perhaps due to the unusual heat of last week. This morning it was exceedingly hot and close for June, and when Letty had worked for a while she began to complain of a headache.

"Let's go outside," she said. "This is one of those days when I can't breathe within walls."

Camilla brought notepaper and pen and ink to the herb garden and sat on the grass in the shade of nearby woods. Using a breadboard for desk, she continued the writing of invitations to the lawn party. Letty rested listlessly for a little while, and then began to cut branches of yellow tansy to fill a pewter jar. Now and then she glanced anxiously at the sky as if she saw some portent there.

Once Camilla paused lazily in her writing to admire the herb garden spread at her feet. "June's a lovely month for herbs. I know what you mean about the garden beginning to look like a carnival. Individually the flowers aren't very impressive, but they're wonderful in a mass."

Thyme had spread its purple blossoms around the sundial, and coriander was dressed in white, shining against gray-green leaves of sage. Bees darted above the scarlet balm, while butterflies preferred the purple. Letty sat down to rest a moment on the marble bench near the sundial, rubbing a finger between her brows to lessen the pain.

"How is Booth's painting going?" she asked. "I haven't looked in on you lately."

"I'm not sure," Camilla said. "Sometimes he seems keyed up and eager to work and pleased with what he's doing. Then the next day he will be dissatisfied and do it all over. I think he'll never finish at this rate. Aunt Letty, why did Hortense go across the river today?"

Letty sighed. "I'm afraid she has gone to see another lawyer, dear. She doesn't give up very easily, you know. She's still looking for some way to break the will."

Camilla was silent, and Letty picked a sprig of mint where it encroached upon the bed of thyme, her thoughts drifting back to her garden.

"How greedy mint is! It would take the whole garden for itself if I let it." She crushed the leaves between her fingers, and the scent was pleasant on the warm air. "I think it's going to storm," she said abruptly.

Camilla looked up at the bright cloudless sky. "Why do you think that? There's not a thunderhead in sight."

"There's a feeling," Letty said. "It's so hot and still and breathless. Don't go riding today, dear."

Camilla laughed. "I hadn't meant to, but you almost tempt me. I'll have to prove to you one of these days how safe Firefly is."

"Ross didn't trust her either," Letty said.

Ross! Camilla thought. Ross was gone and she had firmly dismissed him from her mind. There had been no word from him since he left. That was a book that would be closed shortly, and she did not want to so much as ruffle the pages.

"Tell me, dear," Letty said. "What do you plan to do with yourself from now on?"

Camilla was silent for a moment. She knew only too well

what Letty meant. What was she to do with herself for all the rest of her life? Where was she to find the fulfillment and joy that should be a part of living? When would she ever be loved as a woman hungered to be loved? But she could not say these things to Letty, and tried to answer her brightly.

"It seems to me I'm busy from morning to night. And with the lawn party ahead I have hardly time to catch up with all I want to do. What do you mean?"

Letty was not deceived. "Life," she said quietly, "is loving and marrying and having children. You haven't so much as touched the edge of life as yet. How can you manage it if you bury yourself here? Don't you think about these things?"

Did she not, indeed? And when she thought of them, she saw Ross's face all too clearly, and she did not want to see it at all. She shook her head impatiently and stood up.

"There's time for all that. If you don't mind, Aunt Letty, I'll go back inside. The heat is worse out here than it is in the house."

"What is it you're running away from?" Letty asked.

Camilla stared at her, not answering, and after a moment her aunt went on.

"Once I thought there was plenty of time. But when I look back the years are gone and my life with them."

"I'm sorry," Camilla said softly.

"Don't be," Letty told her. "I've known contentment and happiness a good deal of the time. Though it's of a different sort than I might have had. A lesser sort, perhaps." She rose from the bench and came close to Camilla. "Don't make the mistake I did, dear. The mistake of closing the door on life."

For all that she could be so vague and misty and tremulous at times, Letty saw the truth all too clearly when she chose to. But these were things Camilla did not want glimpsed in her own life, matters she could not discuss. She turned away and went quickly into the house.

As the day wore on, the air grew ever more still and stifling, with the sun burning fiercely through a haze that seemed to magnify the heat. Late that afternoon relief was promised in thunderheads that loomed across the Hudson, bringing gusty winds to tear at the house and set its old timbers creaking. Wind rattled the shutters, wailed down the chimneys of Thunder Heights, and heat fled before the damp onslaught of the wind. All through dinner the buffeting seemed to increase. Nevertheless, the storm held back its expected torrents and was for a time only wind and sound.

Except for the wind noises, dinner was a quiet meal. Letty

ate little and spoke not at all. Booth seemed lost in moody silence. Camilla, deep in her own tormenting thoughts, made no bid for conversation. Thoughts stirred to uneasy life by Letty's words.

Letty's headache had grown in severity, and after dinner she excused herself and went up to bed, refusing Camilla's offer to get her something to ease the throbbing. Camilla watched her go anxiously, and Booth saw her concern.

"She often feels like this when it's about to storm," he said.

The weather had a different effect upon Camilla. She slipped away from Booth and went outside to the ledge above the river. There she stood for a long while in the open, where wind whipped her skirts and buffeted her with rough fingers. Out here, with this exhilaration of the elements all about her, she could lose something of her depression, her loneliness.

Below her the river churned into choppy gray waves, and on the heights above trees thrashed their branches and moaned in the wind. How far above, invisible in the gusty darkness, the stony head of the mountain seemed tonight. Had it been on such a night that Althea had ridden to the crest? Camilla wondered.

She could understand the invigoration her mother might have found in so wild a ride. The racing black clouds overhead, the cold thrust of the wind, even the stinging slap of the first rain against her face—all these were exciting, stimulating.

Cold needles of rain pricked through the thin stuff of her shirtwaist, and she turned reluctantly back to the house. From the lawn Thunder Heights looked dark and somber and cheerless. No one had lighted the swinging lamp above the stairs tonight—that was usually Hortense's charge, and Letty must have forgotten. Lamps had not yet been lit in the parlor, and the dark windows had an eerie look. Camilla remembered her first feeling about the house when she had seen it from the river—that it was a place enchanted and spellbound.

It drew her now, in spite of herself, and she moved toward it just as thunder clapped against the mountain and went echoing from hill to hill up the valley of the Hudson. She did not glimpse Booth in the shadows of the veranda until she reached the steps. His presence startled her. How long had he stood there, watching her?

"It's time you came in," he said. "Don't tempt the spirit of the mountain."

Thunder rumbled nearer now, and lightning flashed, illuminating black towers, striking brilliance from blank windows. Then darkness swept down again, all the more blinding in contrast. Camilla went up the steps, still feeling the strange lure of the house. As she reached the door, Grace came to light lamps in the parlor, and Booth followed her in, locking the French doors against the storm.

How hot and close it seemed inside, once the wind was shut out. Hot and close and alive with rattling sound.

"Perhaps Aunt Letty would like someone with her tonight," Camilla said. "Perhaps I'd better go upstairs."

"Wait," Booth said. "There's no need to go to Letty. I've given her one of her own witch brews and she'll sleep through it all and feel better in the morning. Stay with me awhile, Cousin. It's I who don't want to be left to my own company."

She had no desire to be alone either, in this creaking, whispering house. She sat down in a chair from Malaya, resting her hands upon its ornately carved teak arms. It was too warm for a fire to be lighted, but she missed the bright leaping of flames on a night like this. A fire always made this museum of a room seem more cheerful. Tonight it was a room of oppressive shadows, abounding in its own secrets.

Booth did not take the chair opposite her, but moved restlessly about, tinkling a brass temple bell from India, picking up an ivory elephant and setting it down again. She had the feeling that he wanted to talk to her, and she waited for him to begin. Something in her listened to the storm, tensing to the thunder and vivid flashes of lightning. The fury seemed to be lessening a little now—rolling away toward the Catskills. Rain still lashed against the windows and roofs but the wild vitality was ebbing.

Booth continued his uneasy prowling, and she watched his finely chiseled head as it moved from lamplight into shadow, to emerge again, the face visible in all its dark intensity. Drawn as she had been more than once in the past, she began to wonder about him. It was as if his somber presence made a focus of its own, matching the storm in a strange concentration of energy.

"Why do you stay here, Booth?" she asked. "Why haven't you left this house and found yourself a better life out in the world? What is there for you here?"

Her words brought him about to face her. He leaned

170

against the mantel, one arm stretched along its marble surface.

"How little you know me, Cousin! You don't even know that everything I've wanted in life is contained in this one household, and always has been. Contained, but held beyond my reach. For the moment, at least. But not forever. No, I think not forever."

His eyes were bright with a mirthless laughter that was troubling to see.

"What is it that you want of life?" she asked him.

He ran an appreciative hand along the graceful fluted edge of the marble. "To be a gentleman," he told her. His sardonic smile flashed for an instant and was gone as suddenly as the lightning. "To be a gentleman, to live like a gentleman, to enjoy myself as a gentleman. This has been my purpose for as long as I can remember. Does it astonish you?"

It did indeed.

"I suppose," Camilla said, "that I've never thought of the matter of being a gentleman—or a lady—as being an end in itself."

"That's because you never lived as a child hating your father's butcher shop, longing to get away from the look and smell of it. You didn't grow up watching ladies and gentlemen from a distance, having coppers tossed to you in an offhand manner, being treated as an underling."

He left the mantel and flung himself into a chair, watching her face now, as if he looked for something it it.

"What are you thinking?" he demanded. "What are you feeling about me?"

She sensed a surging need in him, something that reached out to her, almost in pleading.

"Why, surprise, mainly, I suppose," she said, trying to answer him honestly.

"You mean because I've succeeded so well that you'd never have guessed my miserable origin?"

She shook her head. "No—only surprise that anyone should feel as you do. I suppose that all my life I've known people in different walks of life, and if I liked them, their background made no difference to me. It must be easy enough to adopt a veneer of polish, if that's what you want. But how can that be an end in itself?"

"It can easily be an end," he said, "if it coincides with everything you wanted up to the time when you were ten years old. And if it is what you were taught from that time on."

171

"Aunt Letty told me you were adopted when you were ten," Camilla admitted. "Sometimes I've wondered about that. Aunt Hortense doesn't seem exactly—" she hesitated, not wanting to hurt him.

"Don't you know why she brought me here? Don't you know why she snatched me out of my humble beginnings and made a gentleman out of me?"

There was something hard in his tone and Camilla was silent.

He went on evenly, coldly. "She had lost the man she'd set her heart on—your father. She didn't intend to marry and have children. But she wanted to make sure that a good portion of Orrin Judd's fortune came her way. She thought that presenting him with an heir of sorts would safeguard the money she wanted in her own hands. My father was happy to be rid of me. My mother had died the year before and left the whole brood of us to him. Miss Judd had a look at me, talked to me, found that I was bright enough and eager to be part of a different world. I'd shown some talent for painting even then, and she thought me a likely boy to present to her father, who was all for humble beginnings. Unfortunately, old Orrin and I never cared for each other—though she wouldn't see that. Your Aunt Hortense has always believed only what she wanted to believe. She imagines that she has been a doting mother. But all her doting developed after I was twenty and she found she liked a grown young man at her beck and call."

Camilla made a small gesture of distaste, of disbelief. Booth laughed.

"It's not a pretty story, is it? Can you imagine Hortense mothering a boy of ten? And of course she wouldn't take a small baby. She felt I was at least old enough to be of little trouble. I might have run away once or twice, if it hadn't been for Letty. It was Letty who mothered and loved me and brought me up. Of course when I was older I began to see very well which side my bread was buttered on. Sooner or later the old man would die. And whether he left me anything for myself or not, I would have Hortense eating out of my hand and whatever she had would be mine. I've never for a moment lost sight of that. Everything I want is here at Thunder Heights."

Camilla listened, her sympathy aroused, for all that she felt a little sickened. He had, she suspected, deliberately put everything in the worst possible light, driven by some strange need for self-inflicted punishment. The phrase "edge of dan-

172

ger" came to mind. In telling her these things, perhaps he moved a little closer to that edge of destruction that so fascinated him, tantalizing and tormenting himself with his own words.

"How sad and—pitiful," she said softly, more to herself than to him.

He smiled, and his dark face sprang into that strange beauty that she had surprised in it before.

"Scarcely pitiful, Cousin. Though you must admit that my plans and hopes went awry for a time when you appeared on the scene and we discovered that you were to inherit everything that might have come to my mother."

"I should think you would have left then," Camilla said. "I can understand why two women like Hortense and Letty might feel they couldn't leave a security they had depended on all their lives. But you—"

"Tell me, Cousin," he said, "have I been unkind to you? Have I made you feel that I resented and disliked you?"

"No. No, not at all. You've been far kinder to me than Hortense has been." Or than Ross Granger had, for that matter.

"Perhaps I stayed because of you," he said, and there was a gentleness, almost a tenderness, in his voice.

The storm had come rumbling back upon its own tracks, and Camilla saw the blinding glitter of lightning. The windows shivered in an almost instantaneous crash of thunder, and this time she winced.

"A close one," Booth said. "That was on the mountain above us, I think." He went to one of the long doors to peer out through the lashing branches of an elm tree. When he turned and looked at her across the room, his gaze was long and searching.

She was suddenly aware of how closed off they were in this room. She was aware, too, of a change in Booth, of a quickening in him as he watched her. Something in her own blood stirred in response to the urgency she sensed in him.

Because the knowledge left her shaken, she rose uncertainly and walked from the parlor into the antehall. Candles had been lighted in the outstretched marble hands, but the octagon stairway beyond lay in shadow without the usual illumination from above. Intermittently the tall window above the stairs flickered with lightning. All the dark secrets of Thunder Heights seemed to center in the heart of that weirdly lighted stairway, and she dreaded walking up it.

In the moment that she hesitated, Booth came through the

door to find her there. Perhaps she had wanted to hesitate, knowing he would come.

This time he moved toward her with assurance and took her into his arms, kissed her full on the mouth. His lips were cool in the hot and stifling house, and the shock of their touch brought her to herself. She thrust him away, in spite of the response that throbbed in her own blood. Thrust him back instinctively, lest his darkness engulf them both.

For an instant he seemed taken by surprise, as if he had not expected her to resist. Then he drew her roughly against him and kissed her again.

"Never fight me, Cousin," he said as she tried to turn her head away. "Always remember that—never fight me!"

There was a warning in his voice that made her cease her struggling. She went limp in his arms, resting there inert, until he put her quietly away from him.

"Haven't you known the attraction you've had for me from the first, Camilla? There's no cousin relationship between us—that's a pretty fantasy. Don't you know that you are why I've stayed in this house? That I've stayed because I wanted you and mean to have you?"

She found herself moving backwards from him, toward the stairs and possible flight. She no longer feared the darkness. She feared Booth Hendricks more. Or was it herself she feared—the response he had aroused against her will?

"You were drawn to me in the beginning," he persisted. "It was clear enough. What turned you away? I suppose you'll tell me it was Granger?"

"No," she whispered. "Ross Granger is nothing to me."

He laughed with a queer exultance. "Do you think I haven't seen the way you look at him? Not that I mind. There's all the more satisfaction when a formidable opponent is beaten. I don't underestimate Granger, believe me. But I think you both underestimate me."

She had reached the stairs, and she turned and fled up them through the flashing light, with the thunder drowning out any sound of pursuit. She did not look back until she reached the door of her room and flung it open. In a flash of lightning the hall behind her stretched empty and livid. Below, in the heart of the house, she heard a ringing shout of laughter. Booth was amused by her flight, by her fear of her own emotions, but he had not followed her upstairs.

She closed the door and locked it, stood trembling against it in the warm safety of her room. But before she had found matches to light a candle on the stand near the door, she stood alone in the darkness, welcoming the soft gloom that hid her.

Never before had she felt such shame and fear. Not alone because of Booth, but for herself. She knew now that her own loneliness must be watched. It was true that she had always found Booth attractive. But was she, who had been so rudely rejected by Ross Granger, now responding to Booth out of her own need, and because he needed her? Was her fear of becoming like Letty, dry and brittle as herb leaves on a shelf, to drive her to desperate action?

Her hands shook as she lighted the candle. Was it even possible that Booth was what she wanted, after all? Certainly they shared a good deal—a lonely background and the insecurity of the past. What was it then that held her back from him? What was it she distrusted? Booth Hendricks could be artist or devil. She did not know which.

Now she was afraid in this house as she had never been afraid before. She was seized by forebodings that she could not put aside. Booth would not easily be stopped in his purpose. And his purpose was to have her. Only then would he achieve all he wanted of Thunder Heights. Had she the strength to stand against him? Would she always want to?

XIX

IN THE MORNING SHE DREADED THE MOMENT WHEN SHE must come face to face with him again. When she went downstairs to the dining room, Booth was there, as if he waited for her. He stood near the bay window overlooking Letty's herb garden, but he stood with his back to it, as if he were studying the room.

"Good morning, Camilla," he said cheerfully as she paused at the sight of him, trying to hide her dismay. He hurried to draw out her chair, a faint mockery beneath his good manners, as if he knew very well how she felt about seeing him.

"I've been admiring this room," he said. "You've done wonders with it. I can remember how many depressing meals I've eaten in the old room under Orrin Judd's eyes, with dark wallpaper and draperies adding to my depression. You've been good for this house."

She had nothing to say to him. She stared at her plate,

avoiding his eye as Grace brought coffee and oatmeal. He was smiling as he took his place beside her.

"Did you sleep well?" he asked.

She nodded and began to eat in silence. How could she pretend, as he seemed to be pretending, that everything was as it had been before he had kissed her last night?

Plainly amused, he passed her cream and sugar, set the honey bowl by her plate. Then he picked up a knife and made a mark on the tablecloth with the rounded end of it.

"Attend, my dear. I have a problem for you to consider. A theoretical problem. Do you see this line I've drawn? Let's say it represents the life span of a man. The salt cellar here is his birth, the napkin ring his death. Do you follow me?"

"No," she said. "I don't know what you're talking about."

"I haven't explained myself yet," he told her. "The point is this—at certain places in the life line there are forks in the road, choices a man may take. Or a woman. One road may be a pleasant one, with opportunity and safety and very little excitement. The other choice may spell danger, disaster, perhaps. You see the dilemma? The choice of roads a man makes depends, I suppose, on what he is. While I'm not sure there is any conscious choice involved in the matter, I'd like to think there is."

Camilla broke a piece of toast and buttered it, added a dab of honey, avoiding the waxy bits of comb embedded in the amber. She said nothing at all.

He watched her, smiling. "Last night I'd have sworn the honey could melt any wax. What is it, my dear? Do I fail to interest you this morning?"

"I don't know the rules of the game you're playing," Camilla answered.

"I was merely seeking your advice in a serious matter. Which road shall I choose, Camilla? Which way shall I follow?"

"What choice have you decided to make?" she countered.

"I'm not sure that I've decided. In this case both ways tempt me. A man may have his work, even at Thunder Heights. But I am a man who needs more than sufferance, Camilla, and a paid income."

She had no answer for him. When Letty came through the door, she looked up in relief.

"Good morning, children. How well I slept last night!" Letty said. "I didn't waken once. It seems strange that the thunder didn't disturb me, as it usually does."

176

"Booth gave you a sleeping draught, Aunt Letty," Camilla said.

Letty took the chair Booth pulled out for her, and the look she turned upon him was suddenly intent. He spoke before she could question him.

"Camilla is right, dear. I didn't want you to suffer a headache all night long. I know what a spartan you can be, and I thought I could spare you that for once. Besides I wanted to be alone and unchaperoned for once with Cousin Camilla."

A flush came into Camilla's cheeks, and Letty glanced at her and then away. "I see," she said. She turned her attention to breakfast and asked no more questions.

Booth picked up a spoon and crisscrossed the lines he had made on the tablecloth, raising a dark eyebrow quizzically at Camilla as he did so.

"I think I'll do no painting today," he said. "I have a feeling my model is not in the mood."

"But you've only a little more to do on the picture," Letty said. "I'll be glad when it's finished."

"You've never liked that picture, have you?" Booth asked, but Letty did not answer.

They were still at breakfast when Hortense returned from her journey across the river. Booth went to the door to help her with her bag. Camilla heard them talking in the distance, but Booth did not return.

"What happened last night?" Letty asked when they were alone in the dining room.

"Nothing," Camilla said, not meeting her eyes. She wanted no one to know what had happened. "The storm seemed to key him up. I went to bed early."

"Good," Letty approved. "Sometimes I think Booth's high moods are almost as difficult as his low ones. It's best to leave him alone until he gets over them."

When Hortense came in to join them for breakfast, it was clear that this second trip had brought her no more success than had her journey to New York. Her manner was disgruntled, and she seemed unwilling to speak to anyone. Camilla was glad enough to excuse herself from the table and leave her two aunts alone.

Preparations for the lawn party were moving ahead by now, and answers to the invitations were beginning to come in. The affair was to be next week, and there was still a great deal to be done. A big box of Japanese lanterns had been sent up from New York. Caterers had been hired for that day to assist Matilda in the kitchen and help serve refreshments on the lawn. Camilla threw herself into the work of preparation and planning and put away from her the disturbing thoughts that wanted to crowd in. These things she would think about later. Not now.

Some of the little tables that would be used on the lawn needed painting. This was something she could assist with herself. Late that morning she went downstairs to the cellar to find brushes and paint in the room that had once been Grandfather Orrin's workshop.

As she came down the steep flight of cellar stairs, she saw Booth ahead of her and paused, not wanting to meet him alone. But he had not heard her and he moved with purpose toward the larder. When she saw him go into the room where Letty kept her herbs and cooking materials, Camilla darted toward the door of the tool room next door and stepped inside. She would get her things quietly and slip out before Booth emerged. She was curious, however, and wondered what he was doing down here.

As she groped for the things she wanted in the dim room, she heard him utter an angry exclamation: "So! I thought you might be down here."

For an instant she thought in dismay that he had discovered her. Then he went on in the same angry tone.

"You're up to your old tricks, aren't you?"

There was a smothered cry from someone in the larder, and Camilla heard the crash of glass, as if a jar had been dashed to the floor.

"I've warned you not to try that again," Booth cried. "Do you want to find yourself in prison?"

The murmured reply was lost to Camilla's ears, though she pressed close to the wall, trying to hear.

"Tansy!" Booth said and the word lashed like the snap of a whip. "Enough of it can kill, as you very well know. Are you such a fool that you think they wouldn't uncover so clumsy a trick? Clear up that mess and don't try it again."

Once more there came a soft mumbling reply in a voice Camilla could not distinguish. She shrank into the dark space behind the tool room door as she heard Booth stride toward the stairs and spring up them as lithely as the tomcat he often reminded her of. The cellar door closed sharply above, and a soft brushing sound began in the next room.

Camilla slipped out of the workshop and fled upstairs and outside, escaping to the serenity of the herb garden. Here there was brightness and warm, perfumed air. Bees hummed around the balm, and all was quiet and peaceful. Yet not altogether so. For the very herbs in this garden had powers she could not know and did not trust.

She shivered in the warm air. What was she to do? How was she to live with the undercurrent of dark purpose that existed in this house? Hortense or Letty—which one? Oh, not Letty, surely not Letty! Booth would never have spoken so roughly to the woman who had given him love and trust over the years. Or would he, if he were angered? How little she really knew of Booth. And what of his own frightening purpose?

Here in the bright sunlight she tried to tell herself that it was a purpose she need only ridicule to destroy. He could scarcely marry her against her will. Yet she had felt the intensity of single-minded purpose behind him. "Don't fight me," he had said, and there was something in the words that terrified her, even in retrospect. All the more so because a portion of her fear was of herself.

In the days that followed she began to dread the event of the lawn party. How was she to carry it off with the gaiety she had intended? How was she to pretend a pride in Thunder Heights and a desire to throw it open once more to the world, when all the while she knew the very core of it to be sick with evil?

Strangely enough, there was a change in Hortense, and this too made Camilla uneasy. Was it a result, perhaps, of Booth's warning to her in the cellar that day? Or would he have spoken so to the woman who held his fortunes in her hand? At any rate, Hortense became almost cheerful about the coming party and actually began to take part in the preparations. She displayed an interest in the identity of the guests who had accepted and went through the answers Camilla had received, exclaiming about this one and that. She would look forward to seeing old friends, she said, and was pleased that some of those from the best old families had accepted. Only one name caused her displeasure. When she came upon the note Nora Redfern's mother had written, she brought it indignantly to Camilla, who was once more painting lawn furniture.

"Do you mean that Mrs. Landry has actually accepted your invitation?" she demanded, waving the bit of notepaper under Camilla's nose.

Camilla had spread newspapers on the big veranda overlooking the river, and was kneeling there before an upended chair, a pot of green paint beside her.

"Why shouldn't she accept?" Camilla asked, brushing long green strokes down the leg of the iron chair. "Mrs. Redfern is coming, and she says her mother and mine were the best of friends when they were young. They seem to have no wish to keep up an old feud."

"Humph!" Hortense's snort made her red pompadour tremble. "And did she tell you that Laura Landry was horribly rude to us after Althea's death and came near making a public scandal?"

"A scandal about what?" Camilla asked, concentrating on her work.

"Laura took your father's side," Hortense said. "And of course all John King wanted was to make trouble—as we very well knew. He felt he had been slighted by his wife's family, and he wanted his little revenge."

"That doesn't sound like my father." Camilla set her brush down and gave her aunt her full attention. "Just what are you talking about?"

"I've no intention of dredging up something that had no basis in fact in the first place," Hortense said, showing signs of hasty retreat. "But you can take my word for it, Camilla, that Mrs. Landry was extremely rude to Papa and that he told her she need never set foot in his house again. The same went for your father."

Hortense had begun to stride up and down the veranda in her agitation, and Camilla watched her soberly. Once this woman had been in love with John King. How had it been for him—for them all—when he had come back to Thunder Heights for Althea's funeral? What reception had he received?

She asked her question suddenly. "Were you still in love with him, Aunt Hortense? I mean when he came back that last time?"

Hortense whirled about, and the long silver chains she wore about her neck swung and glittered. "In love with him! I have despised your father for more years than I can remember. He led me on when I first knew him, and I would have married him if it hadn't been for Althea and her sneaking ways. It's a good thing I didn't so demean myself, since his true character was revealed when he ran away with her." With that she flounced into the house before Camilla could answer her.

Camilla hurried now with her painting, and as soon as she could pause she went in search of Letty. She found her in the upstairs sitting room, working on a pile of soft lavender

180

material she was making into one of her drifty dresses for the lawn party. Camilla asked point-blank about what trouble there had been between Grandfather Orrin and Nora Redfern's mother. How had it involved John King?

Letty glanced vaguely up from her sewing, and Camilla could almost see her pulling her mists about her, to shut out what she did not wish to consider.

"That was all so long ago," she began, using her favorite retreat.

Camilla persisted. "Aunt Hortense says that Grandfather told Mrs. Landry never to set foot in this house again. And now Hortense is upset because I've invited her to the party."

"Perhaps she won't come," Letty said.

"She has already accepted. Aunt Letty, surely you know what happened between her and my grandfather."

Letty's needle never paused as it moved in and out of her work. "Laura had some foolish idea about what happened to Althea. I don't recall exactly what it was."

Camilla reached out to cover the lavender material with her hands, so that the sewing must stop.

"Are you against me too, Aunt Letty?" she asked.

Letty's lips were trembling. "Please," she said, drawing the goods out of Camilla's hands. "I must hurry if I'm to have this dress ready in time. If you like, dear, I'll play the harp for your guests at the party. Would that please you? I could play all the old Scottish airs Papa used to love. I think they might enjoy my music."

It was no use, Camilla knew. She rose without further pleading and went to the door. At once Letty dropped her work and came after her.

"Don't be angry with me, dear. I've begun to wish there was to be no party. I wish Mrs. Landry weren't coming. I—I'm afraid of what may happen. Please be careful, Camilla. Be very, very careful."

XX

DELIBERATELY AND WITH AN EFFORT OF WILL, CAMILLA focused her attention on her coming duties as hostess. The lawn party must be a success for Thunder Heights, no matter what lay beneath the surface.

The additional servants came in the day before the party

to help with preparations. Hortense was in her element, giving orders right and left, while Letty quietly countermanded those that were too absurd.

Before the servants arrived, Letty had locked the door to the cellar.

"If any of you need anything, come to me for the key," she told the rest of the family. "I'd rather not have strangers moving around downstairs."

It was clear that she was thinking of her precious herbs. Hortense remarked that she was being ridiculously cautious, but no one really objected and the key remained in Letty's pocket.

The day of the lawn party presented clear and sunny skies—a perfect day. The guests would not begin to arrive until four, and at three thirty Camilla and Letty, dressed and ready, sat down on the veranda to rest.

The little tables and chairs set about on the lawn were fresh in their leaf green paint, and Japanese lanterns had been strung the length of the veranda, and from tree to tree on the lawn. At dusk Thunder Heights would be a beautiful sight. Letty's harp waited at one end of the veranda, with a stool drawn up to it, so that she could sit there and play for the guests when the time came. And there were fiddlers coming from the village later on to play the old dance tunes, and even a modern waltz or two.

"After all," Camilla said, "this is a country party. We aren't trying to imitate New York."

She wore a new summer frock of frilly muslin with sleeves that pushed up in soft puffs. Letty's lavender dress was soft and drifty, and the scent of lavender floated about her when she moved.

Booth had absented himself from the house for most of the day, admitting that he detested domestic preparations. He would rather appear with the guests and enjoy himself without responsibility. In these last days Camilla had found his eyes upon her whenever she looked up. He said little, as though he could afford to bide his time, and even though his persistent attention made her uncomfortable, there was a perversity in her that almost welcomed it. If Ross had no eyes for her, at least someone else did.

Only one thing had disturbed this day of the party. Mignonette had disappeared, and no amount of calling brought her to view. For a while Letty did not seem especially perturbed. "She'll turn up eventually," she said. "She's much too clever to let anything happen to her."

182

Only now, as they sat rocking on the veranda, did she begin to fret a little.

"It's not like Mignonette to stay away so long. She's very fond of me, you know."

"Do you think you might have shut her in the cellar when you locked it yesterday?" Camilla asked.

"No, because she was around early this morning. And I haven't been down there since I locked the door."

A voice sounded within the house, and Letty stopped rocking. "Hortense wants you, dear. I do hope she hasn't overdressed for this afternoon. She wouldn't tell me what she meant to wear."

Camilla went inside, to find Hortense at the foot of the stairs striving ineffectively to set spikes of larkspur into a brass bowl. Her gown, as Letty had feared, was on the elaborate side. It was her favorite emerald green color—a somewhat threadbare satin, with an old-fashioned bustle. The skirt was looped up at the side to show a panel of yellow, embroidered in black. Her pompadour was anchored soundly with the little combs studded in geeen jade. Somehow her elegance of a day long past seemed a little pathetic, and Camilla found herself moved by a pity she did not show.

"Oh, there you are!" she said as Camilla reached her side. "No one has fixed any flowers for the post stand here at the foot of the stairs. I thought this brass bowl would do, but it's not deep enough. Do run down cellar and get me a china vase that will be deep enough. Here—take this brass atrocity with you."

The brass bowl was large and heavy and Camilla took it in both hands. Letty gave her the key, and she hurried through the busy workers in the kitchen and down to the landing door and pushed it open. As she stepped down upon the first step something dark leaped wildly past her up the stairs and out the door. Alarmed, Camilla jumped and dropped the bowl. The leaping creature was only the lost Mignonette, but the harm had been done. The bowl bounced out of her hands and down the stairs with a frightful clatter, and Camilla stood looking after it in dismay.

As her eyes grew accustomed to the dim light, she saw that the bowl had done an extraordinary amount of damage in its heavy progress down the steep stairs. The third step, just below where she stood, had splintered and collapsed completely. If she had stepped upon it without looking, she would have been pitched helplessly to the concrete floor, a good twelve steps below. The stairs had no rail, and nothing could have saved her from a dangerous fall.

There was so much noise in the kitchen above that no one had heard the clatter of the bowl, or come to investigate. Camilla stepped carefully over the broken step and made her way to the foot of the stairs. One or two of the other steps had been faintly dented by the bowl as it bounded down, but only the third step, on which she must have dropped it, had been completely shattered.

What had happened puzzled her. The bowl was not so heavy as to cause such serious damage unless the step had already been rotten and ready to collapse. That seemed unlikely. Someone would surely have noticed it. The stairs were of the open kind, and she walked underneath, where she could look up at the shattered step. The board had broken in the middle. One side had fallen through and lay at her feet. The other side still hung in splinters from the steps above.

She picked up the broken tread and studied it. The wood did not look rotten. The splinters of the break looked clean and far from powdery. The step had not rotted through. It was possible that it had been deliberately broken from above, then pushed back in place, to trap the first unwary person to set foot upon it. If Mignonette had not been imprisoned in the cellar and come leaping out to startle her, if Camilla had not dropped the bowl upon the step, triggering what certainly looked like a trap—she would have been flung all that steep flight to the cement below, with nothing to stop her fall.

Her knees had begun to tremble in reaction, and she found a chair and sat down. Anyone who had put weight on that third step might have been seriously hurt. But a deliberate trap would not be set for just anyone. She knew that step had been prepared for one person alone—Camilla King. Yet how could that be? How could anyone know that she would surely be the one to step on it? Carefully, bit by bit, she thought back over what had happened.

Yesterday Letty had locked the door. Yet she herself might have run up and down these stairs a dozen times since if she'd chosen to. Unless it had been prepared at a time when it was unlikely that she would be coming down them again. But how could anyone know that Camilla King would come down them at exactly the right moment?

The pattern grew clearer by the moment. Hortense had sent her down deliberately on an errand. She had waited for the prescribed moment and conceived an errand that would send just one person down these stairs—to disaster.

"Camilla! Camilla, are you there?" That was Hortense now on the landing before the cellar door.

She had only to be silent, Camilla thought, and see what happened. If Hortense came down cautiously, stepping over the broken stair, she would know the answer. She could see her green skirts up there now, see her foot coming down to the top step. Camilla jumped up and called to her aunt.

"Be careful, Aunt Hortense! There's a broken step. Watch out or you'll fall." She had not possessed the steel nerves to try the experiment, lest she risk Hortense's life.

Hortense gasped and drew back her foot. Camilla picked up the brass bowl and went to the bottom of the stairs.

"This bowl saved me from a bad fall. This and Mignonette. Someone must have shut the cat down here by mistake and when she leaped out she frightened me so that I dropped the bowl and it broke the step. Odd, isn't it, Aunt Hortense, that a step should break so easily?"

Hortense said nothing. She was staring at Camilla in horrified silence, and Camilla could not read the cause of her horror. Was it because of her own narrow escape—or because Camilla had discovered the trap?

"Wait there," she said. "I'll get you the other vase."

She went to the shelf where extra vases were kept and picked one out with strange care. It was as though it were easier to concentrate on the matter of the right vase for a spray of larkspur, than to think about how nearly she had met injury, or even death.

By the time she returned to the stairs, her knees were steadier, but she knew her cheeks were flushed, her eyes bright.

"Here you are," she said, climbing the stairs and stepping carefully over the dangerous place. She put the vase into Hortense's limp hands. "I must lock the door so no one will make a mistake and come down these stairs until they're mended. I was lucky, Aunt Hortense. This is the second time Mignonette has practically saved my life."

Seen in the light of the landing, Hortense's face looked as though it had caught something of the reflected color of her dress.

At that moment the knocker rattled on the front door, and Camilla spoke quietly to her aunt.

"The first guests are arriving. Hurry and fix your larkspur. And don't worry about the step now, Aunt Hortense. We have a party to go through."

But as she followed Hortense through the kitchen and back

to the foot of the stairs, her mind was busy with the three corners of a triangle. It could have been Letty, who had the key to the cellar. But access through a window would have been equally possible, and Mignonette could have come in unnoticed by a window. In that case it might have been Hortense. Or the entire plan, including instructions to Hortense and the fixing of the step, could have been managed very easily by Booth.

She could not find the answer now, for there was Nora Redfern at the door, and with her a plump, rather dowdy woman with an air of confidence and authority, whom Nora introduced as her mother, Mrs. Landry.

Laura Landry's handclasp was strong and friendly. "I insisted upon coming early," she said, "so that I could have a bit of a visit with Althea's daughter before the others arrived."

When Grace had taken hats and wraps, Camilla led the way through the parlor and out upon the veranda, where Letty still sat rocking peacefully.

Camilla slipped the cellar key into her hand. "Be sure no one goes downstairs, Aunt Letty. There's a broken step that might injure anyone who didn't see it. It's only thanks to Mignonette that I escaped. She was in the cellar after all."

Momentary alarm flashed in Letty's eyes, and then she was rising to greet Nora Redfern and Mrs. Landry. The key had been hidden, and there was no telling what she thought about the broken stair. If there had been a long-existing animosity between Thunder Heights and Blue Beeches, it was not evident in Letty's gracious reception of the two women.

Camilla turned toward the veranda steps and saw Booth at the foot of them watching her. "Congratulate me!" she said to him brightly. "I came very near killing myself on the cellar stairs a few moments ago. It was only by luck that I saw the damaged step and saved myself."

Did something flicker in his eyes? She couldn't be sure. He had taken her hand to draw her down to the lawn, and his manner seemed truly solicitous.

"You must be careful, Camilla. I'll have a look at the bad step later on."

Then he too was greeting Mrs. Landry and Nora in his usual suave manner, and if he had ever plotted disaster to Camilla King, there was no reading it in his face or bearing.

She walked across the lawn with Nora and Mrs. Landry for a view of the river, and there was no further opportunity for her to be anything but a hostess. Mrs. Landry was more interested in her than in the river, however.

"You're as pretty as your mother was," she said. "Perhaps prettier. But there's a difference. Your mother had a dare-devil streak that could get her into trouble. You look a bit more sensible."

Was she sensible? Could she be, with this trembling at the pit of her stomach that never quite ceased, that urged her toward a blind terror that she must hold off at all costs?

"I'm not sure that's a compliment," she told Nora's mother, and miraculously the trembling did not show in her voice. "I'm so glad you've come, Mrs. Landry. I know you and my mother were good friends, and there's so much I want to learn about her."

But now other guests began to arrive, and there was no opportunity for more talk. Soon there were little clumps of ladies and gentlemen all about the lawn. Hortense and Letty and Booth moved among them, greeting old friends, meeting younger members of river families, whom they had not met before, and all three seemed at ease, slipping easily back into old ways.

Once Hortense stopped beside Camilla, glowering a little. "You know why these people have come, don't you? The old ones are here out of curiosity. To see what we've done with ourselves. The young ones are here to have a look at you and decide whether you'll make a good match for one of their own crowd."

Camilla laughed with a touch of bitterness. There was a time when this party would have seemed like wonderful fun to her and she would have taken part in it wholeheartedly. But that was before the shadow of Thunder Heights had crept across her spirit.

As always, the sun vanished abruptly behind the overhanging hill, though the colors that streaked the sky seemed brighter than ever because of the black silhouette of the mountain. The house stood aglow with lamps, and now servants were lighting the candles in the Japanese lanterns, so that lawn and veranda were soon rimmed in jewels of blue and green, red and yellow. Down toward the river, against the blackness of the bushes, fireflies lit small darting lanterns of their own in the warm night.

On the veranda the fiddlers from the village struck up a tune, and the young people ran up the steps to enjoy a reel. Camilla found herself handed breathlessly from partner to partner. Once she saw the lighted shape of a boat passing their promontory on the Hudson, and knew that the passengers must be watching, perhaps with envy, the festivities at Thunder Heights. Sometime, long ago, she had wanted that very thing. Now it seemed an empty illusion.

When the musicians changed to a waltz, someone touched Camilla's arm and she turned to look into Ross Granger's face. In the happy shock of seeing him, all doubts fell away. The rush of joy that went through her was rooted deeply in pain, but for the moment the joy was uppermost. She no longer questioned her own heart. This was her love and would always be, whether he cared for her or not. In him lay all safety and strength—a haven from peril. The very shape of his chin, the carriage of his head gave her confidence to face whatever she must face. She went into his arms and made no effort to hide the joy in her eyes.

"I'm sorry I'm late," he said. "I hope I'm still welcome. You invited me, you know."

"Oh, you are, you are!" she cried, and joy was there in her voice as well, with only a small stab of pain in her heart.

He held her gently as they danced, and she felt a kindness in him that had been lacking when he went away. Perhaps he had missed her just a little too.

"Did you find what you wanted in New York?" she asked, and held her breath against the answer. "Are you going away soon?"

"I'm not sure," he said. "There are some things I must finish here first."

"Work for my grandfather?"

"Work for you. How have things gone while I was away?"

"Badly," she whispered. "Terribly! I want to see you. I must see you!"

"That shouldn't be difficult. I'm here."

"You don't understand. I must see you away from the house. Where no one will watch me, or hear us."

"Wherever you say."

She thought frantically. "Tomorrow morning at the cemetery, then. Can you meet me there at ten?"

"Of course," he said.

The waltz had come to an end, and she went reluctantly out of his arms, feeling that she gave up all safety until she could be in them again. Now the throbbing of pain and loss came uppermost and joy subsided.

Refreshments were served at the little tables on the lawn, and Camilla, moving here and there as hostess, was drawn at length to Mrs. Landry's table, to sit down with her and Nora.

Up on the veranda Letty had taken her place at the harp and begun to play the old tunes of Scotland. There was a good deal of Scottish blood in the Highlands of the Hudson, and she was listened to with delight, and sometimes with tears, on the part of older members of the group.

Laura Landry was neither Scottish nor sentimental, and she liked better to talk than to listen.

"Nora tells me you're a good rider," she said. "And that you've bought a horse of your own. I'm glad to hear it. We all rode in the old days. Althea especially."

"I know," Camilla said. "I found her gray riding habit in the attic, and I wear the whole costume—top hat, boots and all. I think sometimes the older people around the countryside think I'm her spirit come back to ride Thunder Mountain again. Mrs. Landry—were you at Blue Beeches when my mother was thrown and killed?"

The plump, assured face creased into lines of pain. "I was here when Orrin Judd brought her down from the mountain. Booth came looking for her at Blue Beeches, hoping she hadn't taken the mountain trail. So I came right over and waited here at Thunder Heights."

"I've heard there was some sort of scene after they brought her down," Camilla said.

"You mean I made a scene. You needn't be delicate about it. I did. Althea was too good a rider to be thrown, no matter what that horse did. I felt there was something wrong—more to the accident than met the eye. I wanted it looked into."

"I understand her horse was frightened by the thunderstorm," Camilla pointed out.

"That always seems one of the strange things about what happened," Nora put in. "That Althea went out on Folly in the first place."

"Not if you knew Althea as I did," Mrs. Landry said. "That part I can accept. It was the wild sort of thing she would do. But as you know perfectly well, unless she is taken by surprise, it's practically impossible to throw a good rider from a sidesaddle. After all, if your knee is over the horn and your right foot hooked behind your left calf, you're locked into the saddle and nothing is going to budge you. Althea would have secured her seat and fought her horse to a standstill. The horse didn't live who was too much for her. And I said as much to Orrin Judd. But it was the wrong time."

"What do you mean?" Camilla prodded.

"He was wild with grief, and he thought I was trying to

make trouble of some sort—to blame him. He was blaming himself as it was for not having got rid of the horse long before. There wasn't anyone I could talk sensibly to, until your father got here. He saw what I meant, but by that time it was impossible to get through to Orrin. He took to his bed, except for the funeral, and they stood about him, holding everyone else away. The three of them—Hortense and Booth and Letty. I don't suppose Orrin would have believed us anyway."

"Believed what?" Camilla asked. She felt cold and her hands were clammy.

"Believed that what happened was not wholly an accident," Mrs. Landry said flatly. "Your father believed it, but there was nothing he could do. No evidence of any sort."

"But—but why? I mean why would anyone have wanted to harm my mother?"

"Your grandfather sent for her when he was ill, and once he saw her again he knew where his affections lay. He was at outs with the rest of the family by that time, and he felt Althea had been treated badly. So he was going to change his will. I gather that he meant to do the same sort of thing he did in the will which left everything to you. But he tossed it in their faces. He let them know what he intended ahead of time. So two days before Althea was to leave for home, the horse threw her. Only I don't believe it."

Camilla heard her out in sick dismay. It all sounded so horrible—and so possible. She could believe these things now, as she might not have believed them when she had first come to Thunder Heights. She could believe because she knew what it was like to be the hunted one.

"The thing I've never understood," Nora said, "was why old Orrin waited so long before he sent for you, Camilla. If his feelings had changed toward Althea, why didn't he want to know her daughter?"

"John King took care of that," Mrs. Landry said. "I remember him as a gentle person, with great kindness and sensitivity. He won all our hearts in the old days. But when a gentle person is angered it can be a fearful thing to see. He swore Orrin Judd would never have his daughter, and that neither of them would ever set foot in Thunder Heights from that day on."

Camilla spoke softly. "And he kept his word as long as he lived. Now I understand why he would never talk about what happened to my mother. Now I can understand why his sickness over her death was more than ordinary grief."

Mrs. Landry reached across the little table to cover Camilla's hand with her own. "This is why I had to see you. You must never make the misstep your mother made."

Camilla nodded mutely.

She had forgotten her guests for a time, and she looked around dazedly. Letty had not chosen to join them for refreshments and was still at her harp. Hortense had taken over the duties of hostess in the grand manner and was moving about among the tables with an air of doing what she had been brought up to do. Ross had disappeared after his waltz with Camilla and was nowhere to be seen. Camilla's eyes moved uneasily from face to face, now searching for only one. She found it at length. Booth had withdrawn a little from the scene. She saw him on the far side of the lawn, leaning against an elm tree, the light from a lantern flickering across his dark face.

He was watching her. She met his eyes across the expanse of laughing, chattering people, and she could not look away. It was like the exchange of a lover's gaze, she thought queerly. He was waiting for her. Waiting for the time that he would hold her in his arms. She was aware of the cold sweat upon her palms, and she reminded herself quickly that Ross had returned. She was not alone any more. Tomorrow she would talk to him, tell him everything. He would know what to do.

XXI

IT WAS WELL INTO THE EVENING WHEN THE LAST GUESTS had left and the Japanese lanterns had been extinguished. Camilla went upstairs, only too ready to drop the role she had been playing and let down her guard. Now she could be afraid, if she wanted to be afraid. And she could think about what she must say to Ross Granger tomorrow morning. She must plan an ordered recital, so that he would believe her and not dismiss her words as nonsense.

When she reached her room, she found that the door she always left closed stood ajar. For an instant the feeling she had experienced in the cellar, staring down at a broken step that might have pitched her headlong, swept over her again. Fear was like nausea in her stomach, and she did not want to go in. She pushed the door wide and stepped just across the threshold.

But it was only Letty, waiting there in her room. She sat in the little rocker before the cold hearth, still dressed in her frock of misty lavender, rocking gently back and forth, and twisting a bit of lavender in her fingers. Mignonette slept comfortably in the middle of the bed, none the worse for her imprisonment in the cellar.

Camilla closed the door and went quickly into the room. With the nausea subsiding, she could almost chatter in relief.

"Did you enjoy the party, Aunt Letty?"

Letty sniffed the lavender absently. "I want to talk to you, dear."

"That's fine," Camilla said. "I'd like to talk to you, too. Mrs. Landry told me something about—about my mother's death. I think you should know what she said."

"I do know." Letty closed her eyes and waved the lavender beneath her nose, as if to gain strength from its pungent odor. "That's why I must talk to you. I know what Laura Landry believed at the time. And in part she was right. But only in part. Sit down on the ottoman, dear. Come close so I needn't speak loudly."

Camilla drew up the big footstool and sat down, almost touching Letty's knees.

"Mrs. Landry doesn't know what happened that late afternoon when Althea went riding on the mountain. She doesn't know that it was I who sent her to her death."

Camilla waited in silence and without belief for her to continue.

"Perhaps you don't realize that the horse that nearly killed me several years before was the same horse that killed Althea."

Camilla heard her in surprise. "No, I didn't."

"She was a mare named Folly. As beautiful a little mare as I've ever seen—delicate and good-mannered and affectionate. She was my horse, Camilla, and I loved her dearly. Until I found out that dreadful day, I never knew that she had a wild streak in her that made her go crazy in a thunderstorm."

"She threw you then?" Camilla asked.

"No. I had dismounted to look at the view. There was a storm coming up, and the whole Hudson valley was a queer livid color, with thunderheads boiling up and lightning flashing in the distance. It was frightening and very beautiful. Hortense was riding with me that day, but she didn't get off her horse. She was impatient to get home. I stood on a rock to put myself into the saddle, and just as I set my foot in the stirrup there was a clap of thunder that might have startled any horse. But Folly was more than startled. She went mad. My foot was caught and she trampled on my arm trying to get free of me, dragging me until my foot came loose from the stirrup. Folly ran away, and Hortense managed to get me home."

Letty's voice was quiet, empty of all emotion, but her fingers twined together tightly as she went on.

"I was very ill for a long time afterwards. The doctor feared a brain injury, as well as the broken arm that never healed properly. Papa would have shot Folly, but in spite of the way I was hurt I loved her, and I pleaded for her all through my delirium. To soothe me, he promised that she could live and I could keep her as a pet, providing no one ever rode her. I know she never meant to harm me, and she remained my friend after I was well. But none of us rode her again. All this, of course, was after Althea had gone away and married."

"When my mother came here on that last visit, didn't she know that Folly wasn't supposed to be ridden?" Camilla asked.

Letty bowed her head. "She knew. Booth told her, when he tried to stop her that day."

"He had been painting her, you know. But they didn't hit it off very well, and I think she never liked him. She posed for him, but she made fun of his painting. She was always gay and I think she only meant to tease, but she made him angry. She told him she was a better woman than the girl he was painting in the picture, because she would have had that rearing horse in hand and ridden him if she wanted to. Booth said the horse in the picture was my Folly and that she was a dangerous animal—a killer.

"I was there at the time, and I can remember the way Althea laughed and said she would ride her. And she would do it right then. I heard the whole quarrel between them. I tried to make her understand that a storm was coming up, and she said that was exactly the point she wanted to make. She was a good enough rider to handle a horse under any circumstances."

Letty paused, shaking her head sadly.

"She was always like that—even as a little girl. The moment anyone told her she couldn't do something, that was what she must do."

"Where was Grandfather while this was going on?" Camilla said.

"He had been ill—that's why he had sent for her—and he was in bed upstairs in his room at the time. Booth had been painting outside on the veranda to get the best light. Althea was wearing her habit for the picture, and she laughed in his face and ran down the steps and off toward the stable. I wanted to go to Papa then, but Booth said not to disturb him. I think Booth was really upset by Althea's outburst. Perhaps he thought Papa would blame him. He was so often in the wrong with his grandfather. He said he would go after her and stop her, keep her from riding."

"But he didn't, did he?" Camilla said.

Letty was silent for a moment, as though she were trying to remember something. "He tried. I sat there on the veranda waiting, with the sky growing darker, knowing there would be an early dusk, due to the storm. I waited for Booth to bring her back to the house. But after a while he returned alone with a red slash across his face where she had struck him with her riding crop. They had quarreled out there in the stable."

"Couldn't you have sent someone after her?" Camilla asked.

"The only one who could have handled her in a mood like that was Papa. I should have gone to him then. But I knew he would be wild with Booth, and I was afraid he might even put him out of the house for good, if he knew about this trouble with Althea. So I sat there and did nothing. I can remember my thoughts at the time. Remember them so well. I was thinking that Althea was always the beautiful one, the gifted one, the lucky one. She had led a charmed life, and nothing could happen to her. So I sat there and let her go to her death. And all the while there was a voice speaking to me inside, telling me that this time something would happen. But I wouldn't listen."

Letty's calm had begun to dissolve, and she was weeping gently, a scrap of lavender-scented lace to her eyes.

"You mustn't blame yourself," Camilla said. "The fault was Booth's, not yours. Grandfather couldn't have stopped her either by that time, and he was ill."

"No, no!" Letty looked up at once. "It was not Booth's fault. Even though she had struck him, he was worried and upset about her. I can remember the way he strode up and down the veranda, watching the storm blow up, helpless and frustrated because he could do nothing."

194

"Do you think he might have been acting?" Camilla said. "Mrs. Landry thinks there was something—deliberate about what happened."

"Mrs. Landry is a gossip," Letty said, her tone unusually sharp. "A troublemaker. As I know very well, she tried to make a great deal of trouble afterwards."

"When did you go to Grandfather?"

"When Folly came home with an empty saddle. Booth heard her gallop into the drive, and he ran out to catch her and put her into her stall. Then he sent a groom out to search for Althea, and came running to the house to let me know what had happened and that he would go out searching himself. That was when I went to Papa. When it was too late. He got out of bed and had his own horse saddled. And he rode up the mountain where he thought she was sure to have gone. Booth was out looking for her too, but he chose the wrong route. He thought she might have taken the easier road along the river. He couldn't believe she would be so foolish as to go up the mountain on a crazy horse in the storm. But that is what she did. And it was on the mountain-top Papa found her."

"Where was Hortense?" Camilla asked.

"She had a headache and went up to her room to lie down. She didn't know what had happened until they brought Althea home."

A silence settled upon the room. Letty wept softly, her handkerchief to her eyes, while Camilla sat lost in unhappy revery. A rising wind whispered in the chimney, and Letty looked up uneasily.

"Listen to the wind. It's beginning to blow again. I don't want to stay alone tonight, Camilla. I don't want to get up in the night and go walking about the house."

"You needn't, Camilla said quickly. "Stay here with me. The bed is plenty big enough for two, and I'd like someone to keep me company tonight."

Letty began to speak again in a rush of words, as though she wanted to hold nothing back. "I've suffered for so many years because I didn't act. I could surely have found a way to stop Althea if I had really tried. So I am the one who is guilty. I'm the one Mrs. Landry has a right to blame, if she blames anyone. But you see that I couldn't remain silent forever. A few months ago I tried to tell Papa exactly what had happened. I wanted to gain his forgiveness. But he was so badly upset by what I told him that it brought on his last

195

attack. So I was responsible for his death too. And for his changing of his will—because after what I told him, he said he could never trust any of us again."

That all this unhappiness had existed behind Letty's quiet serenity was disturbing. Yet there was no real comfort Camilla could offer. Any reassurance would sound hollow and meaningless. True, Letty's self-blame was exaggerated out of all proportion to reality, but Camilla knew better than to try to dissuade her in her present distraught state. Later, perhaps, at a calmer time, they could talk about these things, reason them out sensibly.

"I'll go get my night clothes from my room and come right back." Letty rose and slipped out of the room, a slight, frail figure in pale lavender, moving in a faint aura of lavender scent.

Later that night, when the lamp was out and the room dark except for a bar of moonlight from the balcony, Camilla lay awake and quiet beside her aunt. Tree branches soughed in the wind all about the house, and she lay very still, waiting for Letty to fall asleep. But Letty's breathing remained ragged and uneven, and it was Camilla who slept first.

Once during the night she wakened uneasily and stretched out her hand to find Letty gone. But when she stirred and reached for a candle and matches, Letty spoke from the rocking chair by the hearth.

"I'm here, dear. Go to sleep. I'll keep watch. Don't worry about me. I have so much to think about."

And Camilla fell asleep again and did not waken until morning. When she sat up in bed, she found that Letty had taken her clothes and returned to her own room.

But she had other matters to think about now. Today she was to meet Ross at her grandfather's grave. In Ross she centered all hope of escape from the frightening dilemma in which she found herself. She had no actual evidence of any kind to offer him, but she thought he would listen with sympathy to her story. And perhaps he would tell her what to do.

When the time came she gathered an armful of flowers and set off on the road to the village. The day was once more hot and still. Distant clouds in the east seemed to hang motionless, and the morning steamed with humid, oppressive heat.

The cemetery drowsed on the hillside in the warm June sun. Slowly Camilla climbed the path that led to the burial plot of the Judds. She always felt a sense of peace and friendliness in this place. Here all storms had quieted, and those who slept held no rancor against the living.

A tall stand of yew trees shielded her from view of the road, and she sat on the grass beside Orrin Judd's grave and took off her big straw hat. Other than those who lay beneath the stones, no one awaited her. The old man who tended the graves nodded from a distance and went about his own work. All else was still and somnolent in the sun. When the flowers she had brought were arranged, Camilla tucked her white skirts about her, leaned her cheek against her propped-up knees, and closed her eyes.

She knew, however, the very moment when Ross reached the cemetery gate. Though she heard no more than his step, no more than the creaking of a hinge, her quickening senses told her it was Ross. She sat up eagerly and waited for him.

He climbed the path and she watched him come toward her, saw with love and pride the broad strength of his shoulders, the clean length of his stride. But it was his face she sought most eagerly, so that she might read in it his mood toward her. There seemed no antagonism in his look this morning, but only the gentleness she had sensed in him yesterday. Her heart began to thump raggedly, and she had to remind herself of the purposes which brought her here to talk to him.

"A pretty picture you make," he said, "there on the grass in your white dress."

He dropped down beside her, stretching out to his full length, leaning on one elbow. She could not bring herself to destroy the peace of the moment with the words she had to speak, and he did not ask her purpose in bringing him here. It was as if he, too, wanted to preserve this moment of companionship between them.

Idly he began to tell her about shad fishing at night on the Hudson, when the run had been on, and how he had gone out one evening with Toby and they had filled their nets with silver shad and brought the fish home to Thunder Heights and Blue Beeches. She listened with pleasure, wishing that she might go out on the river with him another year.

Then, when she felt lulled and quiet, he sat up so that he could look into her face. "You were afraid of something yesterday, Camilla—what was it? Why did you want to meet me here?"

She began to tell him then what had happened—all of it. About the tea that had made Mignonette sick. About the

197

night when Booth had said he wanted to marry her and she had run away from him. About the words she had overheard in the cellar, and finally about the broken step.

He listened grimly and discounted none of what she told him. She saw the dark blood rise in his face as he listened, saw the anger in his eyes.

"There's only one thing to do," he told her when she came to an end. "You must get away from the house. Break your grandfather's will and do as you please. You have no real obligation to any of these people. They'd never given a thought to you. If you must, settle something upon them so your conscience will be free. But get away from Thunder Heights yourself and don't come back. It's the only way."

"If I went, I could keep nothing of the money or property. I would leave everything behind with the house. If I couldn't live up to Grandfather's wishes, then I would have no right to any of the inheritance he left me."

There was a light in Ross's eyes that she could not read. "Do you really care? Do you want it? You lived without it before—you can again."

"That's not the important thing," she said helplessly. She had hoped he might understand. Knowing that he did not, she felt defeated. She could not put into words her feeling about all this. How could she make him hear the echo of her grandfather's sorrowful voice? How could she convey her tenderness for Letty, whom she could not abandon? Or her conviction that she must somehow pick up life in her mother's place? The ties that held her to Thunder Heights were intangible and emotional. They could not be held up to the cold light of reason.

He saw refusal in her face and sighed. "I was afraid you'd feel this way. It's ridiculous, of course, but the choice is yours and I shan't try to dissuade you. But if you're to stay, you must safeguard yourself and you must do it at once."

"How?" she asked. "What do you mean?"

"You must make a will. Pompton's in New York now, but he'll be home tomorrow. See him then and tell him what you want."

"What good would a will do? If anything happened to me, everything would go to Hortense and Letty. In a will I could make no other arrangement."

He reached out and circled her wrist with his fingers. "Oh, yes you could. In fact, that's the whole idea. The will must leave everything you have to charity—with no more than a bare pittance for Letty and Hortense. And you must let them

198

know the wording of the will as soon as it has been safely drawn up. Then you'll be safe. You'll be worth a good deal to them alive, and they're likely to guard you tenderly."

"They would hate me for it. At least Hortense would. And Booth. How could I go on living at Thunder Heights in an atmosphere like that?"

"How can you live there anyway?" He dropped her hand impatiently, and she could see that he was growing annoyed with her again. "There's no choice, apparently, that is acceptable to you. Don't you understand—this is the only safe move for you to make! That is, unless you do as I first suggested and give the whole thing up."

"I can't," she said. "I can't do that."

"Then think about the matter of the will," he told her. "But do something about it soon. They must realize you might take such a step, so they're unlikely to wait, once they're sure you're suspicious. These—accidents—may grow more deadly."

Camilla plucked a blossom of white clover, twirling it between her fingers. She felt painfully torn between conscience and duty.

"I'd better get back," Ross said. He got up and stood looking down at her.

She stood up beside him, not wanting him to go, but knowing no way to hold him here. The anger had died out of him and there was only pity in his eyes now—and something more. He stepped toward her as if he could not help himself, and she was in his arms where she had been once before, held close to his thudding heart, clinging to him and weeping.

"My dear," he said. His hand was on her hair, and he held her head against him for a moment before he bent and kissed her lips. There was only tenderness in his touch now, only a great sadness.

"Why must you go away?" she wailed. "How can I live if you go away?"

"You must know I can't stay any longer," he said gently, his lips against her hair. "I've given ten years to your grandfather, but they were years of preparation. Now I must get on with my work. I believe I'm ready for it now."

"Build your bridge here," she whispered. "Build it for Grandfather. Build it for me."

"And if I did?"

"Then you could stay nearby. For all the time you were building it you would be a part of my life."

"But after that I'd be gone," he said. "As you've just told

me, you're tied to Thunder Heights, Camilla. You could never come with me to all the places where I'll go. It's better to end this now. It would hurt us all the more later. I didn't ask to love you. Indeed, I've fought against it."

She clung to him more tightly than ever. "No, no! We mustn't ever be apart again. Ross—I'll do as you say. I'll give up the inheritance and go wherever you wish. If only you want me with you—that's all I ask."

He kissed her again. "You know how much I want you. But in the end you'd never forgive yourself, or forgive me. I was angry when I asked you to throw away what you feel is your responsibility. It's not a sacrifice I could accept."

He put her out of his arms, as he had done once before, but this time his hands were gentle and there was pain in his eyes.

"Stay here in the cemetery a little while longer," he said. "Then we won't be seen together outside. It won't help you if the Judds think you've met me here secretly." He started away from her and then turned back for an instant. "Please be careful, Camilla," he said and hurried off toward the gate.

She stood stricken and helpless, watching him go. What was she to do? What was the answer for her? To know that he loved her and wanted her brought a mingling of pain and joy with the knowledge, but pain was uppermost, and she could not tell where to turn.

When she heard the gate creak and knew he was gone, she went to stand for a little while beside the grave of Althea Judd King. How young she had been to die. Yet she had known the fullest meaning of happiness. She had lived with her love and borne him a daughter whom they both had loved. And now that daughter stood beside the place where Althea lay and knew that something of herself must die too soon, as surely as the body which lay beneath the granite slab had died too soon. But in Camilla it must die without the taste of happiness or fulfillment.

Once more her thoughts turned to that stormy night on the mountain and all the dark puzzle of what had happened there. If she could find the full answer to these things, might she not find as well an answer to the problem of her love? Why she should feel this to be a possibility, she did not know, but the conviction was strong within her.

If Althea had been too good a rider to be thrown, how had Folly freed herself and come home with an empty saddle? And what had happened between Althea and Booth out there in the stable before she had ridden off in the storm?

Why had she struck him with her riding crop? What was the basis of the angry quarrel that had flared between them?

She thought again of the crop as she reached the stone lions that marked the gateway to Thunder Heights. How could it possibly have fallen into those bushes? Could Grandfather have tossed it there despairingly after the accident? Yet Grandfather had taken loving care of Althea's riding things in the attic. And why had Aunt Letty taken the crop away, kept it out of sight, said nothing to the others about the finding of it?

None of these questions could be answered, and it was the present she must face, not the past.

XXII

LUNCHEON THAT DAY WAS A SOLEMN MEAL, WITH ONLY Hortense and Letty to keep her company. Letty said Booth was working upstairs on his picture. Only a few touches to the background remained to complete it, and he wanted to work straight through, while the mood was upon him.

"I'll take him something when we finish," Letty said. "I'm glad he's working again. I'll be happy when this painting is finished."

There was something in her tone that made Camilla glance at her. "Why will you be happy?"

"It's as Booth says—I've never liked it," Letty said. "It's too painful a picture to be endured. I can't look at it without seeing Folly's rearing hoofs, striking at me. Just as they must have struck at Althea."

"Do you suppose she dismounted the way you did?" Camilla asked. "Do you suppose that is how she was thrown?"

Hortense said brusquely, "Do talk about something else. We can do without such a gloomy subject with our meal."

They finished the meal in silence.

Afterwards, when Letty had fixed a tray for Booth, she asked Camilla to come upstairs with her to his studio.

"He wants you to see the finished picture, dear," she said, when Camilla looked as though she might refuse. "I think he wants you to be pleased with it."

Camilla would have preferred never to look at that picture again. She felt as Letty did about it, but she had no reasonable excuse to offer. And she could not avoid Booth all the time. Not if she was to continue living in the house.

Up in the nursery, he had set his easel facing the long windows along the north wall. When they came in he had finished the last brush stroke and was standing back to study the picture with critical eyes.

"I've brought you something to eat, dear," Letty said, and set the tray on a table.

Booth hardly glanced at it. His look was on Camilla. "It's done," he said. "Come and tell me what you think."

Letty slipped a hand through Camilla's arm, and they approached the easel together.

With the background completed, the violence of the scene seemed to hurl itself at the beholder. Folly, rearing with wild hoofs, was a deadly sight. Her ears were laid back, her nostrils dilated, her lip curled above vicious teeth. But the girl who stood clinging to her bridle was almost laughing in exultance, as if she had thrown herself into the furious satisfaction of taming this rearing beast. Althea herself would surely have applauded such reckless courage.

Camilla, staring at the picture, could not be sure whether the face in the picture was her own or her mother's, but she knew that the wild emotion the artist had caught in the woman's storm-lighted face could well have been Althea's.

"I think I've never looked like that," she said to Booth.

"But I can imagine you like that, after seeing Althea angry," he said.

Letty had stepped closer to study the picture's details. The background of stormy sky had been completed, and the dark, stony ground beneath the feet of horse and girl had been painted in detail. The scene was clearly the bald top of Thunder Mountain, with the edge of the cliff dropping off not far away. The girl in the picture had dropped her riding crop in her struggle with the horse and it lay a short distance away in the left foreground.

Letty uttered a soft exclamation. "You've painted in Althea's riding crop!" she cried.

"It's a good touch, don't you think?" Booth said. "I needed something to fill that empty spot."

"But the crop was never found up there," Letty said softly.

Booth shrugged. "Aren't you taking this too literally? After all, the entire scene is something I made up. I started painting it before I ever knew what would happen to Althea."

Letty said, "Wait for me here, Camilla. I'll be only a moment."

202

She hurried off and Booth smiled at Camilla. "What's the trouble these days, Cousin? You hardly came near me at the lawn party yesterday."

She wanted to say, "There's the ugly matter of a broken step between us. And how will you explain that?"

But she remembered Ross's warning and suppressed the words. She would not be safe in this house until a will had been made. And she could not go to Mr. Pompton until tomorrow. In the meantime caution was her safest defense. If Booth did not know that she suspected him, she would be far safer than if he did.

"I was busy with our guests," she said quietly. "I had no time for members of the family."

"Yes," he said, "I saw the attention you were paying to Mrs. Landry. I suppose she tried to fill your ears with old scandals out of the past?"

Before Camilla could answer, Letty had returned, carrying in her hands the little riding crop with its head of silver chrysanthemums. She held it out to Booth.

"Here you are," she said.

Booth took it, and the queer, electric excitement kindled in his eyes. *The moment of danger*, Camilla thought. The crop had meaning for him—that was plain.

"Where did this turn up?" Booth asked.

"Camilla found it. She can tell you where."

Booth turned the crop in his hands, examining the polished silver cap, the leather thong that had rotted through.

"Suppose you tell me, Cousin," he said.

The roof of Camilla's mouth felt suddenly as dry as her lips. Booth was watching her. Letty was watching Booth, and there was an undercurrent of sick excitement in the room. Camilla touched her lips with the tip of her tongue and began to speak.

"When I climbed down to that spit of land that strikes out into the river below Thunder Mountain," she said, "I found the crop caught in a crotch of brush."

"As if it had been flung there," Letty puzzled. "But where could it have been thrown from, I wonder? Not from the top of Thunder Mountain—the spit is too far out for that."

"And why, if Althea had carried it up there, would she have thrown it over the cliff?" Booth said easily. "I'm sorry there's been such a mystery about it. I can tell you what happened."

"If you knew, why didn't you tell us sooner, dear?" Letty asked. "Why didn't you tell us when Papa kept wondering about the crop and looking for it to keep with the saddle and bridle?"

"I didn't tell anyone," Booth said, "because Althea struck me across the face with the crop, and that was not something I cared to tell. I took it out of her hands, and she mounted Folly and rode away. I carried the crop to the lawn above the river and flung it out as far as I could throw. Into the water, I thought. I intended that she would never strike anyone with it again."

Letty's sigh was a soft release of breath, as if she had been waiting in dread for his explanation. She took the crop from him and held it out to Camilla.

"You may have it now, dear. Carry it the next time you wear Althea's things. I'm sure she would want you to have it."

"I'll carry it this afternoon," Camilla said. "I've had no time for riding lately. But I've wanted to explore those queer ruins that look like a castle over on the next hill."

"That will be nice," Letty said. "Booth dear, do come eat your lunch."

"You're right about the ruins," Booth said. "They are those of a castle. But they're man made. A few families along the Hudson got the notion years ago that they would give the river a look of the Rhine. They thought a few expensive castle ruins would be picturesque—but the idea never caught on. When I was a boy we used to use Castle Dunder for picnics, didn't we, Aunt Letty? It's a good spot for a view."

He had turned his attention to the food before him, and Camilla smiled at Letty and slipped away from the room. There was in her a growing urgency to be out on Firefly again, riding through the hills. Away from this house she would be safe just that much longer. She could use the entire afternoon for riding and exploring the ruins. Then there would be only dinner, the evening, and one last night to get through. She would lock herself in, perhaps ask Letty to stay with her again. And in the morning she would go to Mr. Pompton's office in Westcliff and await his coming. Ever since she had talked to Ross this morning the need for action had been building within her. She was no longer undecided as to what she meant to do. Somehow, ever since she had looked at the finished picture of girl and horse, she had known that she must fight for her life. She must act swiftly while there was still time, and while Booth was without suspicion of what she meant to do.

The riding crop lay on the bed where she had tossed it,

and as she dressed in Althea's gray habit, she glanced at it now and then. Booth's explanation had been glib and logical, but she did not believe it. He might fool Letty, who loved him as a son, but he could not fool her. His story of what had happened to the crop was a lie. She had seen it in the exultance in his face, in his supreme confidence that he could step to the very knife edge of danger and back away in time to save himself.

Yet, even while instinct told her that he was concealing something about the crop, her mind drew only a blank when she tried to think what it might be. Why had he painted the crop into the picture unless it had really lain there on the ground near Althea when she had struggled with the horse? Had he done it deliberately, playing with danger? Or had he done it from memory, without thinking—with an artist's unconscious observation of every detail?

But there was no way in which Booth could have been on the mountain to see what had happened. He had come in to tell Letty that Althea had refused to listen to him and that she had gone out alone into the rising storm. Then he had remained at Thunder Heights until her riderless horse had come home. After that he had roused the house and sent out searchers. Orrin Judd had gone up the mountain. Booth had chosen the river path for his search. He had never been near the mountaintop that night at all. There was no way in which he could have affected what had happened to Althea. Nor could he have seen the crop on the ground at her feet. That is, if the crop had really been there, and was not merely the imaginative touch Booth claimed it to be.

When Camilla was dressed and ready for her ride, she went to Letty's room and tapped on the door. Someone moved inside, but there was no answer and she knocked again. To her surprise, Hortense opened the door, and Camilla saw that she had been crying.

"I was looking for Letty," Camilla said.

Hortense stared at her in antipathy. "All the trouble that has come to this house since Papa died is due to you. Why don't you go away?"

"Do you know where Letty is?" Camilla repeated.

"I don't want to know. I came here to make her understand something, and she flounced out and left me. You'll have to look for her."

Camilla met Grace on the stairs, and the girl said Miss Letty had gone down to the cellar. Camilla hurried down and found that the broken step had been repaired. Nevertheless, she stepped cautiously as she went down the steep flight. Letty was in the larder, and she glanced up as Camilla came in the door.

"Rosemary and lavender make a lovely tea," she said, busy with her jars of herbs. But Camilla saw that her hands were trembling.

"Did you know," Camilla asked, "that Hortense is upstairs in your room?"

"I know," Letty said. "She came in to see me just now, but I walked out and left her there, I didn't want to listen to the things she had to say."

"About me, Aunt Letty?"

Letty waved the question aside. "Her nonsense doesn't bear repeating. I see you're ready for your ride, dear."

"Yes. I'll go out in a little while. But I wanted to talk to you first, Aunt Letty."

"You, too?" Letty sighed. "I came down here to be busy and peaceful."

Camilla wondered if she dared tell Letty about the will she meant to ask Mr. Pompton to draw up tomorrow. There was nothing greedy about Letty and her advice might be worth seeking, if she were not in one of her vague and evasive moods. But first there were other things to be said, and there was no use trying to approach them delicately.

"I think you ought to know," she said, "that the step that might have killed me yesterday was deliberately tampered with. I'd have shown it to you if it hadn't been mended so quickly. The wood wasn't rotten at all. There was no reason for it to break so easily."

"Tampered with?" Letty's hands went on with their work, and she did not look at Camilla. "For what purpose? By whom?"

"I think it was intended that I should be badly hurt on that step. But I don't think you planned such a trap, Aunt Letty. Nor do I think Aunt Hortense did. It's the sort of thing a man would execute."

Letty whirled to look at her and there were high spots of color in her cheeks. "You're making a dangerous accusation. And without proof."

"The proof is gone," Camilla said. "But I know what I saw."

"I don't believe it," Letty said, her lips quivering as she spoke.

"What about the riding crop then? I know that worried you when you saw that Booth had painted it into his picture.

206

And I think I know why. You were wondering why he saw it there in his mind's eye—just as I was wondering. That's why you brought it in and showed it to him, isn't it?"

Letty shook her head a little wildly. There was no serenity in her now. "I won't listen to such insinuations, Camilla. Ever since Booth came to this house, everyone has been against him. No one has understood him or loved him but me. I didn't expect you to turn against him too. Of course he is—different—and perhaps a little eccentric. But that is often true of the highly gifted."

"Then you don't believe, Aunt Letty, that Booth would ever make an attempt on my life? Or even, perhaps, on my mother's?"

There was a long moment of silence in the room. Letty seemed to be struggling with too strong an indignation for words. In the end she merely shook her head fervently in answer.

"Very well," Camilla said. "I just wanted to know where you stand in all this, Aunt Letty. I'll go out for my ride now."

As she went upstairs, she felt torn and saddened. If it came to a choice between her safety and Booth's, she suspected that there would be only one decision Letty could make. She was no more to be trusted than Hortense or Booth himself. At Thunder Heights every hand was against her, and that was as it would always be. And for such emptiness she must give up her love.

She let herself out the heavy front door and started down the steps. Behind her Letty's voice called out and Camilla turned around. Letty stood on the steps, breathless from running upstairs.

"Don't go riding, dear," she said. "There's going to be a storm."

Camilla looked up at the sky. It was blue and hot and still. What clouds there were still hung motionless on the horizon as they had seemed to do all day. Not a breath of air stirred the leaves in the park before the house.

"There's not a sign of a storm anywhere," Camilla said.

She would have walked on toward the stable, but Letty came after her and caught at her arm in entreaty.

"Please, dear. You must believe me. I have a feeling that something terrible will happen if you go riding today."

"A few moments ago you were encouraging me to ride," Camilla said. "What made you change your mind?"

"I—I don't know." Letty looked as if she were about to

crumple in upon herself. "I never understand these feelings or how they come. I just know they must be listened to. It's a feeling I have about that horse. You know I was against your buying the mare from the first. Just as Ross Granger was against it."

"And I've proved you both wrong," Camilla said. "Firefly and I understand each other. I feel safer with her than I do—in this house."

Letty drew back as if Camilla had slapped her. Then she turned and went up the steps, a drooping, pitiful little figure, her crooked arm held against her body. With a mingling of impatience and sympathy, Camilla walked away toward the stable. There was nothing more she could say to Letty, and it was just as well to leave her with that last thought.

XXIII

SHE HAD NOT SENT WORD TO HAVE FIREFLY SADDLED, SO SHE had to wait for it to be done after she reached the stable. More than once she scanned the sky to see if there was any evidence of Letty's threatened storm, but it burned blue and empty and no hint of a breeze stirred the breathless air. She wondered if Ross were upstairs in the rooms over the coach house, but she could find no reason for calling to him.

Firefly was restless and eager for a run. She stood impatiently, while Billy helped Camilla into the saddle. Out upon the road Camilla gave the mare an easy run as far as the place where the winding trail led up Thunder Mountain. With the horse moving like a dancer beneath her, full of spirit and life, something of the joy of riding returned and Camilla could put Thunder Heights away from her for a little while. For her there would always be both a physical and an emotional release about riding.

They climbed the trail up Thunder Mountain, but this time Camilla did not dismount at the top. Firefly was behaving skittishly, sidestepping, and swinging her hind quarters about in a balkish way. She was like a lady in a state of sulks because no one had paid attention to her for several days. She would be sweet enough after a while, but first she would make clear her displeasure and refuse to forgive the neglect.

Camilla coaxed her, teased her, spoke to her lovingly, but Firefly tossed her pretty head and would not relent.

"All right," Camilla told her, "I'll let you have your fun, but first let's get over to the next hill. There's more room there for your tricks. I don't care for them at the top of a cliff."

Rising on the far hill were the "ruins" of Castle Dunder. From this distance the gray heap of stones looked convincingly like an ancient castle, and rather grim and forbidding.

With her hand firm upon the reins, Camilla urged the mare through the woods that hid a trail winding around the inner curve of hill. They walked now, due to low-hanging branches and the very narrowness of the path. When they merged upon an open slope of hillside, they were just below the ruins, and the clustered stones rose ahead on the crest of the hill. Approached from the rear, the place looked an empty shell and far less picturesque than it seemed from a distance. However, the main tower appeared solidly built, for all that the crumbling walls which fell away behind embraced only an empty expanse of weeds and grass.

There seemed to be a shed built at the rear of the structure, and Camilla let Firefly prance up the slope. Clearly the mare distrusted the gray pile of stones, but Camilla insisted and she gave in, though still displeased. A low wall offered an easy foothold for dismounting, and Camilla stepped down to it, jumped to the ground and tethered Firefly in the shelter of the stable-like shed.

As she started across the grassy field toward the main tower of the castle, a spate of rain struck her head and shoulders. She looked up in surprise and saw that the wind had risen so that trees on the hillside were thrashing their branches. Letty's threatened storm clouds had puffed their sails with wind and were moving up the sky.

She hurried toward the tower entrance where a few stone steps led to an oblong opening and stepped gingerly into the dark lower room. In the dim light she could make out a circling of stone stairs marching to the top of the tower. The room smelled of damp left over from old storms, and the stone walls had the authentic chill of a castle. She had no desire to linger here in the dim light that came through the door.

The circling stone steps drew her, and she followed their spiraling wedges upward in a dizzy climb until she emerged in a bare room at the top. Here several archers' windows, deep and narrow, slit the circular stone walls, letting in slivers of gray light. A rusty iron ladder led upward to still another level and what appeared to be a trap door to the roof.

Now she wanted to reach the very battlements and watch the storm clouds rise. Testing the rungs to make sure they would hold her weight, she climbed up beneath the trap door. At first it refused to give as she pushed with her shoulder, but when she persisted, it creaked open, sending shivers of dust and rotting wood down upon her head.

Up here the air smelled sweet and clean. She stepped out upon the flat, open top of a tower, and stood beside the circling parapet. The spurt of rain was over for the moment, but wind rushed at her jubilantly and tore at her veil and hat. The distant mountains of New England were obscured by mists, and even the nearer Catskills had been hidden from sight, but the rolling panoply of the storm gave in itself a tremendous view. Far below the Hudson was whipped with curling threads of foam, and the entire scene was like one of Booth's wild Hudson valley paintings.

So lost was she in watching the swiftly rising clouds that she had almost forgotten Firefly when the mare neighed. She must go down at once, she thought, and start for home. Letty had been right after all, and it would be raining hard before long. As she hesitated for a last long look, she heard the answering neigh of another horse.

At once she walked to the land side of the tower and looked toward the shed. Firefly was there, and tethered near her a second horse, a man's saddle upon its back. No rider was visible, and she was puzzled and a little uneasy. This was not one of the horses from Blue Beeches, and she wondered what passerby might have discovered her presence. At the foot of the tower a step sounded, and she leaned over the steep parapet to look straight down.

She was just in time to see a man enter the narrow doorway below. It was Booth Hendricks. A shiver ran through her as she shrank back from the parapet. He must have hired a horse in the village and ridden out here deliberately. She could hear him walking about below and wondered helplessly what she must do.

He came to the foot of the spiralling stairs and called up to her. "Camilla! Are you there, Camilla?"

If she did not answer, perhaps he would not come up to search for her. Perhaps he would think she was elsewhere and go away. But almost at once she heard his footfall on the echoing stone of the steps and knew he was coming up the stairs. She was trapped with no means of saving herself and only the riding crop in her hands to fight him with.

With deadly certainty she knew what his purpose would be. There would be no need for indirection this time in his attempt on her life. A fall from the tower could be easily explained later, and Booth's ends would have been met.

In a moment he would emerge in the room at the top of the tower and then it was only a few steps to the roof beside her. As she trembled there, her mind turning this way and that like a hunted thing, a course of possible action came to her mind. Foolish, perhaps, and hopeless. But the only chance she had.

She pulled the gray hat from her head and tossed it to the far side of the tower. Then she dropped to her hands and knees and crouched in the one hiding place the roof offered—the niche made by the trap door where it lay propped against the parapet. The door itself shielded her and he could not see her as he climbed the stairs. He would need only to turn around for her to be visible, but for an instant when he stepped from the top of the ladder to the roof, he would have his back to her hiding place.

Her breathing seemed almost as noisy as the rising wind. Her throat was tight with fear. She pulled herself small in the cramped space as he came up, his feet ringing on the iron rungs.

"Camilla?" he called again—and was out upon the roof.

He saw her hat at once and went toward it. In that instant Camilla flung herself from her hiding place and down the ladder. She had no time to feel for her footing, but used her hands as well as her feet to swing herself down. Caution was impossible. There was no time to be quiet, and she set the echoes ringing. She was on the stone steps now, slipping, stumbling, catching herself before she pitched headlong. Above her she could hear him following—and he was unhampered by a heavy riding skirt.

At the tower door, she did not trouble with the few steps down, but sprang to the ground and fled across the grass to the shed. Firefly heard her coming and pawed the earth, neighing in nervous excitement. But Booth could move more swiftly than Camilla and his hand caught her arm, whirling her about. She saw his face in the gray light. He knew she had guessed the truth. There was danger in his eyes—exultant danger. And death.

She struck at him with the silver head of the riding crop, lashing it across his face. For an instant he was taken by surprise. Pain blinded him and he drew back. She twisted free of his grasp and sped the few yards to the low stone wall beside the shed. In a second she was up on the wall, from there into the saddle, and the reins were free in her hand.

She swerved Firefly about and made her rear, her front feet striking out in Booth's direction. Again he fell back, and Camilla turned the mare toward the woods trail and was away, with Firefly's hoofs pounding the turf. Crouching low over the saddle she gave the mare her head along the narrow trail. Caught up in Camilla's own fear, Firefly hurled herself into breakneck speed, seeking only to flee the unknown terror. At least the curve around the hill was steady and gentle, so no sharp turns need be taken. Camilla could not hear the other horse behind, and she dared not look back, but Booth would be in the saddle by now and after her.

"Hurry, hurry!" she moaned to Firefly. "Hurry!"

Suddenly they were in the open, and she knew they had reached the top of Thunder Mountain. Before she could turn the mare, Firefly was out upon the bare top of the mountain, with cliffs falling away on three sides, and the downward path behind them. Camilla fought her to a halt and turned her about. She could hear hoofbeats now, as Booth ran his horse through the woods, and despair swept over her. Thunder Mountain, with the way down cut off, would be as bad a trap as the top of the tower.

And then, without warning, Ross Granger rode out from the lower path and was between her and Booth. She jerked Firefly about and urged her toward him.

"It's Booth!" she gasped, pointing.

Ross understood at once. He leaned over and slapped Firefly's flank with the flat of his hand.

"Go home!" he shouted. "Ride for home!" With a violent jerk, Ross wheeled his own horse across the path to intercept Booth.

She had no need to urge the mare now. Firefly was tearing down the lower path. But now there was something new and frightening about her gait. She lunged against a tree in passing, and Camilla felt a crushing pain in her left leg. The mare was fighting to get the bit between her teeth, and she was trying as well to rid herself of a rider she now feared.

Camilla ducked low beneath the next branch before it swept her from the saddle, and clamped the toe of her right boot behind her left calf. It was clear what Firefly was trying to do. This was no pretty sulking spell. She meant to dash her rider against a tree, or scrape her off beneath a branch, and she was wickedly intent on her purpose. Camilla could only flatten herself over the pommel, ducking as well as she could the thrashing branches. The pungent taste of pine was in her mouth, and her hands ached with their effort to bring the mare under control.

The trail was steepening and danger lay in a misstep, lest the mare stumble and roll on her. Pinned beneath her mount, she might readily be killed. But the fight was hard on Firefly too, and with Camilla clinging like a burr to the saddle, and never relinquishing her struggle to get the mare's head up and under control, the horse was tiring too. When the road suddenly opened on a level before them and the trees fell away, the fight drained out of the mare and she cantered to a halt a little way down the road. Camilla had won.

The quiet, the absence of buffeting and wild motion was almost shocking. Firefly still on the dirt road, and both girl and horse were trembling. Camilla pushed her tumbled hair from her forehead and spoke in a low, soothing voice to the mare. She was docile enough now, her wild fright drained away, and Camilla turned her toward Thunder Heights.

Only then did she have time to think of what might be happening back there in the woods. Ross, she knew, would stop Booth and engage his attention. But what would happen between the two men? Both had been spoiling for trouble for a long while. If it came to a fight, Camilla knew Ross would handle himself well. But she did not trust Booth. He would stop at nothing if he were pressed, and she was suddenly fearful of the outcome. But there was nothing she could do now but wait. More than once, she drew the mare in and listened for the sound of a horse's passage on the hillside above. Thunder rumbled in the distance and lightning flashed far away. There was wind in the trees, but no other sound. And still it did not rain.

At the gate of Thunder Heights Hortense stood waiting. When Camilla turned off the road, she called for the stableboy, and came forward herself to take Firefly's bridle.

"Get off," she said curtly to Camilla. "If you can. You look beaten."

Camilla's body felt sore from the lashings and her left leg was bruised, but she took her foot from the stirrup and slipped down into the stableboy's grasp. When he set her on her feet, she swayed for an instant, and Hortense gave the boy the bridle and took her arm.

"That mare has a vicious streak, hasn't she?" Hortense

said. "I've been waiting for it to come out. I expect she's killed a rider or two somewhere along the line. That's why Booth had her brought here to Berton's That's why he told me to—'find' her for you in the village. You didn't know that, did you?"

Camilla shook her head wearily. "It was my own fault. I was frightened and I frightened the mare."

"I've been a fool," Hortense said. "I believed that he only wanted to make you afraid—so you'd give everything up and leave. I wanted that myself. I thought if I made you sick with that tea . . . but the cat drank it. Letty knew I'd been down in the larder that day . . . she could have told you."

Camilla could only stare at her numbly. Hortense looked faintly bedraggled, for all her old-fashioned elegance. The lace at her throat was worn, and pins were visible at her belt line. Yet in spite of this outward disintegration, she was more convincing and forceful than Camilla had ever seen her. She was a woman to be heeded

"He means to kill you, Camilla. You must know that now. He tricked me on the matter of sending you down to the cellar on a trumped-up errand. I'd never have been a knowing party to that broken step. I've never meant you serious harm. But Booth will stop at nothing."

"Yes, I know." Camilla's lips barely formed the words. All this was something she must come to later. Now the only part of her mind that still functioned focused entirely on what might be happening on Thunder Mountain. For herself, she wanted only Letty's ministering hands and ointments and a bed to lie upon.

"Where is Aunt Letty?" she asked.

There was a strained note in Hortense's voice. "She's locked herself in her room. She's waiting for them to bring your body to her. Down from Thunder Mountain. The way they did Althea's."

XXIV

THE DRIVEWAY SEEMED ENDLESSLY LONG AS CAMILLA FOL-lowed it, leaning on Hortense's arm. She limped a little as she walked, but bruises were nothing compared to the pressure of anxiety in her mind.

"Who sent Ross after me?" she asked.

"I did," Hortense said. "When I learned that Booth had hired a horse from the village and was riding up the mountain, I knew he meant you harm. So I told Ross. He got a horse from Blue Beeches and went out at once."

"Aunt Letty didn't want me to ride," Camilla said. "She tried to stop me from going."

Hortense tossed her head scornfully. "You mean that nonsense about a storm? It must have surprised her as much as anyone else to have one really blow up. She was afraid to tell you the truth—about that horse. Though she knew, because that's what I went to her room to tell her. She said she didn't believe me. Perhaps she didn't want to believe me. Booth has always been the center of her existence. Or—perhaps she knew all along."

"Letty never wanted to harm anyone," Camilla said. "I know that."

Hortense clutched her arm and Camilla winced. "Look—there on the steps!"

The afternoon was growing dark, and a few lamps had been lit inside the house. Against the light a man stood before the front door of Thunder Heights—a tall, lean, elegant figure. It was Booth, and he stood as if braced, with his legs apart, his arms akimbo. His eyes were alive with a grim mirth as he waited for them.

Hortense ran toward him. "How did you get here? Where is your horse?"

Camilla followed, and as she drew near she saw the jagged tear in his jacket. His tie was gone, his hair disheveled. A cut from the riding crop marked his forehead, and a bruise had begun to swell the cheekbone under one eye.

He gestured carelessly in answer to Hortense. "I left my horse and came down the cliff by way of the short cut."

"Where is Ross?" Camilla demanded—that one question uppermost in her mind.

"We met—if that's what you're wondering." He regarded her almost airily. "Granger managed to interfere with my seeing you home, Cousin. But where he is now I don't know or care."

"What did you do to him?"

"A better question might concern what he did to me. I've never taken to rude physical brawling. But I know the mountain better than he does. I knew it as a boy."

"You went up the cliff the night Althea died, didn't you?" Hortense said. "I always thought you were up there."

"But since you doted on me, my dear mother, you kept your suspicion to yourself? That was kind of you."

A deep, tearing anger began to stir in Camilla. "What happened that night? What did you do to my mother?"

He stepped back from the fury in her face in mock alarm. "You've proved yourself a dangerous woman, Cousin. But I did nothing. Nothing at all. I knew she would go up there, and I tethered my horse at the foot of the cliff while I was supposed to be out searching the river path. I could get to the top easily by the cliff path, while Orrin was taking the long way around by the hill. But I assure you she was already dead when I came upon her body, and she couldn't laugh at me, or taunt me any more."

"Is that when you found the crop?"

"Yes. I'll admit picking it up was a foolish impulse. I wanted to make sure no one would ever strike me with it again. So I carried it down the mountain without thinking. You can understand that I was in a state of some excitement. When I found it in my hand, I carried it out to the lawn and flung it into the river. Or so I thought. I didn't dream it would turn up years later to be used against me in the hands of Althea's daughter."

The bitter light in his eyes was frightening, but Camilla stood her ground. The only thing that mattered now was what had happened to Ross. Before she could speak, a voice called from the upstairs sitting room in the house. The three on the driveway looked up to see Letty at the open window.

"Booth?" she called. "So you're back, dear." Her eyes flicked briefly over Camilla, and the look was without emotion. "Please come up here, Booth. I want to see you."

Booth shrugged. "I'll go see what she wants," he said.

Camilla followed him slowly into the house. The candles in the antehall had been lit, and so had the lamp that hung above the staircase. She moved toward the marble arch opening upon the stairwell, her worried thoughts on Ross, even as she watched Booth start up the stairs.

Part way up the third octagon turn, he paused, one hand on the banister, and looked upward. Apparently Letty had come to the rail above, for Camilla heard her speaking to him softly. Booth cried out in sudden warning.

"No—no, Aunt Letty! Don't!"

There was alarm in his voice and Camilla stopped, with Hortense just behind her. Even as they stared, a sheet of flaming oil streamed down from the great lamp above as Letty's hand must have tipped it. The fall of flame spilled over the wooden steps, encased the octagon railing, and dripped to the floor below. It was caught at once in the strong draft of the stairwell and in a flash the entire wooden structure was a roaring chimney of flame. Letty could escape, above, if she chose, but Booth, part way up the stairs, was trapped.

To her horror Camilla saw that Letty had not moved back from the fire, but was coming down the stairs toward Booth, toward the very heart of the blaze. In the same instant Booth tore off his jacket and leaped up the stairway, to fling it over Letty's head. He picked her up in his arms and came down through the flames, his own clothes on fire, his very hair burning.

Hortense had rushed wildly outside, screaming "Fire!" and a man dashed through the door past Camilla. It was Ross, and he took Letty from Booth's arms, beating out the streak of flame in her skirt. Then he caught up a small rug, wrapped it around Booth and rolled him across the floor to the door. In a moment Ross had him outside on the grass, and Camilla drew Letty down the steps, where she crumpled to her knees on the driveway.

The servants had rushed out of their quarters at the side of the house, and one of them ran off toward the village to summon help. Hortense kept up her screaming until Camilla took her by the arm and shook her.

"Stop it!" she cried. "You can't help anything by screaming." Then she turned to kneel beside Letty.

A patch of Letty's gray skirt fell to ashes when Camilla touched her, but her aunt sat up dazedly and leaned against Camilla's arm. Beyond them the heart of the house was burning like an enormous torch, and the fire was spreading into both wings, even as they watched.

"Booth!" Letty cried. "Where is he?"

She flung off Camilla's restraining arm and sprang up to run to Booth where he lay upon the grass, with Ross bending over him.

"Don't touch him," Ross warned. "He's unconscious. You'd better leave him for the doctor to tend."

Letty stood quietly, looking down at the man who lay at her feet. The extent of his burns was frightful, and Camilla turned away, faint and shaken. No matter what he had been, she would not wish this for him. But Letty did not wince.

"He won't live." She spoke softly, but her voice did not quaver. "It's better that way."

She leaned sadly upon the arm Camilla put around her, and they walked a short distance away beneath the trees.

"He saved my life," Letty said. "He came up through the flames and brought me down. I didn't mean it to be like that. I didn't want him to live, but I meant to go with him."

"Hush," Camilla said. "Hush! You mustn't say such terrible things."

Hortense had come to stand beside them, and she was past her hysteria now. "Let her be," she said. "She means them. Let her say what she pleases."

Against the stormy darkness of the sky the great tinderbox of a house flamed with a wild brilliance. Sparks showered as a center turret collapsed, and Camilla felt the touch of ash upon her face. Suddenly there seemed to be many people thronging the grounds, some shouting and moving about, some watching helplessly.

"Let it burn," Letty said. "Let it burn to the last ember." Tears had begun to stream down her cheeks and she made no effort to stop them. "I knew when I saw the riding crop that he'd painted into the picture. Even then I wouldn't believe such evil of him. I wouldn't accept my own thoughts, or the things you tried to tell me, Camilla. I'd always remember him as a little boy. Such a sad, handsome, unloved little boy. But when I saw the riding crop in the picture I knew that he'd gone up Thunder Mountain the night Althea died, and later I had to face the truth."

"He told us she was dead when he found her," Camilla said quickly. "Perhaps that was the truth."

Letty shook her head. "Only part of the truth. He sent her to her death. I made him tell me today. He taunted her and made fun of her courage until she was so angry she struck him with the crop. But he knew she would ride Folly if he made her angry enough, tormented her long enough. When the time came he saddled the horse for her and he left the girth only partly buckled, knowing it would give if Folly acted up in the storm as she was sure to do. Althea was too angry to check the saddle when she mounted. I think she could have handled Folly in spite of anything if her saddle had been safe. She must have been thrown violently when it began to slip. Folly came home dragging the saddle, and Booth went out to catch her."

The volunteer firemen were here now, with the horse-drawn engine from the village. The play of the hoses made a weak hissing against the tornado of flame. At least they could wet down the trees nearby so the woods wouldn't go.

"Afterward," Letty said, "Booth went up the mountain by the short cut to see what had happened to Althea. I—I don't know what he might have done if she had been alive then. But I believed him when he said she was dead." She looked up in entreaty at Camilla and Hortense. "You see why I had to act? He couldn't be allowed to go on like that. There would be no end to it as long as he lived. Yet in spite of everything, he saved my life."

Dr. Wheeler came, and when he had examined Booth, he shook his head gravely. "It will be only a little while now," he said.

Letty knelt on the grass beside Booth, her eyes tearless, her gaze never moving from his burned and blackened face. Camilla stood with Hortense, waiting. Ross had gone away to work with the firemen. There was nothing to be done. Nothing at all to be done.

Only once did Booth open his eyes, and for an instant the spark of life burned bright with its old intensity. His look moved from Hortense to Camilla, and there was recognition in it, and the old sardonic amusement. Then his gaze was all for Letty.

"Thank you," he said strangely. "We'll all be free now."

His eyelids closed. This time he had stepped across the knife edge of danger.

Toby brought a blanket from the coach house to put over the figure on the grass.

The fire was past its fiercest burning now, though one tower was still in flames and the ruins would smoulder for a long while. Ross had left the futile struggle. He came to draw Camilla away into the deep cool shadow of the trees, and she realized that her face burned from the heat of the fire.

"You're safe," she said. "I worried so. What happened beween you and Booth?"

"We fought." Ross was short. "I think I was getting the best of it, when he broke away. I don't know how he got back, and I didn't much care. The fight was out of him for the moment. I had to take the long way back with the horses. But don't think about that now."

Camilla looked up between high branches and saw the stars in a night blue sky. The storm had rumbled away in the distance, and the rain had never come. She turned in the shelter of Ross's arms and looked into his face.

"Booth spoke the truth," she said softly. "We're all free now. There's nothing to tie any of us here."

He held her closely, and she put her cheek against his. "Will you take me with you, Ross? Wherever you go?"

His kiss answered her, his arm was her support.

The last burning tower crumbled and fell with a great roar and a rush of high-flung sparks. The sound echoed against the mountain above and clapped back and forth across the river. The quiet afterwards was intense. Far below the quiet Hudson waters flowed as they had always done. But Thunder Heights was gone forever.